Praise for

the darkest corners

An ABC Best Book for Young Readers

"Gripping from start to finish . . . with twists
that left me shocked."
—Victoria Aveyard, #1 *New York Times*
bestselling author of *Red Queen*

"As dark as Gillian Flynn and as compulsive as *Serial*."
—Laura Salters, author of *Run Away*

"Will have you questioning the lies young girls tell,

"Yo⟨...⟩ ⟨...⟩ges,
⟨...⟩ough the twists and turns."
—*Bustle*

★ "Thomas carefully crafts the suspense. . . .
An unsettling story of loss, lies, and violence
lurking in the shadows of a small town."
—*Kirkus Reviews*, Starred

★ "Expertly plotted with plenty of twists and turns—
never mind a truly shocking conclusion."
—*Booklist*, Starred

★ "Hand this one to . . . fans of Netflix's
Making a Murderer."
—*Shelf Awareness*, Starred

Books by Kara Thomas

The Darkest Corners
Little Monsters
The Cheerleaders

little monsters

KARA THOMAS

EMBER

Text copyright © 2017 by Kara Thomas
"Wrath" text copyright © 2017 by Kara Thomas
Cover photograph copyright © 2018 by Andreas Kuehn/GettyImages

All rights reserved. Published in the United States by Ember, an imprint of Random House Children's Books, a division of Penguin Random House LLC, New York. Originally published in hardcover in the United States by Delacorte Press, an imprint of Random House Children's Books, New York, in 2017.

Ember and the E colophon are registered trademarks of Penguin Random House LLC.

Visit us on the Web! GetUnderlined.com

Educators and librarians, for a variety of teaching tools, visit us at RHTeachersLibrarians.com

The Library of Congress has cataloged the hardcover edition of this work as follows:
Name: Thomas, Kara, author.
Title: Little monsters / Kara Thomas.
Description: New York : Delacorte Press, [2017] | First edition. |
Summary: When Kacey moves in with her estranged father and his new family, her new friend goes missing and Kacey finds herself at the center of the investigation.
Identifiers: LCCN 2016032457 | ISBN 978-0-553-52149-8 (hc) | ISBN 978-0-553-52151-1 (el)
Subjects: | CYAC: Mystery and detective stories. | Missing children—Fiction. |
Moving, Household—Fiction.
Classification: LCC PZ7.1.T46 Li 2017 | DDC [Fic]—dc23

ISBN 978-0-553-52152-8 (trade pbk.)

Printed in the United States of America
10 9 8 7 6 5 4 3 2 1
First Ember Edition 2018

To all the girls in my life,
who are the furthest things from monsters

CHAPTER ONE

They fire off a round of texts at me five minutes after midnight:

We're coming.

Get ready.

They're not threats, but my friends have a way of making even the simplest demands feel like ultimatums. *Sneak out.* I don't have a choice: if I say no, they'll make sure I'm fully aware of how much fun they had without me.

But then again, it's cold, and not the normal kind of cold. It's Broken Falls, Wisconsin, Dead of Winter cold.

No one warned me about the winters before I moved here. The books and movies are right that Christmas in Wisconsin is magical, with the barns glowing under white string lights, fresh-cut Christmas trees visible through scalloped windows.

But everything that comes after is just cruel. Wind-whipped sheets of snow so thick you can't move through them. Mornings where *above freezing* is the best thing you'll hear all day. Layers of ice on your windshield that take ages to chip off.

And February. February is just the biggest asshole.

February makes you feel like you'll never see the sun again.

My plan was to go to bed early and avoid the inevitable texts from Bailey and Jade. *Are you up? You better be up!* My friends' restlessness is in direct proportion to how miserable and gray it is outside.

Tonight, though: tonight is so clear you can count the stars like they're diamonds.

I text back: *guys I'm so tired* 😔

Bailey: *Stooooop.*

Bailey: *We're doing the thing tonight.*

The skin on the back of my neck pricks. *The thing.* The thing was Bailey's idea; almost everything is Bailey's idea. I take a deep breath to slow my suddenly skittish heart. I could call them, tell them I'm not coming, but they'll just make fun of me for being scared.

There's shuffling outside my bedroom door. The lamp on my nightstand is on. My stepmom, probably, coming to scold me for being up so late.

"Kacey?" A tiny voice. Definitely not Ashley, whose voice carries over hill and sea. My stepmom's constantly talking, sucking up all the air so my half sister can barely get a word in.

I fire off another text to Bailey: *I can't come. Sorry.*

2

"You can come in," I say. Lauren pokes her head inside the room. She reminds me of a doll: Dark, blunt bangs. Porcelain skin. Round head, a little too big for her body. We have the same eyes—wide hazel ones that prompted a particularly nasty freshman at my old high school to call me *that freaky Bambi bitch.*

I fluff out the comforter to make room for Lauren to crawl underneath with me. "You okay?"

Lauren hugs her knees. She's wearing fleece sock-monkey pajamas. There's something about my sister that makes her seem younger than most kids her age; she still cries when she falls off her bike and bleeds. Tonight there's a raw pink strip over her upper lip from the cold.

"Keelie is texting me pictures from Emma's party," she whispers.

I want to fold my sister into a hug. Squeeze the sad out of her. Emma Michaels lives down the road—she's been Lauren's best friend since preschool. But Lauren isn't at Emma's thirteenth birthday sleepover right now, because Keelie March told Emma not to invite her.

Keelie is thirteen, like Lauren, but she fills out her leotards in a way that makes the dance dads want to wait in the car. I saw Keelie in the parking lot over the summer, when I went with my stepbrother, Andrew, to pick Lauren up from her Saturday-morning class. Noticed the way Keelie watched Andrew from the corner of her eye as she lifted her leg onto the ramp railing in a perfect stretch. Sweat glistening between cleavage that even I didn't have. It was sweltering out; Keelie was twelve going on twenty, staring at a seventeen-year-old boy like he was a Popsicle.

"They're drinking wine coolers," Lauren says. "That's why I wasn't invited."

I think of the American Girl dolls still set up in Lauren's room, arranged around a tea set like they're waiting for a party that's never going to happen. I know she won't play with them because the girls at school have already packed theirs up and put them in the attic.

Those girls are thirteen and drinking. I should call Emma's house and tell her mother what's going on in that bedroom. Then I remember the things that went on in my house when I was thirteen.

"Do you want me to block Keelie's number from your phone?" I ask Lauren.

She shakes her head, sending a tear down her cheek. "I just really wish I was there."

I'm about to tell her *fuck Keelie March and those other dumb girls, you have me,* when headlights flash through my bedroom window. My room faces Sparrow Road, the outer edge of our cul-de-sac. It's what Bailey and Jade branded the perfect loading spot for a sneak-out. And it seems that despite my texts, they came anyway.

Bailey flashes her high beams; then there's darkness.

Lauren frowns. "Who's that?"

"Just Bailey and Jade," I answer, fumbling for my phone. I'll tell them Lauren is awake. I definitely can't come out now.

"Are you guys going somewhere?" I hear the hopeful lilt in her voice.

4

"No—we were just—"

Snow crunching outside my window. Bailey's face, illuminated by the light from the phone under her chin. She makes a ghostlike *bwahahaha* noise and I jump, even though I'm looking right at her. Jade appears next to her. Adjusts the messy bun sitting atop her head and taps on my window with one finger.

I dart over and raise the glass. Bailey mashes her face against the screen, makes a pig nose. "Ready to go?" she whispers.

I cringe. Even when Bailey whispers, she's loud.

I think of nosy Mrs. Lao next door, probably perched in the armchair by her living room window with a Sudoku book. A small wooded clearing separates us from the Laos, but in the winter, when the trees are bare, the slightest noise from our house is enough to send Mrs. Lao's Yorkie, Jerome, into a barking fit.

Jade notices Lauren sitting on my bed before Bailey does. She nudges Bailey and flicks her eyes to me, as if to say, *What the hell is she doing here?*

"She came down here because she was upset and couldn't sleep." I steal a glance back at Lauren. She's picking at the pills on her fleece pants, but beneath her bangs, her eyes are on us.

"Can we just go another night?" I whisper.

"No," Jade says. "Put your pants on. Live a little." She wiggles her eyebrows at me and grins.

But when I look at Bailey, she's not smiling. I could swear that there's a hint of fear in her face, and for a second, I think I'm off the hook. Then: "I have all the stuff. Don't wimp out, Kacey."

Wimp out? I never agreed to this *thing* in the first place.

5

Bailcy's eyes are focused on me. Daring me to say no. Her message is clear: if I come out tonight, I'm forgiven for all those times I stayed home.

Across the street, there's faint yelping. Jerome. Mrs. Lao must have let him out to pee.

I turn to Lauren. "We're just going out for a bit, okay? Please don't tell your mom. You can stay in here, okay?"

She looks down at her toes. "I won't."

A bubble of relief. I exhale. Pull jeans on over my fleece PJ pants and throw on the jacket I left draped over my desk chair. The relief doesn't last long when I see Lauren's face. Crushed.

She gives me a halfhearted wave as I pop out my screen and climb up on my windowsill and awkwardly out the other side into the cold night air. I pull the window down behind me feeling like the shittiest person ever, but I have to get rid of my friends before they wake my stepmom up and everything goes to hell.

When I'm tucked in the back of Bailey's Honda Civic, balled-up Taco Bell wrappers under my butt as I fumble for the seat belt, Jade says, "Is she gonna rat us out?"

"She won't," I say.

Bailey looks over her shoulder as she pulls away from the curb. Turns front and slams on the brakes, letting out a little yelp.

Lauren is standing in front of the car, her body illuminated by Bailey's headlights. I nearly slide off my seat. She's wearing her purple down jacket and she's waving for us to stop. Bailey and I both lower our windows.

"Can I come?" Lauren wraps her arms around her waist. "I won't say anything. I promise."

My heart twists. Lauren coming along tonight is a bad idea in a million different ways. "You can come next time."

Jerome starts to bark again, obviously forgotten in the backyard. A light flips on from Mrs. Lao's back porch.

"Shit," Bailey says.

My stomach twists. If Mrs. Lao sees us—"Just get in the car."

Lauren looks at the house, then back at me. "Really?"

Bailey flips her headlights off, chanting *shit, shit, shit* under her breath. I lean over and throw open the back door for Lauren. "Yes! Just get in."

Lauren ducks and climbs into the backseat next to me. "Ride it like you stole it!" Jade hollers.

Bailey accelerates, hitting the curve at the end of the cul-de-sac. My head knocks against the back window. Lauren's breathless, like we've completed a heist.

Jade lowers her mirror. Warm brown eyes winged with black liner meet mine; she's pissed, but what am I supposed to do? They're the ones who decided to drag me out.

I feel the cold in my hands. The vents are pointed away from Lauren and me, concentrating all the heat in the front of the car. Bailey's eyes meet mine in the rearview mirror. I hope she can read what I'm trying to communicate: *It's not too late. We can go back.*

But she grips the steering wheel and looks straight ahead at the road. It's covered in packed snow, the bare trees on each side bending eerily toward the center. Lauren pales when she sees where we are. "Where are we going?"

I hesitate. "Up to the barn. You still want to come?"

Lauren picks at the pills of fleece on her pants again. Lifts her head and nods.

Bailey stops at the foot of Sparrow Hill and cuts the engine. "Let's do this."

Lauren has my hand in a vise grip. We're climbing Sparrow Hill, picking our way around the barren white spruces and trying not to slip on the icy patches of snow.

There was a time when my brand-new half sister was terrified of me. She'd sense me coming into a room and skitter out of it like a cat. Now I'm *her* sister. She won't let anyone forget that, especially my stepbrother, Andrew. *Her* half brother.

Now she trusts me enough to bring her to the creepiest place in Broken Falls—Sparrow Kill. That's what everyone calls it, because of what happened in the Leeds House before it burned down.

Jade, already several paces ahead, looks back at us, a pinch of concern on her forehead when she sees Lauren's face. "If you're scared, you can go back and wait in the car."

"So she can get snatched by some creep?" Bailey says. Something rustles past our feet. "Shit! Something touched me."

I feel Lauren's hand tense in mine.

"It was probably just a chipmunk," I say. I look down at my sister, drop my voice to a whisper. "You really don't have to do this. We can walk home."

She nods. I can see the wheels turning in her head. *Keelie March wouldn't be brave enough to climb Sparrow Kill.* "I want to."

My foot catches a slippery spot and the ground disappears

from underneath me. I fall, taking Lauren down with me. Pain shoots up my tailbone.

Bailey and Jade whip their heads around. See us on our butts. Bailey starts to laugh—a full-on belly laugh that rises into the night, skimming the tops of the trees. I start to laugh too, and then so do Jade and Lauren. We laugh as loud as we want; the nearest house, the Strausses', is more than half a mile away.

It's okay, I tell myself. *We're laughing. Everything will be okay.*

Jade extends a mittened hand and helps me up. Snow seeps into my socks, through the tops of my boots.

Without the moon to guide us, it's too dark to spot the barn. Bailey reaches into her bag and digs out a flashlight—one of those small ones with the name of her dad's plumbing company on it—and illuminates a shallow path for us. "I think it's to the right."

We move together, the crunch of our footsteps in sync. When Bailey stops short in front of me, I know she's spotted it.

The barn has a face. They took the door off its hinges years ago, leaving a gaping hole for a mouth. Two windows, high up, form the eyes. Those are broken, too. I know it's probably because of some kids who came up here to dick around, throw some rocks, but it's still creepy.

The house is gone, but I've seen it in pictures. A red-and-white Scandinavian-style house set behind wrought-iron gates. The scalloped windows reminded me of the dollhouse in my mother's baby pictures, the one my grandfather built her.

I never found out what happened to the dollhouse. Everyone

knows what happened to the Leeds House, though: it burned down.

What no one knows for sure is who set the fire. By the time the fire marshal arrived on Sparrow Hill, there was nothing left of the house but ash and the gnarled bodies of the five children who lived there. Outside, sitting upright on a bench, was Hugh Leeds, the children's father. There was a rifle next to his body and a single gunshot wound to his head.

His wife, Josephine, was never seen again.

The town fought for years to tear the barn down, clear the property and sell it, but without Josephine's body, they couldn't prove she was dead. So the barn stayed, belonging to the Leedses by law. They cleared the wreckage of the house and planted trees around the scorched earth.

Depending on who you ask, Josephine Leeds is still here, walking up and down Sparrow Kill, her white nightdress bloody and filthy at the hem. People call her the Red Woman, and they say she can only be spotted at night.

That's why *we're* here. To see for ourselves.

To scare the shit out of ourselves. Because what else is there to do during a Broken Falls winter?

"You first." Bailey jabs me between my shoulder blades.

Jade snorts. "Are you actually scared?"

Bailey ignores her and steps up to the entrance. Holds up her phone, casting a pale glow on the barn floor. "This is maaaaaad creepy." It comes out as if the breath has been sucked out of her.

I walk through the mouth of the barn, feeling Lauren's sharp inhale as I step away from her. Bailey, never one to be outdone, snaps out of her fear and follows me.

There's hay scattered over the ground, accompanied by the occasional glint of a condom wrapper or beer can. A loft looms on the other end of the barn, its floor beveling under the weight of its age and neglect.

The scraping of feet, and then Lauren and Jade come up behind us. "So now what?"

Bailey sits. Removes the tea light candles from her bag and arranges them in a neat row. Jade tosses Bailey her lighter and smirks. "Do we cut our palms and make a blood oath?"

"If you don't take it seriously, it's not going to work," Bailey scolds. She flicks the lighter and lets the flame hover over the wick on the first candle.

I sit next to Bailey. Next to me, Lauren dutifully lowers herself to the ground, eyes wide, and I lean over and whisper in her ear: "Nothing is actually going to happen. It's not real."

But when Jade sits, I see her shiver. Bailey catches it and raises an eyebrow as if to say, *See?*

Jade wraps her arms around her middle. "It's freezing. Can we just do this and go home?"

Outside, the wind picks up. A draft flows through the door; the flame gutters out. Bailey frowns, tries again. We fall silent, watching her finger skate across the trigger of the lighter.

Finally, a flame. Bailey's eyes are fixed on the candles as she lights them, but I see the quaver in her hand.

The last candle flickers; the flame jumps to life. Bailey sits back. A satisfied look comes over her face. She slips something out of her back pocket: a silver pendulum, a daggerlike blue crystal at the end.

Bailey'd found it in her attic while putting away the Christmas ornaments in January. She'd opened a box of her mom's old things by mistake.

Now, Bailey inhales and holds the pendulum over the circle formed by the candles. A gust of wind passes through the barn, causing the chain to sway.

"How are we supposed to know if it's working?" I ask. "The wind is so strong."

Bailey looks at me and holds her free finger to her lips. The chain goes still; the crystal at the end of the pendulum stops swinging.

Bailey's voice comes out in a hush: "Is there anyone here?"

Our eyes on the crystal, we're silent, until:

"I farted," Jade says.

Bailey leans across the circle and slaps Jade's thigh, hard. Lauren erupts into giggles.

Bailey actually sounds angry as she glares at Jade. "You killed the energy, jerk."

"Oh, what*ever*." Jade rolls her eyes. "You're the only one who believes this garbage."

Next to me, Lauren hugs her knees to her chest. She's still in those sock-monkey pajamas. Her eyes are on the candles. I won't betray her, reveal that Bailey isn't the only one who believes this garbage. Andrew, my stepbrother, told me that Lauren couldn't sleep for days when her friend Chloe said she spotted a strange ball of light on Sparrow Road.

A gust of wind picks up. Something slams against the outside of the barn, drawing a yelp out of Bailey. Jade sits up straight, turns to the noise.

The thrumming in my body zips up to my brain. *Just adren-aline.* "It was only the wind."

Then: the crunch of snow. The wind rises again, howling, taking footsteps outside with it. Running. Someone—*something*—running away from the barn.

Bailey jumps. "What the hell was that?" Lauren's arms shoot around my middle.

Jade stands. "I'm going to check."

I roll onto my knees. Jade shouldn't go alone. "I'm coming."

"Don't," Lauren cries out. "What if someone's out there?"

"There's more of us," Jade says. "It was probably an animal, anyway."

I don't ask what kind of animal other than a human would be spying on four girls performing a séance in the middle of the night. Bailey sits back on her heels, frozen.

I look from Bailey to Lauren. "Stay with her, please?" I don't know which one of them I'm talking to.

Jade is already out the door; I'm at her heels. "This was a stupid idea," she mutters, picking her way through the dark. Her own feet barely make a sound on the snow. She shouts into the trees: "Hey, dickhead! We're going."

I pull my scarf over my face, leaving Jade to shout into the wind, and make my way around the barn to the wall where we heard the slamming. The snow is packed solid. No footprints. No animal, no human.

I make my way back to Jade. "There's no one out here. You can stop yelling."

The wind picks up again, nearly knocking us backward.

That's when the groaning starts. I whip around just in time to see the snow on the roof of the Leeds Barn sinking.

Lauren.

I take off running, shouting: *Get out get out get out.*

A body collides with mine: Bailey. She's got Lauren by the hand. I steady myself, grab on to both Bailey's and Lauren's arms as a *crack* splits the silence. We watch as one half of the Leeds Barn roof falls, hitting the ground with a thud.

That's when Lauren starts screaming.

Bailey's voice is breathless: "We need to get the hell out of here."

I grab hold of Lauren. "Hey. It's okay. It was just the wind."

Lauren's eyes are on the barn. The sound coming out of her is shrill enough to carry over half a mile.

Jade is at our side in an instant. "Shut her up. Seriously. Or we're all screwed."

"Come on." Bailey grabs Lauren. "Let's just get her in the car."

Before I turn to follow them, I poke my head inside the barn. It's dead still, a gaping hole in the roof letting in the light of the moon. On the floor, all five candles are out.

CHAPTER TWO

When we're shut inside Bailey's car, Lauren stops screaming and starts to whimper. I take her ice-cold hand in mine. "You didn't get hurt, did you?"

"She's fine," Bailey says, starting the engine and peeling away from Sparrow Hill.

"I wasn't talking to you," I say, irritated enough to raise my voice. "That roof could have squashed you both."

Jade glares at me. "Brilliant idea. Letting her come."

"What was I supposed to do? You shouldn't have decided we should go to that decrepit old barn in the first place."

Lauren's whimpers give way to short, shallow breaths. She's hyperventilating. My stomach turns as Bailey swerves over to the side of the road and throws the car into park.

Bailey twists around as far as her seat will let her. "Hey. Look at me," she says. She reaches back and gives Lauren's knee a shake. Her voice is gentle. "You have to stop crying. If you go home hysterical, you're going to get us in trouble."

Lauren wipes her face with the sleeve of her jacket. "I know. I'm sorry. I just want to go home."

Bailey sighs, turns forward. Puts the car in drive and pulls away from the shoulder. Lauren hiccups.

"I can't take her home like this," I say. "She's too upset."

Jade reclines her seat into my knees. Props her feet up on the dash. "She's okay. She just needs a minute. Right?" Jade turns to Lauren for affirmation.

My sister nods but won't make eye contact. She has always found my friends ridiculously cool: especially Jade, with her oversized vintage sweaters and armfuls of bangles and impeccably drawn winged eyeliner.

Jade smiles at Lauren. When she turns back around, Lauren lowers her head onto my lap, crying silently. This is just the culmination of her being stressed out—she's still upset about Emma's party, and now she's spooked from the roof collapse. And embarrassed about losing it in front of my friends.

That's what I try to tell myself. But I can't tear my eyes away from Bailey's knuckles, wrapped around her steering wheel, white as the snow on the hill.

I don't bother falling asleep once I'm back in my room, because I have to be up for work at six. Milk & Sugar, Ashley's café, opens at seven on the weekends.

Ashley doesn't look at me funny when she comes to wake me

up. Doesn't say anything about my midnight jaunt. Relief and guilt needle me as I help her chip the ice off the windshield of her SUV and let her prattle on about the storm that's supposed to hit us tomorrow morning.

My nerves are still frazzled from last night, from not sleeping, which leaves me with little patience for the way Ashley and another car at the end of our road sit deadlocked at a stop sign because they can't agree who should go first. Because people around here are polite. Like, the type of polite where if there's one piece of pie left at dessert, the person next to you will give a twenty-minute dissertation on why *you* should have it.

Just last week, Tom Cornwell, an elderly man who always orders one poached egg over toast, slipped on ice outside Milk & Sugar. I've seen people in New York threaten to sue for less, but *Tom* actually apologized to Ashley and refused the free breakfast she tried to force on him.

According to the radio, it's a record low of five degrees today, windchill minus twenty-five. I feel it in the joints of my fingers once we get to the café as I get the coffeepots going, in the ice-cold of the toilet seat when I pee quickly before we open.

The energy is off in the café when the regulars start straggling in. We're not as busy as we usually are on Saturdays, probably because of the weather. The people who do come in grumble over their coffee not being quite right, the heat not coming on fast enough as they wait for their breakfast.

Even old Tom Cornwell is pissy. He must have developed an allergy to gluten in the past few days, because he spends five minutes scolding me for bringing him regular toast. He stops

17

just short of accusing me of trying to kill him and doesn't drop his change in the tip jar like he always does.

Rob, the cook, screws up whatever orders I manage to get right.

Maybe it's me. I'm exhausted. The energy I do have leaches out of me; by ten a.m. I'm a puddle on the stool in the kitchen while I work on the plate of scrambled eggs Rob made me for breakfast. I can't eat without hearing the crack of the barn roof. Without hearing Lauren's earsplitting scream.

If anyone finds out we were trespassing—that we were there when the roof collapsed—we're going to be in such deep shit.

At a quarter after, Bailey strides through the front door. I should be relieved, based on how we left things last night, but the sight of her makes me stumble and overcharge the man I'm ringing up.

I feel her eyes on me as I void out what's on the register and re-ring the order. I hand the man a number to put on his table so I can bring him his omelet when it's ready. Bailey inches up to the counter as he walks away. Yawns, drags her fingers through the strawberry-blond hair that falls to the middle of her back. Her peacoat is unbuttoned, exposing her work polo. *Friendly Drugs* is embroidered on the pocket.

"Can Rob make me an egg white and spinach omelet?" she asks around another yawn.

I shoot a glance at the clock. "Yeah, but you might be late for work."

"It's fine. I'm only going in so Bridget can leave early again." Bailey stretches her arms behind her. "She can wait."

Bridget Gibson is on our Do Not Like list. It's not because

she's dance team captain and salutatorian and universally feared; it's because of Cliff Grosso.

Cliff Grosso is a year older than us. Future poster child for brain damage in the NFL. He had a full ride to Ohio State, until he rear-ended an off-duty sheriff's deputy last spring after he'd been drinking.

Bailey was in the passenger seat. Now, Bridget Gibson is dating Cliff, and whenever his name comes up in the halls of Broken Falls High, she's quick to point out that Cliff wouldn't have even been in that car if he hadn't been about to hook up with Bailey Hammond. Somehow because of this it's become Bailey's fault that Cliff was drunk and behind the wheel of a car.

I shout for Rob to make Bailey's usual and pour her a to-go cup of coffee, black. When she hears the ding of the bell in the kitchen, confirmation that Rob heard me, Bailey jolts a little.

My fingers find the buttons on the sleeve of my shirt and fiddle with them nervously. "Are we okay?"

Bailey lifts her gaze to mine. Her blush is slightly lopsided, like she was in a rush getting ready. "Why wouldn't we be?"

"I just—Lauren could have gotten us busted, with the screaming—"

Bailey cuts me off. "It's fine. Stop talking about it."

The bell over the front door tinkles. Bailey jumps again and turns to see who's come through the door: a woman pushing a stroller carrying a sleeping newborn, a toddler tugging on her other hand. I lower my voice. "What's up? You're so jumpy."

"It's called caffeine, Kace. I've had like three cups of coffee already."

Bailey steps aside while I help the woman with the kids, who doesn't know what she wants and nearly bursts into tears because of it. I want to tell her that Bailey babysits, but Bailey isn't looking at me.

The harried woman decides on a strong cup of coffee, and the bell dings in the kitchen. Rob passes a take-out container through the kitchen window and grins. "For Bailey Bear."

She wiggles her fingers at him and flashes him a smile. None of us actually knows how old Rob is, but he's got five years on us, easily. He grins at Bailey, adjusting the red bandana we all have to wear to hold back our hair.

"Bailey!" Ashley's voice appears before she does. She emerges from the back room, where her office is, the notebook she uses to make the weekly schedule tucked in the crook of her arm. "I thought I heard a familiar voice."

"Hey, Mrs. M." Bailey stands up straighter and brightens, like a switch has been turned on. She's all apple cheeks and smiles as my stepmother comes over and gives her a hug.

"Come over more, will you?" she says. "I'd love to see you around the house. You girls are always out and about."

You have no idea, I think as Bailey's eyes flick to me. "I'd love that," she says.

Ashley beams a motherly smile, then flounces off to fix the crooked chalkboard in the front window. I wonder if maybe I imagined Bailey being weird. She seems perfectly normal now. Then I remember the schedule she made Jade and me for the weekend and realize there's a party tonight.

"Hey," I say quietly, still holding her food. "Isn't Sully's party tonight?"

Bailey's upper lip twitches and her happy face folds into a frown. "You actually want to go to that?"

Of course I don't; I would rather be in bed or playing Mario Kart with Lauren and Andrew than drinking piss-warm beer in the freezing basement of Kevin Sullivan's McMansion, but I nod, because I know Bailey wants to go.

She and Jade make it a point to avoid high school parties. They always say they're stupid, but really everyone knows that's because Bailey doesn't want to run into Cliff—or Bridget, who is bold enough to hiss *go home, skank* at Bailey's back after a few sips of peach schnapps. Rumor has it tonight is going to be a rager, though; Kevin's older brother is home from college for the weekend and allegedly bringing a bunch of hot Canadian college guys with him. Everyone except the losers and mouth-breathers will be there.

I hand Bailey the food and meet her eyes.

"Okay," she says, almost looking amused. "We'll text you when we're on our way to pick you up."

I steal a glance at my phone the second Ashley starts cashing out the register for the day. Normally at the end of my workday, my screen is bloated with group messages from Bailey and Jade. *When are you getting out of work/what are we doing tonight?*

But there's nothing. No mention of the party Bailey said we would go to.

Silence is never golden with Bailey and Jade. I wonder if I'm being punished. If being ignored is my penance for letting Lauren come last night, for almost getting us caught.

On the ride home, I rest my cheek on the seat belt, pulled taut, as Ashley prattles on about dinner plans.

"I was thinking maybe Chinese, since your father's working." There's a silent *again* at the end of her sentence. My dad works night shifts in a pharmacy at a hospital in the city, forty-five minutes away.

At a red light, Ashley examines her part in the mirror. Moves a piece of bottle-brown hair until she finds a pesky gray strand and yanks at it. She's five years older than my father and has a serious complex about it.

But when I saw her for the first time, I thought, *Now,* she *looks like a* mom.

Here's the truth: my actual mom sucks. She's always sucked. Even when I was little, like really little, I could tell that she sucked at being a mom. I remember sitting at my best friend's kitchen table for dinner, because my mother was late picking me up again, mouth watering at the buttery rolls and Tater Tots, and thinking, *This is what a real dinner looks like. This is what a real mom looks like.*

When I think of my mother I think of Happy Meals for dinner, paid for by the change scrounged up in her car, the one that smelled like cigarettes because she let her boyfriends drive it and smoke inside. I think of the surprise on my teachers' faces when they saw how young my mom was, the hot shame in my cheeks at always being the last kid to get picked up from the after-school program.

It wasn't all bad—especially when it was just the two of us, and we did things like drive to get Carvel at midnight in our pajamas, or sit on the living room floor and cut out all the supermodels from her magazines, turning them into paper dolls.

I wish I could say it was my mom who ruined everything, but I was the one who changed. I grew up and couldn't stand the boyfriends anymore—the way they smelled, the way they talked to her, the way they all seemed to use my mom up and leave her in pieces. I got angry, and I took it out on her.

I was thirteen the first time I said *I fucking hate you* and she said she fucking hated me too. The fights always ended with something in the house broken and both of us in tears, with her telling me she loved me and she promised to do better.

The thing is, I love my mom. But I'm starting to think it's possible to love someone and hate them at the same time.

Anyway, how I wound up in Broken Falls with the father I'd never met and the stepfamily I didn't know I had: my mom's latest boyfriend, the one I called Tattooed Douche, was so bad that I decided I would rather live in a friend's basement than my own apartment any longer.

A social worker got involved, phrases like *no possibility of reconciliation* were uttered, and phone calls were made to Russ Markham, the man I only knew by the signature on the checks he sent every year on my birthday.

Ashley welcomed me with a special dinner and a brand-new comforter set from Target; Andrew talked my ear off about my school schedule and promised to introduce me to all his friends—cross-country runners, soccer players, future Ivy League graduates, and girls who wore pearl earrings.

But I chose Bailey and Jade. Or rather, they chose me, drew me into their satellite, which seemed to orbit outside all the usual high school drama. Who was hooking up with whom, who was lobbying to win best smile. None of that mattered to them. They seemed to have their own private world where the only things that mattered were each other.

I really thought that I could be a part of it, the day Bailey pulled up to the curb where I was waiting for Andrew after school and said, *We're going to my house.* I knew that it was an invitation to something much bigger. Two becoming three.

But three is an uneven number.

When there are three, someone always winds up out in the cold.

When Ashley and I get home from Milk & Sugar, Andrew is in the living room, hunched over his laptop. On the TV, the Netflix homepage is frozen, with the prompt: *ARE YOU STILL WATCHING* WHEN PLANES DISAPPEAR? I stop behind the couch. "That's some light viewing."

Andrew looks up at me. Rakes dark brown hair out of his eyes. That, he got from Ashley. The rest of him is his dead father, who was Korean. I'd be lying if I said that it wasn't reassuring that Andrew shares as much blood with the Markhams as I do.

Andrew looks at the TV as if he'd forgotten what he was watching. "Oh. It's just background noise."

I sit on the arm of the couch and skim the screen of his laptop over his shoulder. He's working on an essay of some sort. "What's that for?" I ask.

"Scholarship stuff." He rubs his face with the sleeve of his thermal shirt. I imagine the bags under his eyes leaving black streaks, like mascara. "For Notre Dame."

Andrew applied early action everywhere. He got into Madison, who gave him a full ride, and his dream school, Notre Dame— only they didn't give him shit. They said Ashley and my dad make too much money, even though their combined salary isn't anywhere near enough to cover four years at Notre Dame.

I nod to the laptop. "You want me to read?"

He considers it for a beat, then gives me a sheepish smile. "Yeah, if you don't mind."

I don't remember when we started reading everything for each other, but I like looking over Andrew's essays. I like feeling needed. As I settle into my corner of the couch, I feel Andrew's gaze skirt over me. I turn to look at him. "What?"

He cracks a knuckle. "You seem on edge or something."

A slick of sweat comes to my palms. Could he have heard us sneak out? "I didn't sleep much last night."

"Neither did Lauren," Andrew says. "She didn't even get up this morning."

Ugh. I'm selfish and disgusting. I've been so busy obsessing about my friends being mad at me that I didn't stop to think about Lauren—how scared she must have been when the roof caved in. In the middle of a séance, no less.

"I'll read your essay later. I'm gonna go shower," I say.

"Good. You stink."

He says it to me all the time. It's a running joke between us, what smells worse—his socks after a track meet, my clothes after a day standing around a bacon fryer—but as I turn to head down the hallway, I catch him watching me, still.

I'm not going to shower. I'm going to check on Lauren. I can't get her face, frozen with fear, out of my mind.

That look on Lauren's face: it wasn't too different from the way her eyes went wide when I walked through the kitchen the day my father picked me up from the airport and first brought me here. Me, an urchin with punk hair and a busted lip, pale skin. I don't blame her for being terrified. Because when people in Broken Falls heard that I was moving in with the Markhams, they had a lot to say about me.

They said that I was Russell Markham's love child from some affair he had in college and he hadn't even known about me.

That I'd been thrown out of my mom's house in Rochester, New York, for being a druggie.

That I'd gotten my busted lower lip from a stint in juvie.

That Ashley was going to make me work at her café to earn my keep.

I know that people said all of this because Bailey told me, much later. Murmured in my ear in her *isn't-that-so-funny* voice after we'd passed a bottle of Fireball between us at one of Tyrell Long's bonfires.

None of the shit people were saying about me was true, but it still hurt the way the ones I actually shared blood with— Lauren, and my father—tiptoed around me like I was a ghost. A stranger with their DNA. Lauren took one look at me and ran out of the room.

I know she loves me now, but sometimes I think Lauren was the only one who saw me for what I really am: a stranger wherever I go. Someone with a look in their eyes you just can't trust.

I was supposed to prove her wrong. Supposed to keep her safe.

I tamp down the guilt and climb the stairs. I still feel like an intruder going up them. My bedroom is on the first floor—converted from Ashley's office, as if I didn't feel guilty enough about moving in—and there's a bathroom across the hall from my room. I don't come up here unless Lauren invites me to watch a video on her laptop.

The door to her room is shut. There's a whiteboard mounted on the outside. Scrawled across the top, in Lauren's handwriting, it says: *TODAY'S SEA CREATURE IS THE CLOWN FROGFISH*. Beneath it is a smudged blob of a thing, drawn in yellow and red.

The date on the whiteboard tugs at me. Lauren hasn't done a new drawing in four months. She's wanted to be a marine biologist since she was a little kid; her love for bizarre sea creatures is exactly the sort of thing Keelie March would sneer at. It's always made me sad, how showing enthusiasm for anything in eighth grade is supremely uncool. Like once you go through puberty you're expected to be dead inside and not care about anything.

I raise my fist and knock. "Laur? Are you okay?"

Quiet. I knock again, harder, expecting to hear her whine about how tired she is and tell me to go away. I press an ear to her door. Nothing.

I open the door slowly and slip into her room; the lights are off, and Lauren is a lump on the bed. I step over piles of clothes, my bare foot snagging on something hard. My ankle goes sideways. I grunt and kick aside one of Lauren's pointe shoes.

I give Lauren's shoulder a shake. My eyes adjust to the dark; her face is half covered by her comforter and I move it aside. Her mouth is open slack, and she's limp under my shaking.

My heartbeat stalls out. "Hey. Wake up."

I put a hand to her chest—wait for the rise and fall. When it doesn't come, I grab both her shoulders. I yell her name, my voice drowned out by my pulse pounding in my ears.

Footsteps and shouting from downstairs: Ashley, calling for me. My stomach goes into free fall at the same moment Lauren's eyelids snap open. Her pupils fix on me, and she starts to scream.

"Get off!" The sound is guttural, as if she's possessed. "Get her OFF ME!"

The bedroom door swings into the wall; Ashley bursts into the room. "What happened? What's going on?"

I step backward, stumbling over the pointe shoe again. "I don't know—"

Lauren scrambles backward on her bed, rattling the headboard. Her eyes still have that frantic look in them. When Ashley reaches for her, she starts sobbing. "Don't hurt me!"

"Hey, hey." Ashley wraps her arms around Lauren. "You're dreaming. Shh. It's okay. You're okay."

Lauren blinks. Her expression settles into surprise; she looks from Ashley, to me, to Andrew, now standing in her doorway. Her voice sounds small and far away, like it's trapped inside a bell. "What happened?"

I swallow to clear my throat. "I think I scared you. When I tried to wake you up."

Ashley rubs circles into Lauren's back. "You can't sleep all day, honey. No wonder you're up at night."

A light touch on my shoulder: Andrew. *Let's go.*

Before I cross the threshold into the hall, I turn and look at Lauren, still burrowed into Ashley's shoulder. Her eyes lock on me, her pupils enormous, as if she sees something that terrifies her.

CHAPTER THREE

Lauren won't come down to eat once the takeout arrives—
she insists she's not hungry—and Andrew takes his food into
his room so he can finish his scholarship essay.

I'm not too hungry either, but I don't like to waste food. I
plow through my pile of lo mein and tell Ashley I'm going to do
homework.

"It's Saturday," she says, as if she's embarrassed her children
are such dorks.

"It won't take long," I say. "We can watch a movie when
I'm done."

I shove my leftovers in the fridge and duck into my room,
where my cell phone is charging on my nightstand. My screen
is still empty.

I sit cross-legged on my bed and inhale. It's still early; Bailey and Jade won't be leaving for the party until ten, at least. I suppress the itch in my fingers urging me to text Bailey and tell her about what happened with Lauren.

Get her off me.

Bailey is fascinated with Josephine Leeds and the barn. I close my eyes and think about all the stories Bailey told me about the massacre. How there are people in town who are convinced Josephine Leeds escaped alive and lived out her days in the woods, a reclusive madwoman because of her grief.

According to Bailey, some people even claim that Josephine killed her children, staged her husband's suicide, and set the fire herself before escaping. But the Leedses' closest neighbor—a man who lived three miles from Sparrow Hill— came forward and said a barefoot woman in a white nightgown banged on his door the night of the fire. She was hysterical and covered in blood; the man was so frightened of her that he wouldn't let her inside the house. The neighbor called the constable twice but couldn't reach him; by the time he returned to his porch, she was gone.

These are all stories Lauren has heard, no doubt—she grew up here, after all.

When I close my eyes, I see Bailey holding the pendulum. I hear the roof caving in. I imagine the events from my little sister's perspective and a shiver runs down my spine.

As I finally drift off, it's to the sound of the wind howling, and I can't tell if it's coming from outside or from inside my head.

. . .

Sunlight streams through my window, prying my eyelids open. It's morning.

I fucking fell asleep. I missed Kevin Sullivan's party—I must have slept through Bailey texting me that they were on their way to pick me up.

They're going to kill me.

Outside, a powdery snow is falling. I check my phone—it's a reflex by now. I never had anyone to answer to, before I met Bailey and Jade.

My stomach turns inside out. My screen is empty.

But the party.

Part of my brain shouts, *Maybe they didn't go.* I click open Instagram and scroll through pictures of the party in my feed. I don't follow a ton of people from Broken Falls, which only makes it more obvious that everyone who isn't me was at Sully's party last night.

I stop at JadeInTheShade. Jade and Bailey are standing cheek to cheek over the beer pong table. Jade's the one snapping the picture; Bailey's eyes are off on something in the distance. Full-mouth smiles. Thirteen likes.

I've always been able to sense trouble coming on—almost like a headache. There's a pulsing in the vein above my brow bone. They ditched me.

The house is silent, making the hollowness in my gut grow as I get up. Sunday is my day off.

I pad into the kitchen. There's a note on the island from Ashley.

Dearest children: Please do NOT go out today. This storm is supposed to be a nasty one. Love you!

I head upstairs, check to make sure Lauren's okay, and find her sleeping peacefully. No vivid nightmares of the Red Woman are making her scream this morning.

Guilt needles me. I decide I'll bribe her out of bed with pancakes.

I didn't know how to cook when I first moved here. Didn't understand that food was its own form of affection, that a casserole or a pie was meant to have the same effect as a hug.

I drag Ashley's cherry-red stand mixer out from the cabinet below the kitchen island and get to work.

While the cakes are bubbling in the pan—I added two drops of red food coloring to the batter, since Valentine's Day is in two weeks—footsteps creak above the kitchen. The upstairs toilet flushes. Either Lauren or my dad is awake.

My heart taps out a steady rhythm against my ribs. This is the first time I've had Lauren alone since yesterday, when I asked her what had happened in the barn and she got upset with me. Now her eyes flick up to me as she shuffles into the kitchen, but she doesn't say anything.

"Hey, Monkey."

Lauren plops herself onto the stool closest to the living room—always the same stool, I learned quickly my first week here—and pulls the fleece sleeves of her pajamas up over her hands. "What are those?"

"Pancakes." I flip one of the hearts, realizing with disappointment that it looks more like a lumpy ass. "How many do you want?"

"None." Lauren props her chin on her hands. Her gaze darts around the kitchen, avoiding me, and rests on the window over the sink. Outside, Andrew's dark figure is still hunched over the snow shovel.

I root around in the overhead cabinet for a plate, the edges of my pancakes browning. *What really happened in the barn, Lauren? Did you and Bailey see something?* Such simple questions.

The words are on the tip of my tongue as I set the plate on the kitchen island.

"You made them pink," Lauren says, just noticing.

I pause, one hand on the back of a stool. "Mm-hm."

Lauren squirms in her seat. Tugs at her sleeves. "Do you think we could make pink puppy chow?"

"Yeah. We could tint the cake mix, I think." I allow myself a small smile.

I cut the stack of pancakes in half and pass half on a plate to Lauren. She shakes her head. "I'm not really hungry."

I pick at the pancakes as I remind Lauren where all the puppy chow ingredients are. I set my plate aside; I'm not really hungry anymore, either. Lauren is quiet as we measure out the confectioner's sugar and cake mix, but there are shades of her usual self peeking through; when Andrew comes downstairs, hair stuck flat to his head, and collapses onto an empty stool at the island, she swats him for snatching a handful of our M&Ms.

"You're so *rude,*" she says, and I feel myself thaw a bit. Lauren is okay. We're okay. It doesn't matter if my friends hate me; I have everything I need right here in this kitchen.

And still, a dark voice comes into the back of my head and tells me to enjoy it while it lasts.

• • •

An inch of snow and a couple games of Mario Kart later, my phone rings. It's Jade. My heart goes into my throat, because Jade never calls me. There's never anything so important she needs to tell me that Bailey can't get to me first.

"You guys play." I get up from the couch and leave Lauren and Andrew to battle out who gets to be Toad this round. I hit *accept call,* and Jade's raspy voice fills the earpiece.

"Is Bay with you?" she asks.

"No. Why would she be here?"

"Kace," she says. "Something's wrong."

Junior Year
March

If you're reading this, I'm dead.

Just kidding. Although if someone were to find a notebook with two golden retriever puppies on the cover, pages of my middle school anxieties inside—*What if I get my period while we're running the mile in gym and it leaks down my leg! What if auditions for* The Music Man *are open and I have to sing in front of everyone!*—I might just kill myself.

Anyway, I dug out this notebook because I'm going through Some Shit, and I guess writing about it is a healthy outlet or whatever. I'm not dumb enough to do it on a blog or something—poor Alexa Ryan blogged about how she made herself throw up every day after dance team practice, only she forgot to make it private and the other girls found it. Someone forwarded it to Alexa's parents and they sent her to a psychiatric hospital in Madison and for a while it was literally all anyone talked about.

Now literally everyone in Broken Falls is talking about me. Jade says I'm being dramatic, but the car accident and Cliff's DWI are the very definition of drama, and if there's one thing that keeps Broken Falls going, it's drama. (And Packers Sundays.) I mean really, what else do we have?

I never thought that I would be the source of BFD (Broken

Falls Drama, which also means "Big Fucking Deal," which Jade cleverly realized). But put yourself in my shoes: the summer before junior year you make a vow to yourself to get noticed. You are tired of being Hammy Bailey Hammond, B+ student and all-around nice girl. The type of girl people call a "classic beauty," which everyone knows is code for "you would have been considered hot fifty years ago, maybe." So you have Jade cut four inches off the hair you've been growing since the third grade and spend every summer morning in front of your brother's Tae Bo tapes until you magically have a butt.

And yet still, on the first day of junior year, no heads turn as you walk into homeroom. You feel stupid for expecting them to. And then right before lunch, you plunk down in your assigned seat during third-period local history, and then none other than Cliff Grosso sits down next to you in a cloud of Axe. He checks you out like he sees you for the first time, even though you've gone to the same school for twelve years. He looks at you with those ice-blue eyes and says, *Hey, 'sup?* and you flush from your stomach to your toes, because apparently you are that pathetic. You spend half the year making small talk before the bell, pretending you don't give a shit how he smirks at you whenever Mr. Cannobbio embarrasses himself using the term *historygasm*. With feigned disgust you watch him cycle through girls, because a nice girl like Bailey Hammond would never even *think* about the feel of Cliff Grosso's used-up lips on hers.

Maybe I was tired of being a nice girl. Maybe that's why when I found myself alone with him at Tyrell's party last weekend, I laughed when he made a joke about Mr. Cannobbio and didn't turn away when he leaned in. I decided right then and there that I was okay with losing it to Cliff Grosso, even though everyone loses it to Cliff Grosso. I made out with him even though he tasted like Natty Ice and salsa. When he said he knew somewhere private in Tyrell's house I said no, because I would not lose my virginity while half my graduating class played beer pong outside the door. So I said, *Is anyone home at your house?* even though everyone knows that Cliff's dad doesn't give a shit how many girls he has over.

It would be like ripping off a Band-Aid, this virginity business. That's truly what I thought would happen. I didn't realize how many beers he'd actually had until he failed to slow down at a yellow light, and *bam,* rear-ended some chick who just happened to be a Broken Falls deputy.

Anyway. Now Cliff has a DWI and people are saying that he might lose his scholarship to Ohio State. And guess who everyone blames. I thought maybe it wouldn't be so bad when I got to homeroom and Meghan Constanzo rushed up to me and asked if I was okay, was I hurt? Gosh, I was so lucky the accident wasn't serious. Meghan Constanzo and I have exchanged about a total of ten words since I've known her. I smiled very politely and watched her sit back down at the table with one of her tennis friends, a senior, who glanced back at me before turning to Meg and mouthing, *Her?*

Yes, *her.* Surprise! The painfully average girl whose first kiss was with a nose-picking trumpet player was *the girl* in Cliff Grosso's car. And everyone knows what happens in Cliff Grosso's car. When I was kissing Cliff I really thought that it would transform me, or at least how people saw me. Because it's sexy when good girls do bad things. People still talk about how epic it was when Meghan Constanzo threw up in Sully's pool after homecoming last year. Because that's the type of stuff you can get away with when you're Meg Constanzo and literally everyone adores you. I overestimated what I could get away with, I guess.

Because I'm nothing. There are girls like Meghan, who are adored, and there are girls like Bridget Gibson, who are feared, and then there are girls like me and Jade, who are nothing. People literally have no opinion on us. We're not losers, we're not *nonexistent*—people just aren't aware of us.

I want to go back to being nothing.

Anyway, Meg and her friend sounded sympathetic enough that I thought the rest of today might be okay. Then I was waiting in line at the cafeteria and Axel Schulz, who still has his scholarship to UW, collided with me. His sloppy joe slid off his tray and onto my boots, and it hit me like a punch to the stomach. *He did that on purpose.*

Words were on the tip of my tongue—*Fuck you, asshole*—but he beat me to it. "Fuck you, Hammond."

I paid for my sandwich and left my tray at the table with Jade. I told her I would be right back, nothing happened, I was fine—and marched over to the lunch monitor and asked for the bathroom pass. At the table by the door, Axel looked at me and laughed with his friends. "Too bad Cliff couldn't find out if the carpet matches the drapes." I caught someone else saying *hammered and nailed,* which is the term the football guys use for what is essentially date raping.

When I got to the bathroom I wet a paper towel and dabbed at the oily orange spot Axel's lunch had left on my Ugg. And

I thought, *God, please let there be* someone *in this school who doesn't think I'm a life-ruining whore.*

And then I went to local history—I thought about skipping it, because I still had to sit next to Cliff—and it turned out he hadn't even shown up for school at all. The bell rang, and then out of nowhere this girl walks in. Messy white braid with the ends dyed purple, wearing Vans with strange shit scribbled on the sides, and just sat in Cliff's empty seat. She didn't even ask where she should sit or say, *Hey, I'm new* or anything. I thought, *Who the hell even is this girl?*

And then something clicked—a snippet I'd caught earlier in the week, someone saying that Andrew Kang's stepsister was coming from New York to stay with his family. I hadn't even known that Andrew had a stepsister, and I thought I knew everything about Andrew Kang. Everyone knows everything about everyone around here. People had been talking about the stepsister for the past week once they heard she was coming. All anyone cared about was whether she was hot, because God forbid someone be interesting first.

Anyway, I watched her in the seat next to me—the one Cliff usually occupied—and studied her scrawling inside the cover of a notebook. I couldn't catch what she was writing, but when she saw me watching, she stopped and sat staring straight ahead.

And I thought, *Interesting.*

I watched as Mr. C stopped by the Weird Girl's desk and murmured to her quietly. She nodded, and Mr. C smiled at her and turned to tell us to shut up, he had to explain our quarter project.

Immediately Bridget Gibson piped up from the back of the

40

room and asked if we could work with partners. When Mr. C said no, she started whining: "You *said* we'd get to do at least one partner project." Then the class started rumbling in agreement, and Mr. C flushed like he feared mutiny and told us to knock it off and open our textbooks. But Bridget was relentless. She actually pouted. "But you *promised* we could do something with partners." Because that's how Bridget is: she thinks everyone owes her something, even some poor son of a bitch who's stuck making thirty grand a year teaching a bunch of assholes.

And Mr. C caved just like that. "Fine. But this isn't an in-class project. You have five minutes at the end of the period to find your partner, and then everything is done on your own time."

Bridget smiled victoriously and linked pinkies with Alicia Rivera in the middle of the aisle. A crop of sweat slicked up on the back of my neck. *Partners*. Not a good day to find a partner. I figured I'd tell Mr. C I wanted to work alone, and then I remembered Andrew Kang's stepsister sitting next to me.

When Mr. C wrapped up the lesson and told us to find our partners, I lingered in my seat for a bit, aware of *her* amid the chaos of scraping chairs and bodies. She was looking out the window, flipping her bottom lip with her thumb.

I tapped on her desk with my pen to get her attention. "Wanna work together?"

She twirled her pen between her fingers, looking too depressed to bother sizing me up. "Yeah. Okay."

There were tears in her eyes. I knew then that this girl was going through some shit too.

"I'm Bailey. Are you okay?"

41

"Kacey," she said. "And no. Not really."

I felt Bridget's eyes boring into my back, and I thought about how Kacey had saved me from the humiliation of working alone. *I'm not okay either,* I wanted to say.

Maybe we were meant to find each other today. Maybe we're the Not Okay Girls, and we're supposed to save each other.

CHAPTER FOUR

Something is wrong. I hold two fingers to the throbbing vein at my temple. "What are you talking about?"

"I don't know. Bailey never made it home from Sully's party last night."

"Wait, she went home?" Bailey always stays at Jade's house after parties; she has a strict eleven-thirty curfew, and her mom is oblivious— she really thinks Bailey has kept her promise to be good after the Cliff Grosso incident. She really thinks Bailey spends most of her weekends at Jade's making cupcakes and watching crappy reality television. Not sneaking out to the Culver's in Pleasant Plains or to the occasional party.

"At like ten she said she was busted and had to go home," Jade says. There's a silent *but* lingering there.

"What?" I ask.

"Cathy called me this morning. She said Bay isn't answering her phone and asked me when she was coming home from my house."

"Bay lied to you?"

Jade is quiet. I realize how I must have sounded. *Accusatory.* Because Bailey'd lied to me yesterday too, hadn't she? She said she would text me before she and Jade left for the party.

"I told you," Jade says. "Something's seriously wrong. I've been blowing up Sully's phone, but he's not answering. I'm thinking of driving over there so Cathy can keep calling people."

I can tell she wants me to come with her to Sully's. But Jade never asks for anything. "I can be ready in like ten minutes."

"Okay." Jade's sigh of relief fills the line. "I'll be there in five."

Jade lives on the other side of Sparrow Hill, all the way on the opposite end of town, which means she was already on her way to me when she called.

The thought fills the hole in my stomach a bit. Whatever is going on with Bailey, we'll figure it out together. I haven't been frozen out completely—Jade still needs me.

Whatever my crime was, it's forgiven. For now.

After Jade ends the call, I look at my screen. Bailey had grabbed my phone one night, taken a picture of herself making a grotesque "derp face," and saved it as my wallpaper. I never bothered to change it, because it made me laugh every time I looked at it.

I text her: *Where are you?? This isn't funny.*

. . .

I slip out of the house before Andrew can corner me and ask what's wrong. The answer feels too complicated.

I pause as I pick my way around the spot where Andrew's Mazda is parked. There are fresh tire marks behind the car, the grooves filling up with snow. I didn't hear him go anywhere last night or this morning. I entertain the idea that he went to the party for a half a second and laugh.

Andrew can't drink on his medication, and when I asked him why he doesn't go to the parties anyway, he said he'd rather get his legs waxed than be the only sober person at a party.

Jade's already here. She's idling at the curb in her father's truck. Warren works nights for the power company. When he's sleeping, Jade can take the truck as long as she refills his gas tank. I don't know anything about Jade's mom except what Bailey told me: she killed herself when Jade was five—Jade walked in on her in the bathtub—and I should never, ever bring it up.

"Babe," Jade says as I climb into the truck, "I'm freaking out."

Jade's eyeliner is smudged and her bun lopsided. I reach over and give her mittened hand a squeeze. The picture of her and Bailey from last night pops into my mind—the one I should have been in—and I pull my hand back.

If Jade notices, she doesn't say anything. "When we get to Sully's, I'm going to beat him for not answering his phone. Then I'm going to make him call every single person in his contacts until we find her."

There are plows out already, trying to stay ahead of the storm. When we pass Milk & Sugar, I sink down in my seat. Ashley sometimes wipes down the windows in the afternoon when it gets slow, and I don't want her catching me out gallivanting with Jade in this weather.

Jade doesn't say anything about last night, doesn't ask what I did, and I wonder if they talked about it. If they came to a joint decision to leave me behind.

The first time I snuck out with Bailey and Jade, we went to the Taco Bell in Pleasant Plains. We laughed at the drunken twentysomethings fumbling their orders into the drive-through speaker and imagined having that kind of freedom, someday. In the summer, we snuck down to the lake, waded in up to our midthighs, and laughed under the moon. Bailey never wanted to go home.

Eventually I realized I preferred my evenings by the fire in the den, playing games of Risk with Andrew and Lauren that stretched to midnight. I'd finally found a version of myself I could live with—found a place where I didn't feel like I had to escape.

So I lied to Jade and Bailey and told them Ashley caught me sneaking back in one night. Said I had to cut back, couldn't go out with them every weekend. It didn't stop them from trying to pull me out into the night.

But the night doesn't like to give up its secrets. And if Bailey disappeared into it, there might be no telling what happened to her.

Kevin "Sully" Sullivan lives in a McMansion on Prairie Circle. His mom is always traveling for business, and his brother goes to college in Canada, so Sully is generally left to do as he pleases, which equals instant popularity.

Personally, I think Sully's a creep. He's a squat guy, constantly trying to make up for his size with his easy access to booze. He's always hovering around the girls at his parties like a gnat, snapping pictures for some weird personal collection.

My toes clench in my boots as we pull into the Sullivans' driveway next to a sad-looking beer keg turned on its side.

The Prairie Circle McMansions all have two-car garages. Both of the doors are open and Sully's Ford Escape is on display. Jade parks behind it and we climb out and ascend the long cobblestone walkway.

When we reach the front door, Jade cups her eyes and peers through the glass. She rings the bell. One, two, three times, and then she tries the handle. The door creaks open. No one locks their doors in Broken Falls—something that's always creeped me out.

Sully's house is trashed: there are red Solo cups at our feet and a trash can overflowing with empty liquor bottles by the door, as if whoever was bringing it outside lost the will at the last moment. The contents of what looks like an entire bag of Doritos are crushed into the rug in the living room adjacent to the entryway. We stand in the foyer, listening for signs of life. Then: the rustling of cans, coming from the basement.

"I knew he was home." Jade starts down the stairway leading off the foyer. I pause to shake the snow from my boots before I follow—there's no reason not to be polite.

Sully is bent over the wreckage of what looks like it was once a table for mixing drinks, a Santa's sack of a trash bag in his hands. He looks up and sees Jade and me. "What are you guys doing here?"

47

"*Someone* wasn't answering his phone," Jade snaps.

Sully pats his back pocket. "Oh. I have no idea where that is."

Jade's jaw twitches. "So you haven't heard from Bay this morning?"

"No. Why?"

"She never made it home last night," I say.

Sully's eyes flick to me, like he's just noticing I'm here. "Shit. Well, I don't know where she is." Sully nods to Jade. "You didn't leave with her?"

"She said she couldn't because she had to go straight home. Remember, Tyrell gave me a ride when the party was over?"

Sully blinks. There are freckles on his eyelids.

"You said bye to us!" Jade makes a sound of disgust.

"To be honest, I was blitzed out of my mind," Sully says. "I don't even remember Bay leaving."

"Well, someone must have been outside when she left," I say. "Maybe they talked to her."

Jade pulls out her phone and dials. Moments later, a beer pong cup starts rattling against the table. Sully hurries over to it and fishes his phone out. "How'd that get in there?"

"Are you not understanding what's going on here?" Jade snaps. "Bay is missing, and she was last seen *here*."

Sully's eyes go wide, swiveling to take in the remains of last night's debauchery. "No one called the cops, right?"

I think of the beer keg still out in the driveway. I snatch the phone from Sully's hand. I open up his picture folder. He may have been too drunk to remember Bailey leaving, but there's a chance he caught it on camera if he was outside around the keg.

I flip through, looking for exterior shots of the house. There's a photo of some junior girl, illuminated by the flash of the camera, being held up in a keg stand on the driveway. I zoom in, noticing a spot of blue at the edge of the screen.

Bailey's Honda Civic. *Bailey,* one hand on the driver's-side door handle.

She's not alone. Someone the size of a linebacker is grabbing her shoulder. He's got a shaved head.

"Jade," I say.

Jade yanks the phone from my hand and zooms in on the picture. The color drains from her face as she turns to Sully.

"Call Cliff Grosso right now."

Sully balks. "I don't have his number."

"Then what was he doing at your party?"

"He came with Bridget. I didn't invite him."

Jade's ears go red. "Then call Bridget!"

I cross the basement as Sully fumbles with his phone, Jade towering over him like an angry mother. I run a finger over the surface of the beer pong table—the same one Jade and Bailey were smiling over just last night. Bailey wasn't looking at the camera. She even looked distracted, maybe.

But Bailey wouldn't leave a party just because she *saw* Cliff. It wouldn't be the first time she ran into him; Broken Falls is a small town, and after losing his scholarship, Cliff stuck around to work at his uncle's hunting shop. Bailey had to have known Cliff would show up to Sully's party; she's always calling Cliff the loser former quarterback who has nothing better to do than hang around high school parties with his high school girlfriend.

"No answer." Sully shrugs. "Everyone is probably still sleeping."

Jade runs her hands down her face. "God, you are so useless. Try Val."

Val Diamond, Bridget's right-hand woman. I come up next to Jade as Sully dutifully makes the call. "Do you think that's why she left? She saw Cliff?"

"She would have told me," Jade says. "I would have left with her."

"Maybe she didn't want to kill your vibe or whatever."

Jade rolls her eyes. "If you'd been here, you'd know there was no vibe to kill. The party sucked."

The words hang in the air between us: *if you'd been here.* So casual, like it's the most natural thing in the world that I wasn't there. That they left me out. I swallow to clear away the lump in my throat. "Well, if you guys hadn't ditched me, I would have been here."

"Ditch you?" Jade's eyes flash. "Bay texted you asking what time we should pick you up and you never responded."

My head turns to a fishbowl. No, Bailey definitely hadn't texted me. I slide my phone out of my pocket and show Jade my conversation with Bailey.

Jade gnaws the inside of her cheek and looks up at me. "That's just what she told me. I mean, maybe her text to you didn't go through."

I doubt it. I don't say it, even though I know Jade is already thinking it. Neither of us wants to say out loud what's becoming painfully obvious.

Bailey lied to both of us last night.

. . .

We leave Sully's house with Cliff Grosso's phone number, extracted from a reluctant Val Diamond. I've never had a problem with Val, but there's all sorts of shit between her and Bailey that I never got the full story on. All I know is they used to be best friends, and Val dropped Bailey in eighth grade when Val made dance team and girls like Bridget Gibson started paying attention to her.

When we're shut back in Jade's father's truck, I lick my thumb and wipe away a salty patch on my boot. Jade is on her third attempt to call Cliff Grosso.

"Either his phone's dead or he's hitting the *eff you* button," she says. "Kace, I'm so goddamned scared right now."

"Let's just stick to the facts," I say. "We don't know that something bad happened to her."

Jade eyeballs me, as if to say, *Really?* Because the facts are this: Bailey lied about why she was leaving the party. Cliff Grosso followed her to her car. She somehow never made it home.

An idea springs into my head: "Why don't we just *go* to Cliff's?"

"Like his house?" Jade blinks. Her eyeliner has gone grimy, and there are gold curls falling from the bun atop her head. "Do you *want* to get shot?"

Cliff Grosso lives alone with his father, Jim, and even *I* know what happened five years ago when a bunch of high school kids tried to cross through the woods behind Jim Grosso's house. He took his hunting rifle off the mantel and shot one of the boys in the ass. I guess it was a miracle the kid could walk again, but nothing happened to Jim over the whole thing because apparently in Wisconsin you're allowed to defend your property.

"We can just drive by," I say. "To see if her car is there."

51

Jade picks at a remnant of plum lipstick flaking on her mouth. "Okay. But we're just driving by."

And then she makes a right, toward Pleasant Plains, up Cypress Hill, where Cliff Grosso lives.

We don't talk on the drive up the hill. Jade has to focus on the bad conditions outside, and I am trying to come up with an alternative to Bailey being dead in a ditch somewhere.

There is the smallest chance she went home with Cliff Grosso. She almost hooked up with him once, and it's been nearly a year. Cliff might not blame her anymore for the accident. What if Cliff got into a fight with Bridget last night and decided to hook up with Bailey as payback?

Bailey might just have gone along with it—either because she wanted to relish the chance to piss off Bridget or because she was bored.

The thing about growing up in a town like this is that some people catch boredom like a virus. Bailey has it bad— bad enough to get into that car with Cliff Grosso last spring after he'd been drinking. Bad enough to sneak out every weekend in search of something—what it is, I don't even think she knows.

I think of her idea to hold the séance in the barn, and a shiver runs through me. I roll up my window.

When we reach the top of Cypress Hill, Jade parks at the bottom of the Grossos' driveway. It's too risky to drive up it in this weather, even with four-wheel drive. I climb out of the car and shade my eyes; atop the hill, a row of cypress trees blocks my view of the house.

"We're trespassing," Jade says.

"We're already here," I say. "He's not going to shoot us for ringing his doorbell."

We're panting by the time we get to the top. The head of the driveway loops around the cabin. There are no cars in sight, but smoke puffs out of the cabin's chimney, white as gauze against the orange-pink sky.

Jade climbs up the shoveled path and I pull out my phone and follow her. I feel dramatic, but I type 911 into my keypad, just in case. A tawny cat, almost as pale as the snow, darts past us and around the back of the cabin. The sound makes my heart lurch.

Jade shields her eyes and peers through the garage window. "Cliff's Jeep is here."

In the woods off the side of the house, there's a low-pitched shriek. Snow owl, maybe. I shiver in place. Jade climbs up the porch and rings the doorbell.

No footsteps. Just silence. Jade rings the bell again, then jangles the knob. Locked.

The wind carries toward me, bringing a sour, metallic smell with it. I pull the front crook of my scarf over my mouth. Jade steps around to the side of the cabin. I follow. A high window—bathroom, probably—is cracked open. Jade calls "Hello" into it.

The ensuing silence ripples through me like a current.

Jade gets out her phone, peeling away her mitten to scroll down the screen.

"What are you doing?" I ask.

"Calling Bailey. If she's passed out inside, we'll at least hear her stupid-ass ringtone."

"But her car's not—"

Jade shushes me. It's so quiet on the hill I can hear the first ring leaking from Jade's phone clearly. But there's another noise, farther away.

"I hear something," I whisper.

Jade points to the house, brow furrowed. I shake my head. It's a tinkling sound, like a bell, coming from the woods adjacent to the Grossos' cabin.

I take off after the sound. *It's not Bailey's ringtone.* Still, it's a phone, and it's ringing, at the same moment Jade is calling Bailey's phone. The thought makes my toes curl.

I pick my way around the trees. Step over brown, soggy leaves weighed down with melting snow.

"Call it again," I say, just loud enough for Jade to hear me. She frowns, starts to come toward me.

The tinkling starts up again. Wind chimes. I turn—the sound is behind me—coming face to face with a barren balsam tree. A phone in a case with a peeling photo of the northern lights is on the ground, resting on dead pine needles.

We were with her when she bought it—Bailey is obsessed with the northern lights, and when she saw the phone case at the Pleasant Plains flea market last summer she freaked out, even though Jade told her it looked like shit quality.

Blood pounding in my ears. I reach for Bailey's phone. I'm prompted for a passcode. I type in Bailey's birthday—0427. Access granted. The phone is clinging to life with a five percent charge.

I peel off a mitten and open Bailey's call log. She has dozens of missed calls and texts. All from numbers with the Broken Falls area code, except mine. I open my text.

Where are you?? This isn't funny.

My number is displayed above the text, but not my name. My heart lurches. *Why would she delete me from her contacts?* I flip through to her phone book.

All of Bailey's contacts are gone. Deleted. My pulse picks up.

I thumb through to the next screen. Pull up the camera. No pictures. I know for a fact that Bailey had a minimum of four hundred pictures on here. Selfies. The three of us, making stupid faces. Something delicious she'd eaten.

I look up at Jade, who's staring down at the needles covering the forest floor, her face white. "Someone erased everything."

"Kacey. Do you see this?"

I follow her eyes to the ground, several feet away from us. The pine needles, shielded from the storm by tree cover, are stained red, and the snow around them has been flattened.

Something was dragged here.

Jade looks paralyzed. I follow the tunnel in the snow the body made—it had to have been a body—avoiding stepping too close to the streaks of blood. *Don't touch anything. Crime scene.*

"Kacey, stop."

I ignore Jade and leave her in the woods. That smell wafts my way again. The metallic smell. I cover my face, following the blood around the side of the house.

The snow in the Grossos' backyard comes up to my calves. I hold on to the side of the house for support. On the deck, the snow is stained with a spot of red. Even though my face is covered, I gag when I take a breath.

I climb the deck. On the far end of it, pushed against the side of the house, there's something boxy and covered with snow. I keep one hand pressing my scarf to my mouth, afraid I'll spray vomit everywhere if I smell any more of the blood.

A freezer. The top has been wiped clean of snow. Someone's been in it recently.

I squeeze my eyes shut, snow seeping through my mittens as I lift the top.

I force myself to look and let out the breath I've been holding. Inside is the body of a doe, a puncture wound at her neck. Her eyes are wide open in shock. Like she never saw the arrow from the crossbow coming.

"Kacey!"

I drop the lid of the freezer as Jade emerges from the side of the house. She looks from me to the blood and comes to a full stop.

"A deer," I say. "It's just a deer."

"I called her mom." Jade pulls her coat around her tight. "She says get the hell out of here. Bring it straight to the sheriff's station."

It. Bailey's phone, she means. Which I am still holding in my unmittened hand. "My fingerprints are all over it."

Jade's mouth hangs open. "What does that matter?" She plucks the phone from my hand, staring at me with a strange look on her face.

I feel frozen in place. Sick from the smell of the dead deer. I force myself forward, knowing full well Jade will leave me behind if she has to. I trudge through the snow, my heart hammering so fast now I'm afraid it'll shatter.

CHAPTER FIVE

I haven't been inside a police precinct since an officer from the Syracuse Police Department recognized me as a runaway outside a 7-Eleven last January.

I'd run away a month before that, right before Christmas, but I was a dumbass about it and got caught by Dawn, my social worker. She saw my split and infected lower lip. I lied and said my mom's latest boyfriend did it and got sent to New Beginnings Home for Girls while social services worked out the details of me going to live in Broken Falls, a town I'd never heard of, with Russ Markham, a man I'd never met.

My roommate at the group home, Missy, had been bounced around foster homes from the time she was two weeks old. I could tell why no one adopted her as soon as I met her and she snarled at me to stay out of her shit. In the weekly group therapy sessions, she bragged about going to juvie for the first time when she was twelve, for pulling a box cutter on a classmate.

My first and only night at New Beginnings, I woke up with Missy on top of me, her knees digging into my chest. Someone had most definitely been in her shit, and even though I insisted it wasn't me, she said she could go to jail for felony possession and if I breathed a word to anyone she would cut my throat in my sleep.

I had been planning to make a run for it, before the thing with Missy. I thought hiding out with friends in New York and sleeping on their basement floors was better than being shipped off to Bumblefuck McCow-Town to live with strangers who would take one look at me and decide I was trouble.

But I knew I wasn't smart enough or strong enough to make it on my own until I turned eighteen. I would wind up some-where like New Beginnings again, some girl breathing in my ear that she would cut my throat while I slept.

My social worker took the flight to Madison, Wisconsin, with me. It was the first time I'd ever been on a plane. Dawn was silent throughout takeoff.

"Don't you have your own family to deal with?" I asked. Dawn was flipping through one of those magazines selling things like patches of grass so your dog can pee in the house. I already knew from looking her up on Facebook that Dawn lived with her girlfriend, Renee, a woman who rescued retired greyhounds.

Dawn's jaw set. I prayed to God I hadn't accidentally said something horrible—like maybe she and her girlfriend wanted kids but couldn't have them. "I'm not leaving you."

It was all she said. My chest was tight as I went back to reading my book, one of the few possessions I'd managed not to lose over the years of constant shuffling back and forth between houses. A compilation of fairy tales that had belonged to my mom as a child, even though I don't know why anyone would give this shit to a kid.

They weren't the Disney type of fairy tales, where everyone gets a prince—they were the real stories, the ones that came first. The story where the sea witch cuts out the little mermaid's tongue and she decides to throw herself over the side of a boat rather than stab the sleeping prince. The version of Cinderella where she commands her birds to peck out her evil stepsisters' eyes.

I guess I got attached to the book because I knew all the other stories were bullshit, even as a kid. There was no prince waiting to rescue me—only a social worker with lipstick on her teeth and a crate full of files in the backseat of her car.

Girls are not princesses, and I know all the possible endings to the stories about the girls in peril. They're rarely happy.

The door to the sheriff's department is frozen. Jade punches down on the handle. The noise rattles my brain. *How is this happening? How is this for real?*

The woman behind the desk doesn't look up from her stapling. Like most of Broken Falls, the sheriff's office hasn't gotten an upgrade since the 1970s. The walls are wood panels. Plastic trees in planters, the rocks inside covered with a visible layer of dust.

"Excuse me." Jade taps on the counter. The woman keeps

stapling. Her dark hair is pulled back so tightly it looks like it hurts. Overplucked eyebrows to match. She's wearing too much foundation that she probably doesn't need. She's younger than I first thought. Early, maybe midtwenties. Her badge says *Ellie Knepper*.

Jade hisses in my ear: "Is she deaf or something?"

Ellie Knepper sets down her stapler. Looks up at Jade and smiles. "No, hon, I can hear just fine."

I set Bailey's phone on the counter, which is piss-yellow. It matches the tiled floor.

Ellie looks at the phone, then at me. "Whatcha got there?"

"It's our friend's," I say. "Her mom called you guys to report her missing."

Ellie looks at Bailey's phone again and says, "Huh."

I feel Jade's pulse ticking beside me, like a bomb. Jade is one of the smartest people I know, but she was not blessed with a Midwesterner's patience. Her face goes red, the snowflakes clinging to her curly bun dissolving. "Her name is Bailey Hammond."

"Ah, sounds familiar. Yes—I talked to her mom this morning."

"Then why aren't you guys looking for her?" Jade asks.

Ellie Knepper folds her hands together and rests her chin on them. "If we sent someone out for every teenager who didn't come home on time, we'd have no one for real emergencies. Ninety percent of the time, kids come home in twelve hours."

"She obviously didn't go off on her own, because she would have this with her." I point to Bailey's phone.

A curious look crosses Ellie Knepper's face. "Where'd you say you found that again?"

"Cliff Grosso's house," Jade says.

"Oh," Ellie says. "That's the boy who rear-ended me."

Jade and I share a look. Of course Ellie is the deputy that Cliff hit. You can count the number of law enforcement officers in this town on one hand.

Broken Falls doesn't need much more than that. The only reason anyone here calls 911 is because they hit a deer. The last person who went missing here was probably Josephine Leeds.

The thought makes a chill skate up my spine.

"So you know who Bailey is," Jade pleads. "She wouldn't just run off on her own. You have to send someone up there to look for her."

"Hon, I don't have anyone to send up there," Ellie says. "It's a Sunday afternoon and we've got people keeling over from heart attacks left and right on their driveways. There's already been a pileup on Main Street because of the storm. You need to get home before it gets worse."

"Are you seriously not hearing us?" Jade looks at me for affirmation. "Our friend has been missing all day."

Ellie sighs. "As soon as I have someone free, I'll send them up to the Grosso house, okay? But you two need to *get home*."

"What about her phone?" I say. "Someone deleted everything off it."

Ellie Knepper gives me another curious look. My deep mistrust of cops kicks in.

"I'll check it out," she says. "You girls be careful, okay?"

Jade is rooted to her spot. I've never seen her cry, but the expression on her face scares the shit out of me. Says that tears are imminent—that what's going on is very, very bad.

"Trust me," Ellie says. "The only thing you can do for her right now is go home."

The sheets of snow falling outside the sheriff's station are picking up speed. I've seen storms like this before; within the hour, the roads will be in whiteout condition. The fear of getting trapped, freezing to death in this truck needles my brain.

"We really should go home," I say. "If we get stuck in this—"

"I'm not going home." Jade stares straight ahead. "I have to go back to Bay's and talk to her mom. I'll take you home if you want, but I'm not listening to that woman inside. She didn't even take us seriously."

I gnaw the inside of my cheek. "Maybe she was just overworked."

"Call me crazy, but I think a missing person is more important than a couple dumbasses skidding off the road."

Missing person. "Jade," I say, trying to sound calm. "It's only been a few hours. Maybe she'll come home."

Maybe saying it out loud will make it happen. Maybe she left her phone at the party and someone stole it, wiped everything off it with the plan to pawn it off. They could have changed their mind, panicked, and dumped it.

My stupid theory collapses like a Jenga tower when Jade speaks: "She never lets that phone out of her sight." She's right: Bailey's phone is always within a few inches of her. Her pocket, the cup holder in her car. Under her pillow when she goes to sleep.

"What about her phone bill?" I ask. "Can't her mom go on-line and see who she talked to last night?"

"That was the first idea I had when she called me. She tried that but doesn't have the password to Bailey's plan, and the phone company wouldn't give it to her. Said they had to prove it was part of a police investigation, and obviously there is none."

Bailey's parents are old-fashioned; their cells are still bulky flip phones. After years of battling with them over the necessity of a phone with Internet access and unlimited texting, Bailey finally got permission to get her own plan once she could pay for it. And she did.

Jade's hands are shaking as she coughs into them. "The phone thing is really freaking me out. How it was *wiped* or something."

I hold my fingertips in front of the heating vents. The word pings in my head. *Wiped.*

Like someone was trying to erase every trace of Bailey.

Lauren must have heard Jade's truck pull up to the house; she's waiting for me in the foyer when I get home, her fleece blanket draped over her shoulders.

"Did you find Bailey?" Lauren asks.

I feel my brow furrowing. "How did you find out that's where I was?"

"You just disappeared without saying anything." Lauren frowns. "I heard you talking to Jade before you left. What's going on?"

I strip off my hat and scarf; my neck and ears ache from the cold. "I don't really know what's going on."

Lauren shrinks away, hurt by my dismissal.

"Just let me check something out first," I say. "Then we'll have hot chocolate."

I kick my boots off and bypass Lauren, heading straight for my room and my laptop. I pull up the local news's website, but there's nothing about Bailey. Just a thick red banner at the top splaying *STORM TRACKER!*

Moments later, there's a knock. Andrew opens my door and leans against the frame, frowning at me.

I swallow. "Did you hear what's happening?"

Andrew nods. "Were you at the party?"

"No. They were supposed to pick me up and take me, but they never texted." I don't know why I'm telling him this part. I don't know if it's important.

"Were *you* at the party?" I ask.

Andrew's eyebrows shoot up. "Me? Seriously?"

"I saw the tire tracks. You went somewhere."

"Yeah. To pick up my prescription this morning." He's watching me now, his eyelids heavy. "Where did you guys go Friday night?"

I crack a knuckle. "How did you know I went somewhere?"

I wait for him to correct me, say that he knows Lauren went, too, but he doesn't. "I heard a car door slam outside."

"It was nothing," I say. "We just drove around."

I can't tell if he believes me. But when he turns to leave my room, I think I see something like disappointment cross his face.

. . .

64

Ashley has already heard about Bailey by the time she gets home. Apparently it's all anyone at the café could talk about; Paula Schulz, the stripy-haired gossip Ashley hired this summer, heard from her kids.

Paula's oldest son, Axel, is Cliff Grosso's best friend. *Such a shame,* Paula tutted to me when the Grosso family came up in her daily gossip. *One mistake ruined that poor boy's future.*

I could hear it in her voice, what she was too cowardly to say: *That Bailey Hammond ruined that poor boy's future.*

I stay in my room until it gets dark, looking out the window into the storm. I think of Jim Grosso, shooting that boy in the ass just for stepping onto his property.

I've known men like him—ones who get violent when they think someone has taken something that belongs to them. I remember the boyfriend who came home from a bar with a swollen eye. He'd punched out another man just for looking at my mom.

I've only seen Jim Grosso in passing—mostly I wait in the car whenever Ashley goes into the butcher's after work to pick up a cut of meat for dinner. But Cliff's face is vivid in my mind. His mouth, always twisted with rage.

I don't want to think about what he's capable of when that rage comes to the surface. What he'd be capable of after a night of drinking and running into the girl he thinks took everything from him.

The hours tick by, and I stay in my room, watching the empty screen of my phone. I don't want to face the thousand questions from my family. I'm hiding again, like I did those first few weeks after I moved to Broken Falls.

For my first month or so in town, my strategy was to stay out of everyone's way. As if maybe the Markhams would forget I existed. I'd sneak into the kitchen when I knew no one would be there, like some burglar who'd broken in just to drink their expensive almond milk and eat handfuls of farm-fresh cherries.

Ashley was too busy with running Milk & Sugar and my dad was too absorbed in work-sleep-repeat to breathe down my neck much. Lauren was like a cat, skittering out of the room when she sensed me nearby.

Andrew, on the other hand, wasn't content to let things be. He'd decided that the right thing to do was be my friend, and he wouldn't stop until I relented. I was washing my cereal bowl one Saturday morning when he bounded into the kitchen, skidding to a stop when he saw me. "Hey. What are you doing?"

I felt my face redden. "Cleaning up after myself?"

"Want to go for a run?"

"Like, on purpose?" I never ran unless someone was chasing me or if New York State required it for me to pass gym class.

"Yeah, why not?" Andrew zipped his fleece up to his chin. "It's a beautiful day."

It's not like I had anything better to do. He'd scolded me when I came back into the kitchen wearing my Vans, telling me they were terrible for my feet. I had to borrow Ashley's running shoes—we're both a size eight.

I felt his eyes on the scribbles alongside my shoes. *I was born with the devil in me.* Heat went to my cheeks; it was a stupid lyric from some band I was obsessed with in ninth grade. I would loop the song on those nights where music was my only escape from my mom and the boyfriends and the awful things coming out of their mouths.

"So you like running?" I asked while I was lacing up Ashley's *tennis shoes,* as Andrew called them. Desperate to change the subject from my ratty, creepy Vans.

"It's okay. I feel like I have to do it."

"Why?" If he was going to say to stay skinny, I was going to punch him in the nuts. I had about ten pounds on him despite being six inches shorter.

"I'm going out for cross-country in the fall," he said. "I used to play soccer and I'm afraid colleges will think I'm getting lazy."

"Why did you stop playing soccer?"

"I got kicked off the team for missing too much practice."

I couldn't fathom Andrew being kicked off anything; he was so type A, so hyper-focused on success. Before I could ask why he missed so much practice, he nodded to my feet. "Those fit okay?"

"Yeah. Sure."

I followed Andrew as he made a right outside the house. I realized we were heading west and would pass Sparrow Kill.

I saved my breath to say something once we approached. The barn wasn't visible from the road, but the hill was still covered in snow at the top.

"Do you believe the Red Woman stories?" I asked Andrew.

Andrew hadn't even broken a sweat; I realized he was running under his usual pace for my benefit. "I mean, everyone knows the massacre was real. But I don't think there's anything, like, supernatural going on."

"But the Red Woman," I said. "For her just to disappear."

"People disappear all the time." Andrew shrugged. "Most of the time, they're dead. Sad but true."

For some reason, the thought put a deep sadness in my gut. A sense of loss I couldn't describe.

"What if it's not always true?" I said, the cold air cutting through my lungs.

Andrew turned to look at me. "What do you mean?"

"Hold up." I stopped by a wooden rail guarding the Strausses' property. I sucked in air, greedily, one hand over my heart. Andrew's chest rose and fell evenly.

"I mean, maybe it's crazy to think the Red Woman got away and lived happily ever after," I said, when I got my breath back. "But all those other people who go missing . . . it's not like the whole world looks for every person who disappears."

I'd never felt stupider in my life. But I went on: "I don't know, maybe the world sometimes just swallows people up. Maybe people just *get away*."

"I hadn't thought of it like that." Andrew leaned against the guard posts. I pulled at a blade of grass near my sneaker.

"Can I go up there?" I asked.

"The barn? Why would you want to?"

"Curiosity."

"It's pretty disappointing during the day. It's just a barn. No evil spirits lurking." He wiggled his eyebrows and made his voice deep. "Those only come out at night."

But I was already leaving him behind. The sun was coming

up over the hill, bathing everything in gold. My calves ached until I reached the top and collapsed on a stump, chest heaving.

I thought of what had happened up here—the brutality of what Hugh Leeds had done to his family, and I felt sick. I thought of the things I had almost done to my own mother.

A chill passed through me as I imagined Josephine Leeds, trapped in the barn. Her screams as she heard the gunshots from inside the house. That was when I decided that all the ghost stories got it wrong: evil isn't a spirit or a monster or a ghost. It lives inside regular people, and it doesn't know the difference between night and day.

CHAPTER SIX

The shrill sound of the house phone invades my sleep. I turn over and see the time on my cable box—four-thirty a.m.—and snap to attention. There's only one acceptable reason for someone to be calling this early, and that reason is death.

My heart hammers. *Bailey. They found her. Or she's home.*

The landline stops ringing; I swing my legs over the side of the bed and pat my nightstand down, searching for my phone in the dark. The screen lights up, but there are no calls or texts from Jade. If they found Bailey dead, Jade would know, and she would tell me—

I flip on my bedside lamp and scan the carpet for my slippers, slip them on, then fly out of bed and throw my door open.

Ashley is standing outside my door, one hand poised to knock. The other is holding the house phone. Her eyes are red.

I swallow. "Was that about Bailey?"

"Oh hon, no. I'm sorry. But a bit of good news." She sits on the edge of my bed. "There was a pipe burst at the high school. You don't have to go to school today. Probably going to take the rest of the week to fix it, actually."

I don't know if she expects that to make me feel better. Still, my mind is on Bailey and the fact that she hasn't come home.

"Did you hear anything from Mrs. Hammond?" I kick off my slippers and crawl back into the cocoon I made for myself with my comforter and sheets, pulling them taut over my body. It's so cold.

"The Diamonds printed thousands of flyers with Bailey's picture in their shop last night. Free of charge," Ashley says. "Val has been getting the word out online to get volunteers to help hang them everywhere."

"I'll bet Jade is having a stroke over that. Bailey and Val don't even talk anymore."

Ashley watches me. Opens her mouth, and closes it.

"What?" I ask.

"I just . . . remember being a teenage girl. All the secrets. Things I told my friends that I would never, ever tell my folks."

I'm quiet, because I realize what she's getting at. She thinks I'm hiding something. Something Bailey might have told me that could help find her.

"Are you sure Bailey didn't say anything to you?"

A flicker of a memory lights up my brain. We'd worked to-gether on the local history project: "Design and budget a road trip of Wisconsin's landmarks!" We were pricing out gas and tolls when Bailey dropped her pen and said, *Sometimes I wish I could just get on the freeway and fucking drive.*

But I don't tell Ashley that. It might give her hope that Bailey is okay. And hope is the most dangerous thing you can give someone.

I brush my teeth and park myself in front of the living room TV. The local news channel is dominated by the storm; however, a search for her name on my phone reveals that Cathy and Ed Hammond have managed to get Bailey's picture onto the website for the *Broken Falls Register*.

Eighteen-year-old girl missing from Broken Falls since late Saturday night

The picture Ed and Cathy chose is an odd one. Instead of one of her million selfies or her school photo, they picked the one of Bailey lounging in an Adirondack chair in our backyard. Taken at the birthday barbecue we held for Lauren.

Bailey's rosebud mouth forms a smile, teeth hidden. She hates her bottom row of teeth. Bailey thinks she's hideous, a troll, but I've always wished I looked more like her. Creamy skin, like she slathers it with milk and honey. A smattering of gold freckles on her nose to match her strawberry-blond hair. There's just something naturally wholesome about her looks.

I am the opposite. People stare at me and I feel like I did something wrong. No matter how I style my hair or what I wear, I seem like the type of girl who'd get caught shoplifting eyeliner at Walmart.

I think of the conversation I had with Andrew that day on

Sparrow Hill: *It's not like the whole world looks for every person who disappears.*

A surprising thought roots in my brain: *At least if Bailey's really gone, she's the type of girl the whole world will look for.*

By early afternoon, all the roads are plowed, the downed lines from the storm intact, partially thanks to Jade's dad, who worked overtime to get them up again.

Jade and I are in the backseat of my stepbrother's Mazda. I let Tyrell, Andrew's best friend, sit up front with him; we're going to Pleasant Plains to hang Bailey's *Missing* posters. A box full of them is wedged between Jade and me, and the reason for Jade's scowl—*DIAMOND'S PRINTING CO.*—is stamped on the side.

When we picked up the posters from the Diamonds' printing shop, Val's mother said she and Bridget were already organizing a candlelight vigil. Jade's eyes practically crossed.

"They just want to help," I say to Jade now.

"Wolves in sheep's clothing, Kace." Jade's head pricks up, like a dog that's heard a whistle. She smacks the back of Tyrell's headrest. "What did you just say to him?"

Tyrell's shoulders hike up. He runs a hand over his dark, smooth head, but he doesn't turn around. "Nothing."

"Bullshit. If you can say it to him, you can say it to us."

Tyrell sighs and turns so he's facing us. "People are saying that Bay may have killed herself."

I see Andrew's knuckles go white around the steering wheel. I'm the only one in this car who knows that he didn't really miss a week of school and soccer practice his sophomore year because he had strep throat; he was hospitalized because he was so depressed he couldn't get out of bed.

"Who's saying that?" I demand. "That's a shitty rumor to start."

"I don't know. People," Tyrell says.

Jade's eyes flash. No doubt Tyrell means Val and Bridget. "Well, *people* don't know shit and should shut their stupid mouths. Bay wasn't depressed."

We spend the rest of the ride to Pleasant Plains in silence. Andrew parks in a municipal lot. As we climb out and he locks the car, I catch him cracking his knuckles. His nervous tic.

I put a hand on his shoulder and squeeze. Tyrell and Jade are on the other side of the car, out of earshot. "Are you okay?"

"Yeah." Andrew shrugs me off. "Why wouldn't I be?"

Andrew's dismissal stings; is he really that upset by the rumor about Bailey, or is he pissed at me for last night, for not telling him where we really went Friday?

"It might be faster if we split up," Tyrell says.

"Sure," I say, a lump sitting in my throat. "Divide and conquer."

Tyrell suggests he and Andrew take the businesses west of the main intersection while Jade and I move east. My morning coffee sloshes like acid in my stomach as Jade and I break off from the guys and wait to cross the street.

Bailey's dad reminded us to always ask before we hang a poster in the window of a business. People from Pleasant Plains, in my experience, have not earned their name. They're rougher than the people from Broken Falls, more business-oriented. More likely to kick you out of their sports bar for being rowdy.

In a few hours, when it gets dark, Main Street will be bustling with families out for dinner, hurrying past the homeless man stationed outside the dollar store. Twentysomethings who had too many margaritas at Tex Mex, looking for a fight. It's the type of town people from Broken Falls call "sketchy."

Jade and I came here together alone, once, to go to the art supply shop our teacher, Mr. White, was always talking about. *You will die and go to heaven when you step through the door,* he'd warned us. Jade and I decided to go one day over the summer when Bailey was working. Jade spent half an hour in the paint aisle while I looked at the colored pencils and a rainbow spectrum of polymer clays, indeed feeling like I'd found heaven.

When Bailey discovered we went somewhere without her, she didn't text either of us for two days. Then, out of nowhere, she was bugging us to go to the flea market, as if nothing had ever happened.

Walking through the doors of the art supply shop now doesn't feel very heavenly. The owner does not appear interested in Bailey or our situation, and shrugs when we ask if we can hang her poster in the vestibule. When we step back outside, a neon sign across the street catches my attention. *PSYCHIC READINGS INSIDE.* The store is called Enchantment Crystals and it's next to a head shop.

"Hey." I nod toward the store. "Look."

"No," Jade says. "There are some sketchy-ass people in there."

"Well, aren't we supposed to make sure everyone sees her picture?"

Jade shifts. Pulls her scarf up around her mouth. I can only see her eyes, but she mumbles something inaudible, which I take to be a concession.

We cross the street when it's safe. When I open the door to the small shop, the smell of incense brings water to my eyes. I want to cover my nose so I don't start sneezing, but I'm afraid of offending the big-haired woman behind the counter whose gaze is locked on us.

"Good morning, ladies," she says. "Are you shopping for yourselves, or for a friend?"

Jade's eyes narrow at the jangly metal bracelets on the woman's arm—rows of copper, bronze, and silver, almost up to her elbows. I step forward, Bailey's poster in my fist.

"Our friend is missing," I say. "Can we hang this somewhere?"

The woman slides the poster from my hand. Peers at Bailey's face. "Pretty girl."

They all are, I think. I stomp the thought down, not entirely sure where it came from. Jade coughs into her shoulder. Says in her gravelly voice: "Can we hang it or not?"

The woman hands the poster back to me. "Of course. Maybe one in the window and one on the board?"

She gestures to a bulletin board by the door we came in. It's papered with flyers in shades of neon, advertising Reiki sessions and tantric healing. As I pin Bailey's poster among them, one catches my eye. MEDIUM FOR HIRE—COMMUNICATE WITH THE DEAD VIA A PROFESSIONAL SPIRITUALIST. WILL COME TO YOUR HOUSE!

I run my finger over the strips with a phone number stamped on them.

"I also offer similar services." The woman is behind me. "You know, I could read cards for your friend. The missing one. It could provide some insight to her situation."

Jade snorts. "You've got to be kidding."

The woman rounds on Jade. Gives her a sad smile. "You miss her so much. But you have to stop beating yourself up."

Jade scowls, but there's the slightest flash of something in her eyes. Curiosity, maybe. "What are you talking about?"

"You think that if you were with her the other night, she wouldn't have disappeared." The woman takes a step toward Jade. "You didn't want to be split up from her."

I stare at Jade, who shakes her head. "You read the news. They're saying Bailey left the party alone."

I put a hand on Jade's arm, ready to herd her out the front door. She pulls away from me as bony fingers clasp my shoulder.

The woman is looking at me. "Your aura is brown."

"Okay," I say, stupidly.

The woman is still clutching my shoulder. "You know what happened to her. Deep in your soul, you know the answer."

I pry myself away and muster up my best dirty look. "What are you talking about?"

Jade yanks me and drags me out the door. Her eyes demand answers. "What the hell was that about?"

I shake my head. My tongue has gone numb. "I don't know. I honestly don't know."

When Jade's head is turned, I look back at Enchanted Crystals. Through the window, I see the woman, still standing at the bulletin board, frowning at the poster with Bailey's picture.

Jade and I don't say anything to Andrew or Tyrell about the

woman in the spiritualist shop. But when we get back to the car, Jade leans against the side. She's crying silently.

I start toward her. "Hey—"

Jade shakes her head. "Just give me a minute, okay?"

I nod and stay back, breathing warmth into my hands. Does Jade really blame herself? If Bailey insisted on leaving the party alone, Jade shouldn't feel guilty—

—or maybe it's not guilt. Maybe it's the fact that our best friend is *gone,* possibly not coming back. Jade is crying because she's sad, and that's what normal people do when they're sad.

I put a hand to my cold, dry cheek. *What is wrong with me? What kind of person doesn't cry when their friend goes missing?*

There is something broken inside me. That creepy woman in the store—those types of scam artists are really good at reading people, right? That's why she made that comment, about my aura and my knowing what really happened to Bailey. She could see the ugly thing that lives in me, the thing that only makes me care about myself and my own survival. I wonder if Jade sees it too.

What kind of girl doesn't cry when their friend goes missing?

Junior Year
April

I have a new friend! She's very weird, but I'll get to that part.

First let's take a moment to appreciate how strange that is, *making a friend junior year*. Especially a friend who's a girl. Girls are so weird. They have their cliques and their squads and trying to break in once they're set will only get you laughed at or pitied.

It's really just been Jade and me since eighth grade, since Val dropped me once she made dance team. And no, I'm not over it. You don't get it: Val and I *showered* together when we were little. We spent hours in my basement playing house; I was the father, banging away at Wonder Brother's play work bench with a plastic hammer while Val cradled her Just Born baby doll, her free hand smoothing her stomach, swollen with a pillow under her shirt.

And then when she had the chance to become popular, I was Val's six pieces of silver. I spent so many nights crying and listening to Dad's old sixties folk albums, and then years after that wondering what I did wrong to deserve to be dropped by my best friend in such a callous way. I'll never get an answer, I guess. Sometimes I imagine cornering her, grabbing her by the shoulders, and shaking her, *demanding* one. Why? Why wasn't I good enough for you?

Thank God for Jade moving to Broken Falls, or I would have been absorbed into whatever social group would take me. And being a loser or a freak is worse than being Nothing. People might think Jade and I are aloof because it's always just the two of us, like we think we're too good for Broken Falls, but really, they're the ones who decided we're Nothing. We're fun at parties (if we get invited) and they laugh at our jokes in class (when we crack them), but otherwise, we don't exist.

And that's fine: we're BaileyAndJade. JadeAndBailey. Always one. Just the way we like it.

But now there are three of us. Bailey and Jade and Kacey.

Jade and I've been hanging out with her quite a bit now that I'm not grounded for what happened with Cliff anymore; my parents let me out of my one-month sentence early for being a Very Good Girl. How I convinced them I am a Very Good Girl: come home after school and my shift at Friendly Drugs, do my homework, then numb my mind with reality television until I pass out. In other words, become my dad.

So yesterday at lunch, Kacey kept twirling the faded purple end of her braid over her finger. Jade paused from slurping her iced tea and pointed. "I can fix that for you."

Kacey stopped twirling. Studied the end of her hair as if it weren't attached to her.

"The drugstore sells that shade," Jade said. "I can re-dye it for you. Or not. It's whatever."

"No . . ." Kacey resumed twirling. "It's just that I kind of want it gone."

"Jade cuts my hair," I piped up. "She could just trim the bottom off, right?"

I looked at Jade, who just shrugged. Kacey kept fiddling with her braid, nervous, as if I'd suggested an appendectomy and not a haircut.

But she was waiting by my car after school, a *let's do this* look on her face. We went to Jade's; freshman year Jade gave me bangs in my bathroom and my mom bitched for weeks about finding my hair under the sink, so I knew better than to do it at my house.

Once we were nestled in Jade's bathroom, Kacey started looping the tail of her braid over her finger again. Jade grabbed it from her gently. "I'll only take the purple off. It's, like, two inches."

"Okay." Kacey sat on the toilet, knees up to her chest, while Jade produced a pair of silver scissors from beneath the sink. I sat in the corner of the bathroom, shifting around the loose tiles at my feet like they were puzzle pieces. Jade's dad had started the renovation project months ago and lost steam, like the pothead he is. He and Jade would eat nothing but Oreos and instant noodles if she didn't do the grocery shopping.

Kacey flinched as the shears closed around her hair. Snip, snip. Purple locks fell to the floor like a My Little Pony getting a hack job. Jade patted Kacey's back. "Mirror."

Kacey got up and stared at herself, water spots on the mirror forming a circle around her face. She hesitated: "Can you cut more? I want it all gone."

I'd only ever seen Jade do trims, so I didn't want to be around for the inevitable train wreck. "I'm gonna grab a Diet Coke," I said. "You guys want one?"

Jade nodded, her tongue poking out between her lips as she rearranged Kacey's hair.

I lingered in the kitchen for a bit, lamenting the empty cabinets—it meant Jade was probably eating all her meals at the taqueria on her lunch and dinner breaks. I'd have to sneak some ramen and mac and cheese into the cabinets. I grabbed three Diet Cokes from the fridge and arranged them in my arms pyramid-style.

That was when I noticed Kacey's bag, just sitting there on the kitchen table, next to mine. I shot a glance down the hall; Jade and Kacey were quiet.

I eyed the notebook sticking out of the bag, the one she was always sketching in during history. I set the cans down and ran a finger along the exposed spine. Without removing it from the bag, I lifted the front cover.

Inside was an ink drawing on the cardboard. Intricate calligraphy. I had to turn the book slightly to make out the words: *I WAS BORN WITH THE DEVIL IN ME*

Jade's voice rang out: "Bay! I'm thirsty!"

A chill ran through me. I shut the cover and arranged the notebook exactly as it was before I touched it. The words rang in my head as I padded down the hall. *I was born with the devil in me.*

What the fuck?

"So what do you think?" Jade was beaming in the bathroom doorway, spinning Kacey around like a rag doll on display. Kacey came to a halt, a blush creeping into her cheeks. Jade had given her a shaggy bob, the now freshly blond ends of her hair grazing her chin at a jaunty angle.

"You look hot," I said.

Kacey smiled, no teeth, and tugged the ends of her hair along her jaw. She looked innocent. She looked *transformed* from the girl who walked into history last month. The girl with the dirty hair with purple tips and the stud in her nose.

Later, when I got home, I Googled that quote: *I WAS BORN WITH THE DEVIL IN ME.* You know who said it? H. H. Holmes. As in, the serial killer.

Kacey's face took shape in my mind as I tried to sleep. I thought of the Markhams, asleep in their beds, while Kacey stayed awake, inking over those disturbing words in the front cover of her notebook.

What are you hiding, Kacey Young? And who are you trying to convince everyone you are?

CHAPTER SEVEN

I have two new emails when we get home from Pleasant Plains: one is from the school, informing us of "two separate yet unrelated incidents in the Broken Falls community." The first: the burst pipe in the high school from the blizzard, and an assurance that crews are working around the clock to get the building "up and operational so school can resume as normal." The second issue is Bailey.

We are deeply concerned by the situation regarding one of our seniors. When normal school days resume, our guidance counselors will be available to students to help process any difficult emotions. Anyone with information regarding Bailey Hammond's whereabouts is encouraged to call the Broken Falls Sheriff's Department. This is a very serious matter and all emails with tips sent to this address will be forwarded to the police.

I haven't even gotten the chance to strip my sweaty socks off when the doorbell rings.

"I'll get it," I shout.

The deputy from yesterday—Ellie Knepper—is standing on the front steps. I unhitch the lock latch and open the door.

"Hi there. Is your mom home?" She removes her gloves and breathes into her bare hands.

"Stepmom," I say, but Ashley is already in the foyer.

"Good afternoon, ma'am. I'm Deputy Ellie Knepper."

Ashley steps forward, tentative, and shakes Ellie's hand. "Ashley Markham."

"Oh, I know. I see you around the café when I come in for my cinnamon latte fix."

Ashley puts two fingers to the pendant on her neck. A small smile. "Really? Most of the force is loyal to Pete's Dinette."

"Yup. Personally, I find Pete's food so greasy it'll give you an ulcer. Could I trouble you for a cup of coffee now, actually?" Ellie shifts, looking uncomfortable. Like asking for a cup of coffee is part of a script.

It makes me dread what the next scene is going to be.

Ashley smiles. "Sure. I have regular and dark roast," she says.

"Dark sounds great." Ellie breathes into her hands again and invites herself into the dining room. I guess I am supposed to follow.

Ellie plops onto one of the chairs and unzips her parka while Ashley fusses around in the kitchen. I sit across from Ellie, happy she's here but irritated it took her so long. "So you're taking this seriously now?" I press. "It's already been almost forty-eight hours."

Ellie's mouth forms a tight, chastised smile. I wonder if this is her punishment for dismissing Jade and me yesterday: trekking out in the cold to interview a bunch of high school brats.

From the kitchen, I hear the single-cup coffeemaker gurgle and spit into a mug. Officer Knepper gets out a small yellow legal pad and uncaps a pen.

Ashley comes up behind me and nudges me, hands me a steaming mug of coffee. I hand it to Ellie, who holds it up to her nose. Inhales and smiles like I've given her liquid gold. "Oh. This is great."

"Do you have people out there looking for Bailey?" I blurt. I balance my heels on the rung of the stool and hug my arms around my middle. "I mean, if you're here, who's supposed to find her?"

"The snow's making it tough to do a ground search." Ellie taps her pen against the legal pad. "But don't worry. We're doing everything we can to find Bailey."

Ashley sets a carton of milk and a bottle of vanilla creamer in front of Ellie. "I didn't know which you'd like."

"Milk is fine. Do you know what I could really use, though?" Ellie gives Ashley a placating smile. "A recent yearbook from Broken Falls High."

Ashley's forehead forms a V. "I think my son has his upstairs. I'll go get it."

"That would be so helpful. I've been searching for one all day."

I study the curve of Ellie's lips around the rim of her mug as Ashley hurries out of the kitchen. What are the chances she's been looking for a yearbook all day and couldn't find a single one?

"What do you need a yearbook for?" I ask once Ashley's out of earshot.

Ellie sets her mug down and huddles it with both hands. "There are a lot of names being thrown around right now. I'm better with faces."

She's probing *my* face right now, searching my eyes with her beady brown ones. "So you've been friends with Bailey since you moved here?"

I nod. "Pretty much, yeah."

"How does she get along with her family?"

"Fine, I guess. What do you care about her family? Shouldn't you be asking about Cliff Grosso?"

Ellie taps her pen to her chin. "Bear with me. I've got to cover all the bases. Even the boring ones. How about Bailey and her parents?"

"They're fine, I guess."

"What about her mom, in particular?"

"What do you mean?" I pick at the hangnail cornering my thumb. Realize that's gross. Stop.

"Did they get along?" Ellie asks. "When I was your age, my mom and I used to fight like cats and dogs."

For as long as I've known her, Bailey liked to bitch about her mom—not like how it is with me and my mom, which would be like saying Israel and Palestine don't "get along"—but she and Cathy argue about curfew, and Bailey's B average in school. Typical teenage girl stuff.

I shrug. "They argue every now and then, I guess."

"What about?"

"Usual stuff. Stupid mother-daughter stuff."

"And her older brother?"

"Is at college." I have to take a deep breath. Stop myself from reaching across the table and shaking Ellie by her collar. "Again, why are you focusing on her family when she was last seen with a guy who hated her?"

Knepper looks at me for a long beat. Blinks those short, dark lashes. "So that's why you and Jade Becker went to the Grossos' house, right? Whose idea was that?"

"We both decided, I guess. Did you see the picture on Kevin Sullivan's phone? It was definitely Cliff. *That's* why we went there—he was the last person who saw her before she left."

Ellie blows on her coffee. "We're working on interviewing everyone who was at the party. Big task. Apparently it was quite the rager."

She must sense my eyes flicking downward. "You weren't at the party, huh?"

I shake my head.

"Why not?"

For some reason, I don't want to see Ellie Knepper feeling sorry for me. Or maybe I'm just too embarrassed to admit it: *My friends ditched me.* "I was tired from work. And I heard about the storm—I don't know, I just didn't feel like going out."

"Responsible kid."

I can't tell if Ellie is being sarcastic. She seems too pure, too incapable of sarcasm. Guilt digs at my ribs. I *should* have been at that party.

"What about Cliff Grosso?" I blurt. "How can he explain her phone being on his property?"

Ellie taps her pen against her pad. "I can't comment on that.

It's an active investigation." In other words, she's not telling me shit about Cliff. "When exactly was the last time you spoke to Bailey?" she asks.

"She stopped by the café Saturday before she went to work."

"Did she seem upset? Agitated?"

I've become mute. I can't tell Knepper that Bailey was probably pissed at me without telling her why: that we were trespassing, and for the stupidest reason ever—to perform a séance in the local haunted barn. And while we were at it we were almost crushed by the roof. Oh, and that my little sister tagged along and almost got us caught with her screaming.

If Ellie knows that Lauren was with us, she might tell Ashley and my dad. They'll know that *I'm* the reason my sister isn't eating or sleeping.

My throat feels tight. "Maybe she was a little weird. I don't know. Honestly, I don't know."

Knepper leans closer to me. "I know you're worried, but anything you can tell us, anything Bailey said or did that didn't feel right, it might help."

A flicker of a memory—lounging in the passenger seat of Bailey's car with a passion-tea lemonade, parked outside the Starbucks in Pleasant Plains, after we'd finished our road trip project last year.

I would just get on the highway and go.

"She hated it here," I say. "She told me if she could, she'd just leave."

Ellie Knepper stares at me. "Okay. That's helpful."

I feel like there's a bomb timer ticking down to go off in my brain. I must be staring, because Knepper writes it down on her pad. "I won't keep you much longer. But I have to ask . . . the three of you. Sounds like from everyone we talked to, you're inseparable."

I swallow. "Yeah. We do everything together."

"Did you girls ever fight?" Ellie bats those lashes. I wonder if it's her nervous tic. My toes clench.

"No," I say. "Never. We weren't like that."

Ellie nods, her hand on the mug of coffee she's taken a total of two sips from. "Well, you've been very helpful, Kacey. I'll be in touch."

"Wait." I think of Ashley upstairs, rooting around in Andrew's room for his yearbook. "The yearbook."

Ellie looks at me curiously. "Oh, that's okay. Next time we talk."

She stands up and she's already to the front door when I glance at her coffee, barely touched, and I feel sick. I feel tricked. She just wanted Ashley out of the way so she could talk to me alone.

Did you girls ever fight?

I hadn't lied, exactly. The answer is just too complicated for Ellie Knepper to understand.

Bailey could be moody, prone to snap at Jade and me if she was hungry or bored. Her cruelty was always like a spanking, though; she had a way of making me feel like she was doing it for my own good. *Quit being such a baby. People are gonna think you're uptight.*

She did get mad at me once. It was the night of Lauren's dance recital at Sun Prairie High School. Andrew, Ashley, and

I had met her backstage with a bouquet of rainbow carnations. Lauren's eyes—wide and doll-like from false eyelashes—flicked between the three of us. "Where's Daddy?"

The lilt to her voice said she'd noticed the empty seat in our row during her first dance number.

"He got stuck at work. He's coming to both shows tomorrow." Ashley planted a kiss on her forehead; Lauren wiggled away, her eyes on the group of girls to our right. I recognized Keelie March. Caught the words *diner* and *get a ride from Emma*.

"Hey, you did awesome, Monkey," Andrew said, his voice loud enough to drown out Keelie and her peons. They'd wanted Lauren to hear about their plans, the ones she was excluded from. I stuck my hands in the pockets of my cardigan, afraid of how I wanted to walk over and use them to shake Emma Michaels. *Don't you see they're using you?*

Lauren peeled the stick-on rhinestone from the corner of her eye, one of the ones I'd helped her apply backstage during intermission. They were a part of her tap costume: a navy velour sailor's outfit and matching hat that she was mortified of because a boy she liked would be in the audience, the younger brother of one of the senior girls.

"Can we please just get out of here?" she'd said, and by the time we'd made it to the car she was crying silently.

Andrew cleared his throat. "I don't know about you guys, but I'm starving."

He looked over at me. "I could go for ice cream," I said, playing along.

"You three go." Ashley's mouth formed a sad little smile, like she understood that being seen getting ice cream with her mom after the recital was worse than being left out of the diner trip. "I'm exhausted."

Once we were inside Culver's, sundaes ordered, Lauren had brightened a bit. She told us how one of the kindergartners from the ballet class she cotaught had wet her tutu right before her dance number, even though Lauren had asked them three times whether anyone had to go pee before going onstage.

We were laughing so hard I didn't notice that Bailey and Jade were standing at the edge of our table until Andrew said, "Hey, what are you guys doing here?"

Bailey smirked at me and said low enough that only I could hear: "Way to text us back."

I patted my cardigan pocket, where I'd forgotten I'd tucked my phone. "My phone was on silent."

The morning came rushing back to me: Bailey, stopping in for her egg whites and latte, asking me what I was doing tonight. When I'd told her I had to go to Lauren's recital, she said, *So text us after.*

"So what are you guys doing?" I asked, hoping my panic hadn't crept into my voice. *It's not a big deal; you didn't* say *you would hang out with them.*

"Just chilling," Bailey said. "We got hungry."

"I'm getting onion rings," Jade said. "You guys want anything?"

Andrew swirled his spoon through the syrup on his sundae. "Nah, we're good."

Bailey gave me a little wave over her shoulder as she followed Jade to the counter. Andrew's voice was low in my ear: "What was that about?"

"I don't know." I didn't say what was niggling at me: had they followed us here?

Neither of them brought that night up ever again, but now, I can feel the way Bailey looked at me like a pit in my stomach. The same way Ellie Knepper looked at me when I told her that I never fought with my friends.

It feels like I'd failed a test I hadn't even known about.

I call Jade as soon as I'm closed in my room. She picks up on the first ring. "Have you heard anything?"

"No. But that cop—the woman from yesterday—she just left my house." I glance out my window at the driveway, watching snow fall on the rectangle of pavement where Ellie Knepper had parked her cruiser.

"I talked to her today too." Jade's voice is ragged. "They're supposed to make a statement on the news about it tonight. Announce she's officially a missing person and tell people there's gonna be a vigil. Did you hear about Cliff?"

My stomach drops to my toes. "No. What happened?"

"Apparently someone heard him and Bridget get into a huge fight at Sully's party. Bridge confronted him after someone saw Cliff outside talking to Bailey by her car." Jade's voice goes warbly. "Cliff left the party alone, all pissed off."

My head is cottony. I think of the deer blood in Cliff's backyard. In Cliff's mind, Bailey had cost him his scholarship, and now probably his girlfriend too. Could he really have hated Bailey enough to get rid of her, though?

"I hate myself so much," Jade whispers. "I was upstairs

93

smoking a stupid joint while all of this was going down. If I hadn't listened to her, made sure she got home okay—"

"There's *no way* you could have known." I think of Ellie Knepper's reluctance to talk about Cliff. The way she seemed to be grasping at something bigger. I pull at a loose thread of yarn in the blanket draped over my bed. "Hey—did you tell the cop what we did Friday night?"

"No. She didn't ask."

I glance at my bedroom door. "I need you to do something," I whisper. "If the police ask about the barn, don't say Lauren was there with us. If Ashley knew, she'd flip out."

"Hold up." There's rustling on Jade's end, then the sound of a door closing. "Why would they ask about what we did Friday night?"

"I don't know, if they're trying to retrace all of Bailey's movements—Jade, promise me. It's one thing if I snuck out, but if I brought my sister—"

"Jeez, okay, slow down. So we just don't say we were ever there at all. I mean, technically we were trespassing, and we could get in trouble for the roof. If they ask what we did Friday night, we just say we drove around like we always do."

A slick of sweat comes to my hands. Lying to Ashley is one thing, but lying to the police is another. It's a dangerous road to go down.

"Hey, I gotta go," Jade says darkly before I can answer. "Bay is about to make her TV debut."

CHAPTER EIGHT

Everyone has seen the news.

Bailey's social media pages are flooded with comments.

Please come home!!

Praying for you . . .

Jade and I are tagged in some of them. *Thinking of you guys. Stay strong!* Messages of support, from the dance team girls to underclassmen I don't even know.

Bailey has suddenly become the most popular person in school.

I'm in bed, compulsively refreshing the news story about her disappearance on my phone. The TV spot was useless—just a flash of Bailey's school photo, then a selfie pulled from her profile picture. A plea for anyone with information to call a special tip line the sheriff's office has set up.

The news story doesn't tell me anything I don't know. *Police are still searching for Bailey Hammond's car, a blue Honda Civic. She was last seen wearing a gray scoop-neck sweater over black leggings. The sheriff's office is treating her disappearance as suspicious.*

There's no mention of Bailey's phone, or that someone wiped everything off it.

The cable box below the TV in my room says it's midnight. There are footsteps outside my door. My heart climbs into my throat; Lauren's voice saying my name in that tiny voice of hers stops me from leaping out of my skin.

"Come in," I say, quietly. Lauren is silent as she crawls into my bed.

"You can't sleep?" I ask.

She shakes her head.

"Why can't you sleep, Monkey?" It's such a pointless thing to ask. Obviously it's because of what's going on with Bailey, or because we traumatized her in the barn. She pulls the sleeves of her pajama shirt down over her nails, which she's bitten ragged and bloody. I pull her sideways into a hug.

Lauren looks up at me from under her dark lashes. "Chloe said she saw something."

Chloe Strauss lives on the farm at the end of the road, on the other side of Sparrow Hill. She's a year older than Lauren; Ashley told me the two of them played when they were little— play dates that always ended with Lauren in tears.

Once Emma and Lauren's other friends stopped coming over, Chloe began popping up like a rash. The first time she came over while I was home, Ashley made the girls grilled cheeses for lunch; Chloe sat on the stool, pumping her legs back and forth while she watched Ashley cook, interrogating every step of the process. *Is that Muenster? My mom uses regular cheese.*

Chloe is a know-it-all and a brat, but worse, she's a liar. The type of kid who will shamelessly make shit up so people will give her a moment of attention. I feel my body curl up defensively at the thought of Chloe saying something about my friend.

"What did Chloe say she saw?"

"She saw the Red Woman," Lauren says. "Sunday morning."

A jolt of panic. "Did you tell Chloe we went to the barn?"

Lauren shakes her head. "I didn't. I swear. That's just what she said."

"What exactly did she say?"

Lauren gnaws her bottom lip. "She got up at three a.m. to feed Snowflake, and when she was going out to the stables she saw someone running from the barn on Sparrow Hill. She was covered in blood."

It's no different from every other alleged Red Woman sighting. And it smells like shit from Chloe's stupid horse. "Why was she up at three a.m.?"

"She and her dad had to drive all the way to Minnesota to meet the man who bought Snowflake. You can *ask* her. She's not lying."

Lauren had mentioned that the Strausses had decided to sell Chloe's beloved horse. Chloe very well could have been in the stables early Sunday morning like she said.

"If Chloe saw a bloody woman running around Sparrow Hill, why didn't she call the police?"

Lauren frowns, her bottom lip jutting out in protest. "You're not supposed to tell anyone if you see the Red Woman."

"Well, then it wasn't very smart for her to tell you." I feel my patience thinning. There is something else nagging me—the way the creepy-ass woman at the spiritualist shop had looked at me.

"Hey. If Chloe really saw something, she should tell the police," I say. "It could help find Bailey."

Lauren gnaws the inside of her bottom lip. "Everyone is saying she's dead."

I remind myself that my sister is thirteen, and not completely a child. "She might be."

Lauren tucks herself into me. "Do you think—do you think it has something to do with the footsteps outside the barn?"

I swallow. "Laur, Jade and I checked. There were no footprints. I think the wind was playing a trick on us and made us hear things."

Lauren looks unconvinced. "Can I stay in here tonight?"

"Your mom might think it's weird if she finds out," I say. "She'll get really worried, and might figure out what we did."

"She won't find out. Please." Lauren blinks; there are tears gathering at the corners of her eyes. "I can see the barn from my room. I'm scared."

"Okay." I give in. I can't stand to see her so upset. "But only tonight."

Lauren plops her head on my shoulder, relieved. I feel hollowed out—it takes all the energy I have left to pull her closer to me, to comfort her.

I don't have the words she needs to hear—that whoever took Bailey can't hurt us. Because I'm not so sure I believe it anymore.

Go back to the barn.

I sit up, my back rattling the headboard. Hand to my chest; my heart's beating like a lab rat's. Lauren is gone. She must have gone back to her room before Ashley woke up.

Upstairs, I hear the dull roar of Ashley's hair dryer. The cable box says it's 5:45 a.m. Through the slits in my blinds, I see that the sky has lightened to a pearly gray, which means snow is threatening.

I creep out of bed. Leave my light off in case Ashley comes downstairs for breakfast. I root around in the dark for my running shoes, realize the snow is too deep, and opt for my clunky boots instead. I zip myself into a fleece and pull my clava over my face. I used to joke to Andrew that his made him look like Bane from Batman, so of course he got me one for Christmas. Now, I can't imagine going out in the cold without it.

I move the fleece from my ear and open my door, slowly, listening for the hair dryer upstairs. When I hear it, I slip down the hallway and out the front door.

The trek up Sparrow Road is unforgiving, and I'm still half a mile from the hill itself. I feel the incline in my thighs. I start to warm under the layers I'm wearing. I peel my clava off and stuff it in my jacket pocket.

The sun is coming up over the hill. There's rustling in the

larch trees above me, followed by clacking. I look up in time to see a gray-and-white owl take off, wings stretched wide.

I'm sweating by the time I reach the top. I unzip my coat and give it a flap, desperate to get some ventilation. My cheeks sting from the cold. I pick my way over pine needles and cones, veering as far right as possible to avoid the clearing several hundred feet from the barn.

They razed what was left of the Leeds House and planted spruce trees—seven, one for each member of the family—that form a macabre circle.

The barn rests behind the trees, where the house once stood. Gold light streams through. For a moment I can't believe that this is what we're all so afraid of; right now, with the sunlight spilling onto the snow, washing the walls in amber, the Leeds Barn looks stunning.

A shiver cuts through me. I don't know what I came here looking for. Maybe I just needed to see it in the unthreatening light of the morning.

Go. The snow comes up to my ankles, seeping through the tops of my boots. I wince, but I don't stop. I step through the entrance of the barn.

The boards creak under my feet. It feels as if the barn is one heavy snowfall away from collapsing completely. I shield my eyes from the sun streaming in through the gaping hole in the ceiling.

The circle of tea lights from our séance is still in the middle of the room. The sight of them makes my stomach fall to my toes. We left so many traces of ourselves here.

There's a flash of something by the window at the back of

the barn. Probably the light playing tricks with my vision. I swallow and step forward, my boots rustling the hay scattered on the floor.

My heartbeat picks up. Closer, closer. I blink, hard, trying to wipe the sight from my mind. It can't be real—I must have spooked myself into seeing it.

I open my eyes, and it's still there. A rust-colored streak on the wall next to the window. One that definitely wasn't there Friday night.

A blood smear.

I step back, hand covering my mouth, and a loose board below my feet collapses. I go down, hard. The hay around me is dotted with dried blood. A strangled yelp of fear slips out of me. I dig my heels in and push myself away. Scramble until I'm standing, and then I'm running to the door.

Outside I tear a glove off one hand with my teeth and root around until I find the card in my jacket pocket. *Deputy Eileen Knepper, Broken Falls Sheriff's Department.*

The line rings and rings. I look at my phone and consider hitting *end call*. I shouldn't be here.

"BFSD, Knepper." A gummy sound fills the line. I picture her eating breakfast, something like oatmeal. "Who do I have the pleasure of speaking to?"

"This is Kacey Young. Bailey's friend—"

"Of course! We spoke yesterday. Everything all right?"

"Um, I don't think so." I press a hand to my chest. *Breathe.* "I'm at Sparrow Hill. I went inside the barn, and there's blood in there."

The line falls silent. I feel that word crackle between us. *Blood.*

Knepper's voice sobers. "How much blood?"

The sound of a twig snapping. I whirl around. Nothing there.

"Kacey, you there?"

"Yeah. Um, there's a . . . smear of blood. It's dry."

The line falls silent. I hear clacking, at a keyboard, before Knepper speaks again. "I'm gonna need you to just simmer while I send someone over, okay? Can you head back down the hill for me? Wait by the road?"

Something glints at my feet, catching my eye, and I bend down for a closer look. The pendulum. Bailey must have dropped it on our way out the other night. I pick it up and put it in my jacket pocket.

"Yeah," I tell Ellie Knepper. "I can do that."

One hand on the pendulum in my pocket, I go back into the barn, pick up the abandoned tea lights from our séance, and take them outside. I bury them in a drift of snow under the closest tree.

I'm at the bottom of Sparrow Hill. The sun is at a forty-five-degree angle to my face. A flock of geese fly overhead, their honks volleying back and forth. I've been standing here for a while. I thought about going home and waiting for the police there, but Ellie Knepper said not to move.

My phone says it's almost seven. No messages from Ashley or my dad. I picture Ashley over the counter at Milk & Sugar, licking the pad of her thumb and counting out change to start the register off. She didn't even notice I was gone when she left for work. She must have thought I was still sleeping after a night of worrying about Bailey and didn't want to disturb me.

The crunch of tires on snow. A sheriff's cruiser bumps along, hugging the shoulder even though Sparrow Hill is a one-lane road. As it gets closer I can make out a walrus of a man with a white-blond mustache behind the wheel.

He cuts the engine. Pours himself out of the car and makes his way toward me.

"Sheriff Bill Moser." He sticks out an enormous gloved paw.

The sheriff. I called the *sheriff* away from the search for Bailey.

"Kacey Young." I shake Moser's hand.

Bill Moser frowns. "I thought Ellie said Ashley Markham's daughter called."

"I'm her stepdaughter. Different last names . . ."

Moser turns pink. "Well, let's see what we got here."

Moser starts the trek up the hill and I follow, keeping a polite pace alongside him.

"So," he huffs. "How old are ya?"

"Seventeen."

"Ah, so you're a junior."

"Senior."

Moser stops to take a breath. "I got a great-niece your age, goes to BFH. You know Bridget Gibson?"

I nearly trip over my feet. Suddenly it's clear why Ellie Knepper seemed hell-bent on not discussing Cliff Grosso. He's the sheriff's great-niece's boyfriend.

"I know Bridget," I say. "She's in my grade."

"So. Whatcha doin' all the way out here, alone? Considering what's going on."

A warning flares in my brain, telling me not to say anything about Chloe Strauss and the bloody woman. "Morning walk. I live down the road."

Beside me, Moser wheezes. "Ya walked all the way up to the barn?"

"I thought I heard something. Like an animal. So I came up to look inside."

I can't tell if the sheriff doesn't buy my story or if he's asking all these questions for the sake of asking. He keeps his eyes on the ground. People here don't like unpleasantness. They look their deer in the eye and apologize before shooting.

It's likely why Moser hasn't said anything about what happened up here all those years ago.

"The blood," I say. "It's like, smeared on the wall. And there's some on the ground"

"Well, we'll check it out."

I hang back when we get to the top of the hill, watch as Moser sputters over to the barn. He leans against the entrance, catching his breath. "You know, there's a lot of animals up here," he says. "The blood could've come from one of them. You said you heard an animal, huh?"

The blood drains from my head. Lying was bad, but I'm already in it.

Moser collects himself. Enters the barn. His voice echoes off the walls. "Yup, lots of hunting animals up here. Foxes, stoats, ermines, coyotes. Even saw a bobcat once." A beat of silence. And then: "Oh jeez. That's not good."

. . .

I'm sitting in the front of Moser's cruiser. *No need to freeze half to death,* he said. *Just promise not to drive off on me.* A nervous chuckle. I've been sitting here for over an hour. Lauren and Andrew should be awake by now; if they've noticed I'm not in my room, they probably think I'm at the café working. I gave one of the deputies Ashley's cell phone number, but he must not have called her yet.

The cruiser's vents blast hot air in my face. I press a hand to the cool window. My socks are damp. The deputy Moser called for backup took my boots and wandered off, sealing them in an evidence bag. To eliminate tread marks, he'd explained. I'll get them back eventually, he said.

I peel off my socks and slip my feet into the paper booties the deputy gave me. Drape the socks over the dash, hoping the heat from the vent will dry them.

Tread marks. We walked all over Sparrow Hill Friday night. The snow's covered our footsteps outside, but inside the barn— the tread marks from my boots won't match my story that I only stepped inside the barn today. If they find the other sets of footprints, they'll know I've been to the barn before. With three other people.

But there should be a fourth set, too. From whoever left the blood there. The thought calms my nerves, although I can't put my finger on the reason why.

Two more cars—one cruiser marked *WISCONSIN STATE POLICE K-9 UNIT,* one black with tinted windows—come down Sparrow Road. The drivers each do a three-point turn to park on the same side as Moser's cruiser.

A uniformed man in a wide-brimmed hat steps out of the

state police cruiser, accompanied by a woman who leads a German shepherd on a leash. When they pass by the cruiser, I catch a glimpse of the words on the dog's orange vest: *SEARCH AND RESCUE*.

I fix my eyes on the black car. Its driver is faceless behind the windshield.

My hands fog up the screen of my phone. I wipe the sweat off the screen. Maybe I should tell someone why I really came up here—Chloe Strauss said there was a bloody woman. Even if Chloe was full of shit, there's real, actual blood in the barn now.

The slamming of a car door jolts me. The driver of the black car finally steps out: a man, probably midforties. Curly hair slicked down, cheekbones for days. He's wearing a suit, no jacket. His gaze rakes over the scene, resting on the windshield of Moser's cruiser. Making eye contact with me.

I shrink into the seat. Look down. There's a lima bean–sized tear in the upholstery near my thigh.

Minutes later. Rapping at the window. Moser's face, his breath fogging up the glass. He motions for me to come out. I hesitate. "That guy took my boots."

"Oh. Yes, he did." Moser makes a phlegmy noise. He waves the man in black over to us. I turn in the passenger seat as Moser clamps a hand down on my shoulder. "Detective, this is Kacey Young."

I didn't know Broken Falls had detectives. But then, the man doesn't look like he's from Broken Falls. He doesn't introduce himself. "Good to meet you, Kacey. Can you tell me what happened this morning?"

No accent there. Definitely not from Broken Falls, then. FBI? "I—told Sheriff Moser. I was out for a hike. I went up to the barn, and I saw the blood."

The detective tugs a pair of latex gloves out of his pocket, holding eye contact with me as he slides a hand into one of them. A shiver rips through me.

"You're aware there's a girl your age missing?" The latex glove snaps against his wrist.

"She's my friend," I say.

The detective's eyebrows lift. "I didn't know that."

The sheriff turns pink. "Well, to be perfectly honest, I didn't either."

I think I spy a bead of sweat above his mustache. I don't like the way the detective is looking at me. "Bill, could you check to see how the road blockade is coming along?"

Moser frowns and putters off. When he's out of earshot, the detective squats so we're at eye level. "Kacey, I need to know, were you out here looking for Bailey when you found the blood?"

"What?" The sounds on top of the hill roll around in my head like pinballs. Shouts back and forth. Radios crackling.

"Kacey, look at me, sweetheart. I'm over here." He waggles a finger in front of his face. I bite back the urge to swat it away. "Why did you come up here?"

"I just did. It's quiet up here. Sometimes I come to get away and think."

He nods. I can't tell if he's buying the grief-stricken-friend thing. "See, Kacey, if you have a reason to believe that Bailey might be up here, I need to know. You won't be in trouble.

You understand the most important thing right now is finding her, right?"

My toes clench in the paper booties. "Of course I know that."

Barking, up on the hill. Frenetic, loud, *found something* barking. The detective acts like he can't hear the dog, but I can see it on his face: the slightest quiver in his upper lip. "I'm gonna need you to sit tight for a minute. I'll be right back."

I watch the detective trot up the hill, meeting the deputy who took my shoes and two other officers.

The deputy says, loud enough for me to hear: "We called the crime scene unit from Madison to come swab the blood."

One of the other officers, a woman, says: "You think it's gonna match what we found on those clothes yesterday?"

My blood freezes. I forget I'm in paper shoes and stumble out of Moser's cruiser. Yell over to them: "You found bloody clothes? Where?"

Three heads prick up. The detective turns to look at me, then back at the big-mouth deputy. *Nice job, asshole.*

"Kacey, why don't you get back in the car so you don't get frostbite."

I can't move. "I heard her—how much blood was there? Is Bailey dead?"

The detective drops his voice. "Please get her out of here."

The deputy who took my shoes starts coming toward me. A flap of panic in my chest. *Cornered.*

"C'mon, sweetheart." When the deputy grabs me by the elbow, something in me snaps. Everything I've been tamping down comes flowing up.

"Get the hell off me." The voice doesn't even sound like mine.

It belongs to the ugly thing that lives in me. The creature that goes berserk when it's cornered. One I haven't seen since I left New York.

"Hey!" The deputy steps back, but he doesn't let go.

I start to scream. "Don't grab me—get *off*."

More shouting—the other deputy, the woman, comes running toward us. Everything goes black—if I fight back, I'm going to be arrested for assaulting a police officer. I let my body go limp and I fall to the snow.

I'm not here anymore—I'm in my mom's old apartment, I'm lying at the bottom of the stairs, and all of the fight is leaving my body.

"Get off her." A firm voice.

Two pairs of hands release me. I regain my breath, numb to the cold seeping through my thin pants. Off to the side, Moser is watching me, his jaw open, his stoats, foxes, and ermines forgotten.

I am the only animal up here.

CHAPTER NINE

Sheriff Moser insists on driving me home, even though navigating the blockade the police have set up takes as long as it would have taken me to walk.

My father answers the door. He's in his scrubs; he lives, breathes, and sleeps in them. I'm the one with the last name Young, but my father looks like a well-preserved blond frat boy. A college student playing doctor in those scrubs.

He looks like he must have when he met my mom, a waitress at a hole-in-the-wall wings place in Buffalo, where he was getting his degree in pharmacology.

My father's eyes move from me to Sheriff Moser, and his jaw goes slack. "Kacey. Are you okay?"

My teeth are chattering and my feet are numb. "I n-need to warm up."

My father's hand goes to his chin. Runs a thumb along his jaw nervously as he turns to Moser. "What on earth happened?"

I can't stand around and hear how the sheriff fumbles to relay my lousy version of why I was in the barn. Why I was at a *crime scene*. I rush past him, not even bothering to take off my jacket.

I'm so cold I feel like I'm drunk. I stumble into the bathroom and strip. Turn on the faucet and wait until the water starts to steam. I sit in the bathtub and pull my knees to my naked body as the tub fills with hot water. It shoots up my nose, making me choke and sputter. I rotate the handle all the way to the right until the water scalds my skin, until it's almost unbearable. But maybe if I stay like this for long enough, I'll disappear into steam too.

When I burn all the cold from my body, I get out of the tub. Lock my bedroom door behind me and crawl between my comforter and sheets, naked. The house is silent, Moser's cruiser gone from our driveway.

The worst moments of my life have always managed to creep up on me when everything is quiet. I'll be watching TV or trying to read and then bam, my brain is all *Hahaha bitch, here's that painful memory you'd sell your soul to forget*. Most involve my mother.

I know that the way the detective and Sheriff Moser looked at me is going to be one of those moments. I was an animal that needed to be tranquilized. I wasn't me: I was the beast inside me that breaks free when I'm cornered. The thing that makes me freak out.

Black out.

I was twelve the first time I threw something at my mother with the intent to hit her. I don't even know if I succeeded; the second the glass left my hand, her boyfriend had me pinned down on the floor.

One of his arms was as big as my entire body. It hardly seemed fair, how easily he kept me down, like I was a rag doll. The more I fought to get away, the worse he pushed.

I remember the feel of the scratchy carpet on my chin. How I'd howled like a wild animal.

"You need to calm down," he'd said, in his deep baritone. "Y'all can't fight like this anymore."

The following week, he moved out.

My phone buzzes from the pocket of my jacket, where I left it before getting into the shower. Texts have filled up the screen— some from numbers I don't recognize.

Unknown: *hey it's sully true they found bay's body??*

Andrew: *what is going on?? There's a cop car outside.*

Jade: *fucking call me back.*

I grip my phone. Feel myself coil up. *Leave me alone, get off me—*

When it vibrates again, I hurl it at the wall.

"Shit." I leap out of bed, run over to where the phone has clattered to the floor. Thunderous footsteps down the hall.

"Kacey?" My father. "What was that banging? Are you okay?"

"I'm fine. I fell." I run a finger along the spidery crack at the corner of my phone's screen. It'll be hard to hide that, but thankfully, the phone still works.

My doorknob jangles. "Why is the door locked?"

I sit back on my heels, fully aware of my own nakedness, and there's a hole in the drywall where my phone hit it. I'm going to have to find something to cover that up.

112

"I'm fine. Please leave me alone."

More jangling. I curl onto my side, paralyzed by shame at what I've done to the wall and the screen of my phone. Damaging something just because I was angry—it's not who I am.

It's exactly who I can't be, now that everyone seems to be watching me.

I am still under my covers, wrapped in the towel from the shower, when I hear Ashley's SUV rumble into the driveway. The pillow is wet beneath me from my soaked hair. I can't bring myself to get dressed, or to do anything else, really.

A knock at the door. Ashley jangles the knob; the clicking sound of a key inserting into the lock. She has a master key for all of our bedrooms, in case of major tantrums. Or in my case, a complete meltdown.

Ashley silently comes to my side holding a mug of tea. Unfolds her other hand and reveals a half moon of a white pill. "It'll help you sleep," she says.

I swallow it with a sip of the chamomile tea she hands me.

"Do you want to talk about it?" she asks, stroking a lock of hair from my forehead.

I shake my head. I just want the nothingness that the pill will bring me. By the time I'm falling into a cloudy sleep, I finally remember that the vigil is tonight.

When I wake up, it's almost seven and I realize that no one woke me up to get dressed. At some point, they must have decided to leave me at home, to go to the vigil without me. They haven't left yet—I hear Lauren's footsteps overhead, thunderous when Ashley calls for her to put her coat on.

I can't go. Jade will never forgive me, but the thought barely registers as a blip on my conscience. I can't look all of those people in the eyes—people with their candles and purple ribbons pinned to their coats and their prayers of hope.

Because I think I get it now: what that psychic in Pleasant Plains meant when she said that deep down, I know what happened to Bailey.

She's dead. What other answer is there?

That deputy said they found bloody clothes. I saw the blood in the barn for myself.

When I shut my eyes, I'm there all over again. The image triggers dread in my gut, but I try to think about the blood logically.

There was a smear of it on the wall, but nowhere else in the barn, except for a few droplets on the hay. I've lost more blood from a bloody nose than what was on the wall. Which means—I swallow the thought like a pill—that no one was *killed* in the barn.

Pictures of Bailey emerge in my mind. Bailey, bloodied and injured, running in the woods from her attacker. Bailey, hiding out in the barn. Leaning against the wall for support, and leaving that blood smear herself.

Bailey, running into the night, too hurt to press on. Bailey, curling up on the ground, the snow covering her body by the next day.

I feel sick. I don't even know that the blood in the barn was Bailey's, or that it was real at all. Someone who knows about the Leeds crime scene photos could have made the blood smear as a cruel prank.

But who would do something like that—especially with a girl missing?

Unless someone saw us in the barn.

Impossible. Jade and I went outside and looked for human footprints—there weren't any.

Thinking about that night in the barn makes me feel the cold in my bones. I'm suddenly uneasy with the fact that my family has left me here alone. No doubt Ashley called Mrs. Lao, who never leaves her house, and told her to keep an eye on things. But still. I feel the emptiness of the house in every corner of my body.

I see the blood in the barn whenever I close my eyes.

I wish we had a fucking dog.

My phone buzzes on my nightstand, startling me. There's a text from Jade: *you here yet? can't find you.*

Moments later, another: *I see your family.*

Hand to my stomach, I force a breath in, and out. A full five minutes go by before Jade texts again: *what the actual FUCK, kacey??*

There's pressure behind my eyes. Jade's going to find out, if she hasn't already, that I was there with all the cop cars and flashing lights on Sparrow Hill today. She won't forgive me for not telling her what I saw; missing the vigil is just something else to add to my list of crimes.

I climb out of bed and slip into my flannel pajamas, some of the fog from my brain lifting. It's past seven-thirty now; the vigil will be starting any minute. The local news will probably be streaming it live; I force myself off my bed and head for the living room.

I pause in the hallway. Music—the delicate strumming of a guitar. It sends gooseflesh rippling down my arms.

I am hearing things now. The sedative made me trippy and I'm hearing things.

I stand still, one finger pressed against my pulse beating in my neck. The music comes to a crescendo. It's above me.

I follow the sound upstairs, my knees unsteady.

The music is coming from Lauren's room.

Her door is open a crack. I nudge it open more with my toe and slip inside the empty room.

Lauren's furniture is littered with things: ninety-nine-cent bottles of nail polish from Friendly Drugs, a brand I never saw until I moved here, on the nightstand. Jelly pens, a half-empty Nalgene, earrings shaped like sushi on the dresser. Dance shoes and dirty tights on her desk chair. She and Ashley fight over the state of this room weekly, especially the laundry strewn across her bed and carpet.

Some kids don't even have warm clothes and you treat yours like they're trash.

Her laptop is open on her desk, a video playing.

It's Bailey. Bailey looking even rounder-faced and bright-eyed, like a baby. Bailey in a flowery peasant top, alone onstage with a microphone. *Singing.*

I move Lauren's ballet shoes aside so I can sit in her desk chair. The video ends and begins looping. I click around—the video is embedded in an article. *Missing Wisconsin Girl Planned to Attend University of Indiana at Bloomington.*

Bailey has made national news.

The caption explains that the video is from Bailey's eighth-grade talent show, where she sang "Can't Help Falling in Love." I let it play from the beginning again. Bailey has a sweet voice, a scrappy alto you might hear in a coffee shop. Her hands hug the microphone so tightly you'd have to peer closely to see that she's shaking.

I had no idea she could sing.

I can't bring myself to watch the video again. I feel like a gawker, watching some news story about a girl halfway across the country. The Bailey I knew didn't sing, didn't wear peasant tops. I pick up the jewelry holder on Lauren's desk. It's the macaron I sculpted and painted pastel green in Mr. White's class last year.

I thought beginner drawing and painting would be a nightmare. But art at Broken Falls wasn't like the art class I'd taken as a kid in New York, in stuffy rooms with crayon stubs and paintbrushes slimy from sitting in water overnight.

I'm not great at drawing and sketching—I have a long way to go—but this macaron, my first assignment in his class, convinced Mr. White I was ready to take AP art.

When I brought it home, Lauren locked eyes on it like a ferret on a shiny necklace. "That is *so cool*."

I let her have it without question. She was hesitant, didn't know what she'd owe me in return. I insisted she take it; I knew I'd win her trust eventually.

And here I am, at her computer, alone.

I switch tabs and open Lauren's browser history. The first site on the list immediately catches my eye. *HAUNTED WISCONSIN—THE RED WOMAN SIGHTINGS*

No wonder she won't sleep alone. Bailey showed me this site when she was trying to explain the Red Woman to me. Some of the stuff on it will keep you up at night no matter where you live.

117

I click through to the forum topic, where Lauren is logged in as *mookie*. I swallow to clear my throat. Mookie is on her bed; the nearly decapitated chimpanzee was Lauren's first stuffed animal. She was too little to say *monkey,* so she branded him Mookie.

I scroll past the posts: Stories about the Red Woman jumping out in front of motorists. Stories about her slapping a bloody palm on the windshields of stalled cars, leaving behind a ghoulish handprint. Stories about brave souls going up to the barn and reporting hearing sobbing and children crying.

Nausea wells up in me. That streak of blood in the barn—it could have been a handprint.

I click on the navigation bar until I find Lauren's profile. Apparently, she registered on Haunted Wisconsin on Monday—almost two days after Bailey disappeared.

Lauren's only made one post, in a subforum called THE RED WOMAN—GENERAL DISCUSSION.

It's time-stamped at 10:31 this morning.

Mookie: Do you think the Red Woman made the girl from Broken Falls disappear just like she disappeared?

A chill settles over me. I dig my socked toes into the carpet and scroll through the responses.

badgerboi209: Josephine Leeds didn't disappear. She's a pile of bones somewhere and that girl from BF is probably dead by now too

princess_of_darkness: I heard that the girl from broken falls died of a drug overdose at that party and someone dumped her body. sad

The latest response came three hours ago:

anthropomorphist: Mookie, what makes you think the missing girl has anything to do with the RW?

I scroll down, but Lauren never responded to anthropomorphist's question. I toggle back to her search history, the pit in my gut growing when I see everything Lauren has looked up in the past few days.

the red woman
Josephine leeds murder
séances
how do you make the dead mad
And:
can ghosts kill people?

I click out of the window and leave Lauren's desk and computer exactly as I found it.

When I get back to my room, I lock the door behind me.

I'm in bed, counting the minutes until everyone gets home from the vigil. When I hear the crunching of tires on snow in the driveway, I turn off my light.

Moments after the front door creaks open, there's a soft

knock on my door. I pretend to be asleep. I don't want to know how the vigil went. It's just a reminder that I should have been there. Should have gotten my shit together and shown up, like a real friend would.

But I can't handle the inevitable questions from everyone. *What did you see in the barn?* I can't answer them, and not because Sheriff Moser told me not to when he drove me home.

I can't parse out what's real and what's not anymore. Lauren isn't stupid—she might be a little naïve—but she's one of the smartest kids in her class. She watches *Dateline* with Ashley on Friday nights. She knows that girls disappear all the time: not at the hands of murderous spirits but at the hands of humans.

So why that post on the message boards about the Red Woman? Could she really believe that Bailey's disappearance has something to do with Josephine Leeds?

I can't turn off her scream, looping in my head.

On my nightstand, my phone starts buzzing frantically. Jade's picture fills the screen; her judging stare has never seemed more appropriate. A tear rolls down my neck as I let the phone ring and ring.

When it's done, I reach for my phone. A text message from Jade pops up on the screen.

Look at the goddamn news.

I scoot from my bed to my desk. Shake my laptop out of hibernation. The default news site on my computer shows all the usual misery—bombings halfway around the world, a fire at a Brooklyn apartment complex, and historic snowstorms headed for the East Coast. I let my fingers fly across the keyboard, typing *Bailey Hammond* into the search bar.

I've bitten my thumbnail nearly clean off by the time the top hit loads.

BREAKING: Police discover missing teenager's car

Wisconsin State Police confirm that a vehicle found in an abandoned garage in Broken Falls belongs to Bailey Hammond, 17, who has been missing since late Saturday night. Police have not commented on what they found inside the vehicle but have said that a full forensic examination is under way. A source close to law enforcement says that the discovery of Miss Hammond's car comes off a suspicious discovery earlier today, and that police are ramping up their search for the missing teen.

I lean over the wastebasket under my desk, but all I manage is a dry heave. I spit on top of a discarded draft of an English paper.

Abandoned garage. I think of the bank-owned old farmhouse behind us, the one my father says will never sell because no one is looking to buy ten acres of property in this market. I've seen the enormous double garage out back, its doors rusted from years of weather and neglect. It *has* to be that house.

Because that house—that garage—is less than half a mile from Sparrow Hill. Of course the police would look there after finding that blood in the Leeds Barn. After *I found* the blood in the Leeds Barn.

There's a ringing in my ears, nearly drowning out the thoughts forming: I hand-delivered Bailey's phone to the police. I led them straight to the blood.

And I can only imagine what that detective is thinking now: *What is Kacey Young going to find next?*

CHAPTER TEN

I must fall asleep at some point, because I wake up to the sound of pots clattering in the kitchen. The cable box says it's after nine; I sit up in a panic. I've overslept. *No, the school is still closed.* I blink away the fog and rub my temples.

I check my phone to make sure the news story about Bailey's car wasn't a terrible nightmare. My stomach sinks to my feet; the story is still there, with an amended headline: *Forensic examination of missing teen's car to begin today.*

A chill skates over me. I climb out of bed and drape a fleece blanket over my shoulders. Ashley should be at work by now, so it must be Andrew making that racket.

I open my bedroom door to the smells of cheese and onion, but it's not Andrew who greets me when I get to the kitchen.

Ashley's crouched with her head inside the lower cabinet. Her entire set of cookware is strewn across the counter.

"Sorry I woke you," she says. "I asked your father to fix this pot rack five times."

"What are you doing home?" I ask.

"Paula and Rob can manage the café for today." Ashley lifts the cover of the slow cooker and uses the wooden spoon to transfer the casserole to a pan. "I thought I'd get this over to the Hammonds. You know, give them our best."

My stomach tucks into itself. Of course Ashley made a casserole. It's what people do in the Midwest when someone dies. And everyone thinks Bailey's dead because the police found her car, and she's not in it.

"Kacey?"

My head snaps up. Ashley is watching me as she sprinkles shredded cheese over the casserole in the cast-iron pan. "I asked if you wanted to come to the Hammonds' with me."

I know I have no choice, after ditching the vigil last night. But the thought of looking Cathy Hammond in the eye nearly makes me sick all over the kitchen floor.

And Jade: she's never, ever going to forgive me for leaving her alone.

"Okay," I say. "Let me change."

It's half past ten when Ashley pulls up to the curb outside Bailey's house. The cast-iron pan in my lap is hot through the towel draped across my thighs.

"Um," I say. "Does Cathy know that I'm the one who found—who was there at the barn?"

Ashley looks at me. If I'd blinked, I would have missed her lower lip quiver. She forces a smile like someone's beating it out of her. "I don't—I wouldn't worry about that right now, okay? Let's get inside before you burn yourself."

Ashley rings the doorbell, since I have to carry the pot with both hands. A flit of panic—I should have made Ashley carry the casserole, since she's the one who insisted on making it. I can't wrap my head around how this is supposed to help.

Then Cathy Hammond answers the door. She sees Ashley and collapses into her arms, nearly taking her down, and I'm grateful my hands are occupied.

The Hammonds' house has a stale smell to it, even though it's clean. It's as if all the grief and uncertainty inside is polluting the air. Bailey was always embarrassed by the house; her parents haven't done a thing to update it since they bought it in 1989.

"Oh, you shouldn't have gone through all the trouble. I haven't eaten a thing in days." Cathy smiles weakly and takes the casserole from my hands so I can remove my boots. It looks like she'll break under the weight of the pot. She's all bones, bird arms jutting out from her too-big cardigan. Once I asked Bailey how her mother stays so skinny, and she said, "From obsessing."

I always thought it was endearing, how her mom worried. The Hammonds aren't religious; instead, Cathy abides by the prophet of the nightly news anchor and worships in front of the TV every Friday night. Filling her brain with every possible bad thing that could happen to anyone, ever, but especially to her kids.

She and Ed grounded Bailey for a month for getting into that car with Cliff Grosso last spring. Cathy still brings it up, still tells Bailey, *Someone was watching over you that night.*

The irony now makes me sweat under my jacket. I tear my eyes away from the television in the living room and follow Ashley and Cathy into the kitchen.

I stop short when I see Jade sitting at the kitchen table. Her eyes meet mine. She puts an elbow on the table and props up her chin with her hand, never moving her eyes from me. They are blank, expressionless. Like I'm nothing.

Cathy drops into the seat at the table like she just *can't* anymore. Ashley sits across from her and takes her hand. "I've been praying. Every night. We all have."

Cathy stares at me, as if for confirmation. I nod. Rest my hands on the table. The vinyl tablecloth protector sticks to my palms. I don't think I've prayed since I was a child. I prayed for my mom's boyfriends to go away, for her to change, and for us to live in a normal house where there was no screaming or ugliness.

I learned really quickly that praying doesn't do shit.

"The vigil was lovely." Ashley gives Cathy's hand a squeeze.

"Mm-hm." Cathy uses her free hand to smooth out a wrinkle on her cardigan sleeve. Rakes her gaze over Ashley and me. "Thank you both for coming."

I realize that she didn't even notice I wasn't there last night. I'm torn between relief and feeling inconsequential. Jade is still

125

staring at me, letting me know my absence *was* noticed. And unforgivable.

Cathy jerks; she starts to stand. "Oh my, I haven't offered you anything. What would you like? Coffee? I don't have any creamer—Ed is actually out grabbing a couple things now—"

Ashley tugs Cathy's wrist, bringing her back down to her seat. "Cathy. Sweetheart. Sit and breathe for a bit, okay?"

Cathy plops back down, and it's as if something in her cracks. She starts to sob. Ashley drags her chair closer and envelops her in a hug. I feel like some creepy voyeur, watching them like that. I move my gaze to the fridge; Bailey's school photo from last year is tacked up with a Badgers magnet. Her brother, Ben, goes to Madison; Cathy and Ed want Bailey to go too, but she always said anywhere in Wisconsin isn't far enough from Broken Falls.

The look Jade is giving me now cuts even deeper. Whenever Bailey talked about her lofty plans to go to school out of state, Jade would roll her eyes toward me. *At least you'll be stuck here with me.*

I'm really all Jade has left now. And I'm not enough.

Cathy gives a wet sniffle and pauses her sobbing. "They have a special investigator from the state managing the case now. Said the sheriff's department can't handle an investigation like this. The detective—he has a high solve rate."

The detective from yesterday—the one who made my skin crawl. It has to be him Cathy's talking about.

"That's good," Ashley strokes Cathy's hair. Cathy gives a wet sniffle and pulls away from Ashley. A strangled sound comes from Cathy's throat. "My baby. My tiny, little baby. Where is she?"

"Shh." Ashley strokes Cathy's wrist. "There's always hope. Miracles do happen. Think about those girls who come home—"

Ashley stops herself. I look over at Jade, who has her hands covering her mouth. The thought is horrific: those girls who come home from being locked up in some creep's basement after ten years. *If* they escape at all.

I think of that deputy talking about the bloody clothes they found, and I feel faint. Blood means Bailey probably isn't being held somewhere against her will.

Cathy dabs at her eyes. "I should have done more."

Ashley takes Cathy's hand again. "Sweetheart, don't say that. You don't know what you could have done."

"I shouldn't have let her out of my sight Saturday," Cathy says. "Late Friday night, while Ed was sleeping in Ben's empty room—he snores—Bailey crawled into bed with me. She hasn't done that since she was a baby."

Jade and I share a look. Obviously she didn't know about this. Goose bumps spring up on my skin.

"She was scared of something," Cathy says. "She wouldn't tell me, said she wanted to talk to a therapist. I thought it could wait until Monday—maybe it was that awful Grosso boy harassing her again—"

I think of the doe in Cliff Grosso's freezer again. Think of Bailey, running bloody through the woods like prey. I stand up from the table. The legs of my chair screech against the linoleum. "I have to—bathroom," I choke out. "I'm sorry."

"I'll walk with you," Jade says.

I open my mouth to protest, but Jade's already digging her

nails into my wrist. She pulls me down the hall and shoves me into Bailey's bedroom.

Jade is quiet as I sit on the edge of Bailey's bed. Bailey would be seething, bitching me out if it were her that I'd ditched at a vigil for Jade. Jade hides her anger under apathy. I've never been on the other side of it before.

It's terrifying.

I smooth a hand over Bailey's chenille bedspread. It feels strange, being in her room without her here.

"Can I explain myself?" I ask.

Jade looks like she wants to stab me. "Whatever."

"I freaked out—I wanted to go to the vigil, but I couldn't."

"So you just *left* me?" Jade drops her voice to a whisper.

Pressure, behind my eyes. *I didn't know you needed me.*

"Do you know how infuriating you're acting?" Jade says. "Like, I'm trying to give you the benefit of the doubt. But you're hiding shit from me. Everyone knows you were on Sparrow Kill when they found something yesterday."

"The cops told me not to say anything to anyone."

"I'm not just *anyone*." Jade looks like she's going to cry. "God. I can't believe you."

I inhale. "There was blood in the barn."

Jade's chin snaps up. She's not wearing her eyeliner. It makes her look tired. Sad. "I figured it was something like that if it wasn't her body."

"There wasn't a lot of it." My voice comes out hushed, like river water. "It was like, smeared next to the window, but there wasn't blood anywhere else. J, it looked exactly like it does in the pictures from the Leeds massacre."

Jade blinks. I can't tell if she believes me or not. I feel helpless, like I'm clawing at the dark.

"Why were you even *at* the barn yesterday?" Jade's voice is quiet.

I inhale. Bunch up a piece of Bailey's bedspread between my fingers. It smells like her—store-brand fabric softener and the jasmine perfume she makes a bi-yearly pilgrimage to the Sephora in Madison to buy. "I was there because Chloe Strauss told Lauren she saw someone covered in blood running from Sparrow Hill the night Bay went missing. She says it was the Red Woman."

"And you believed her?" Jade gapes at me. "Jesus, Kacey."

The fact that she doesn't ask why I didn't call the cops and tell them about the bloody woman confirms what I feared: Jade thinks this—a connection to Josephine Leeds's disappearance— is all bullshit. A distraction from the fact that our best friend is missing, maybe even dead.

"I overheard the cops," I say quietly. "They found bloody clothes."

Jade's face doesn't change. She's not surprised.

"How'd you know?" I whisper.

Jade swallows. "I stayed here after the vigil last night. My dad was working, and I just couldn't stand the thought of going to an empty house—Cathy said I could sleep in Bailey's bed. She said *she'd* sleep better knowing I was here."

Jade closes her eyes. Her lids are shiny, like she didn't sleep at all. "When the cops came to tell her parents about the car, they said they had something they needed to show them. I came in here, but I left the door open so I could hear what they were saying."

I suck in a breath.

"They must have shown Cathy a picture," Jade says. "Because she said, *No, that's not one of Bailey's sweatshirts.* And then the cops asked her dad if it could belong to him or Ben."

"So it was a men's sweatshirt," I say.

Jade nods. "Probably. Kace, I think there was blood on it. After they showed her the picture, her parents started crying."

A tug in my chest. "Have the cops talked to Cliff? His entire wardrobe is sweatshirts—"

My voice falters as I see how Jade is staring at me. She smooths out a wrinkle in Bailey's comforter, her eyes avoiding mine. "That cop with the busted teeth, Ellie whatever, she came to talk to me again. I asked her why they hadn't arrested Cliff, and she said they were exploring *all angles.*"

"Okay," I say. "What's that supposed to mean?"

"Think about it, Kace," Jade says. "If Cliff did something to Bailey, why would he be dumb enough to ditch her phone right outside his house?"

"I don't know." But I hear what she's saying—someone could have planted the phone on the Grossos' property to make it seem like Cliff had something to do with Bailey's disappearance.

But Cliff hurting Bailey is the scenario that makes *sense.* Shouldn't it be the theory Jade believes?

Unless she's come up with one of her own. My stomach drops.

Jade plucks at a pill of fuzz on Bailey's bedspread, avoiding my eyes. "I have to ask you something. Did you tell Ellie that Bailey probably ran away?"

My thoughts blur together. I hear Ellie's voice, gently probing me. Monday seems so far away.

"That's not what I said at all," I say. "I said that Bay hated it here and wanted to leave."

Jade stuffs her hands in the pockets of her oversized sweater. "Why would you say something like that? Bay would never *leave* us."

"I didn't make it up." Annoyance flares in me—at Bailey, I realize, for being so delicate with Jade. For never telling her the truth, how she really felt about Broken Falls. I open my mouth to tell Jade everything: our project for local history, how we'd gotten Starbucks afterward. *I would just get on the highway and go.*

There's a knock at the door, stomping down my angry thoughts. *I would have told you about the times Bailey and I hung out alone but she said* you *would be jealous.*

Jade doesn't look at me as she jumps up and opens Bailey's door. Ashley is standing in the doorway. "Kacey, hon, we have to go."

The color leaches from Jade's cheeks. "Did something happen?"

"No, nothing like that." Ashley wraps her arms around her middle and looks at me. "The—the sheriff wants to talk to Kacey."

"Why?" My head feels fuzzy. Of course I know why—they want to talk about Bailey—but why just me? Why not Jade too?

"Sweetheart." Ashley's voice is strange; she's staring at my face. "You're bleeding."

I put a hand to my nose. It comes away red. I feel the blood drip down my upper lip, Jade's gaze boring into me like a question mark.

CHAPTER ELEVEN

Sheriff Moser is waiting for us up front at the station. The desks behind him are eerily empty, save for a woman in a bulky sweater clacking away at her computer's keyboard. The heat is cranking; underneath my jacket, my sweater sticks to my spine. My nose has stopped bleeding, my pocket full of tissues from the Hammonds' bathroom, just in case.

Moser shakes Ashley's hand. "I appreciate you coming down here. Busy lady, managing three kids and the café."

Ashley gives Moser a tight smile. Wiggles her hand out of his paw. "I—should I be in the room with Kacey?"

"Well." Moser's mustache lifts. "I think the detective would prefer to chat with her alone. More honest answers."

A breathy chuckle. Ashley's face is grim. I swallow and touch her hand with my pinky. "It's okay. I'll be okay."

"All right," she says. "I guess I'll wait out here."

"It might be a few minutes," Moser says. "The detective is just finishing up another interview."

Ashley looks down at me.

"It's fine," I say. "Go home. I'll call you when they're done."

When Ashley's gone, I sit in one of the empty waiting room chairs. Moser brings me a tepid cup of water. Mercifully, the phone rings, and he scuttles off to get it.

A door opening. Muttering. Ellie Knepper steps out of the room next to the coffeemaker. After her, a hulking guy steps out, shoulders slumped forward.

Cliff Grosso.

Ellie spots me. Nods. "We'll be right with you, Kacey."

Cliff looks up when Ellie says my name. His gaze skims over me. I pull my jacket tight around my body. I feel the rage bubbling up inside me; why are they letting him just walk out of here? He was the last one seen talking to Bailey before she disappeared.

Are they cutting him a break because the sheriff's great-niece is dating him?

I call out to Cliff: "Hey. That's a nice doe you shot."

He pivots. I see the gears in his head turning. Cliff's stupid, but not that stupid. Good. I want him to know I was in his backyard; I want him to feel violated. He should, for all the shit he talked about Bailey behind her back after the accident. *She was dying to fuck at my house. I couldn't talk her out of it.*

Cliff raises his hands. Gives me two middle fingers.

He opens the door, sending a gust of cold my way. Stands there for a beat, like he's doing it on purpose, then lets the door slam behind him. The sound echoes in my head until someone inside the room calls my name—but this time, it's not Ellie Knepper. It's the man from yesterday.

"I never formally introduced myself. My name is Detective Steven Burke," he tells me. "Why don't you come inside?"

We're in a room that feels much too small for three people; there's a counter with a sink and microwave in the corner. Detective Burke sits across from me at the table. Knepper stands in the corner, arms folded. Supervising. Which one of us, exactly, I don't know.

"Before we start, I want to make it clear you're not in trouble," Burke says. "Technically, you were trespassing yesterday, but we're willing to overlook that in exchange for your cooperation. You seem like a good kid."

Burke gives me a grim smile. I lower my eyes to the cup of water Moser gave me. I'm not stupid; I know Burke is trying to get on my side. Make me trust him enough to tell him why I was really at the barn.

"Does this have anything to do with you guys finding Bailey's car?" I ask.

Burke glances at Ellie. "We'll get to that."

Panic corners me. "I already told Ellie everything I know."

Burke rests his forearms on the table. The sleeves of his dress shirt are rolled up. "See, I have trouble buying that. I have daughters. I know how girls are with their best friends—always covering for each other, not wanting to sell each other out."

"I'm not covering for anyone."

"I believe that, Kacey, I do. I'm just trying to get the whole picture. Find out how a girl with no enemies goes missing in a town as small as this one."

"Bailey had enemies." The words spill out of me, a knee-jerk reaction. I want to kick myself.

Burke cocks his head. Even Ellie Knepper shifts in the corner. Heat comes into my face. "I mean, you *know* that Cliff Grosso hated Bailey. You just talked to him."

Burke nods. "We've spoken at length with Mr. Grosso, and other witnesses at the party. They don't think the disagreement by Bailey's car was physical."

"But he left the party not long after Bailey did. What if he followed her?"

I pick up the cup of water and hold it to my lips, because I don't like how Burke is studying my mouth. Like everything that comes out of it is a lie.

"I'm going to ask you something," Burke says. "You seem like a really smart girl. So I want to know, in your honest opinion, what you think happened to Bailey Saturday night."

I blink, startled. "You want, like, my theory?"

Burke sits back. Crosses his arms across his dress shirt. The top two buttons are undone. "Let's take Cliff out of the equation for a minute. Say he had nothing to do with this. Where would Bailey go if she was upset?"

"I don't know," I say. "She would normally go to Jade's, but she obviously didn't want Jade with her wherever she was going."

"So you think she was headed somewhere with a specific place in mind."

"I didn't say that. Maybe she just drove around, to clear her head or something."

Burke nods for me to continue. "You're doing real good, Kacey. Go on."

It's a thousand degrees in here. I unzip my jacket, shrug out of it. "Maybe while she was driving around, something happened. She could have had a beer or two at the party—if she got into an accident, she may have panicked. I mean, she would never call her parents in a million years. She'd sooner wait by the road for help, I guess. And maybe she ran into the wrong person?"

Burke holds up one hand, twirls his pen through the fingers on the other.

Burke is watching me. "I know this is hard. Would you say that Bailey was the type to trust a stranger who pulled over to give her help?"

"Not really. I mean, it's a small town. There aren't a lot of strangers." I realize I'm making Bailey sound naïve. "She—she knows there's bad people out there. She's just the type of person who thinks that nothing bad is ever going to happen to *her*."

The corner of Burke's mouth tugs upward. "You remind me of my daughter a bit, Kacey. You notice a lot about people. That's something special."

A swell of pride. I tamp it down, but not before a smile quivers on my own lips. That's when I see something flash in Burke's eyes. It's the look of a hunter with a rifle cocked and aimed. The satisfied tug in his expression when he knows he's got a perfect shot at his prey.

He is playing me. He wants me to feel important. I grip the

edge of the table. He thinks everything I just said is bullshit. "Is there, like, a point to this?" I ask.

Burke's smile flickers. "I'm just comparing theories. Most folks I talked to figured if Bailey was upset, she would have sought out you or Jade Becker."

"Are you asking if she was on her way to see me when she went missing?" I ask. "Because she definitely wasn't."

In the corner, Ellie's spine straightens. I've said the wrong thing; I imagine her piecing everything together. My not being at the party. How I was so quick to say that Bailey and I never fought.

"Okay, refresh my memory," Burke says. "The last time you saw Bailey was Saturday, at your stepmom's café?"

"Yes."

"What'd you talk about?"

I swallow. "Nothing, really. She got breakfast and left."

"And what did you do Saturday night, again? From what I hear, you spent most of your Saturday nights with Bailey and Jade. Why was this weekend different?"

"I already told her"—I nod to Ellie—"that I had dinner with my family and went to bed around ten."

Burke takes a sip from his coffee. "Your statement to Deputy Knepper over here says that the next morning, after you paid a visit to Mr. Sullivan's house, you and Jade decided together to drive by the Grossos'."

Had I said that? "I said maybe we should check and see if she was at Cliff's, and Jade agreed. I can't really remember whose idea it was."

"So *you* suggested looking for Bailey at Cliff's. Why?"

"Because I thought she might be there." My tongue feels dry. It's stifling in here. I want to gulp down the water in front of me but don't want to give Burke a reason to think I'm nervous. "He was the last person to talk to her at the party. It made sense. At the time."

I hate the look in Burke's eyes; it's like he's trying to see past me, figure out what he's missing. Like he suspects I'm nothing but a carefully constructed act: the compliant, quiet one. The reasonable friend. It's who I've built myself up to be over the past year, because if the Markhams knew how I used to be, my happy new life would crumble around me.

"Okay, and instead of finding Bailey at Cliff's, you found her phone. How'd y'all find it again?"

"Jade called it and it started to ring. We followed the noise to the woods."

"Here's what I can't wrap my head around. If Bailey's phone was lying out in the cold, how was the battery not dead?" Burke glances at Knepper. "I don't know about you, but if I leave my phone in the car for even an hour in this weather, it's done."

Ellie gives a noncommittal nod.

"I don't know," I say. "Maybe it wasn't out there that long."

"Okay. So you found Bailey's phone while you were looking for her at Cliff Grosso's. Makes sense." Burke leans on his elbows, toward me. "Now, showing up at that barn and finding the blood? That makes less sense."

Of course, that's why I'm here. Does he think that I'm the one who left that blood smear in the barn?

Just tell the truth and nothing bad will happen. My mom said that to me when I was a kid, after I'd gotten into a scuffle with a girl during a kickball game in elementary school. She'd said I kicked the ball into her face on purpose because she and her friends wouldn't let me sit at their lunch table. I remember sitting in the principal's office waiting room, my mom's hand in mine.

Just tell the truth and nothing bad will happen.

It's such a load of bullshit. If I start from the beginning, tell Detective Burke everything, Ashley and my dad will definitely blame me for what's happening with Lauren.

There's only so much people are willing to forgive. That's the truth that trumps everything else.

"I already told you why I was at the barn," I say.

Burke leans forward. "You want to know what I think, Kacey? I think you're not telling me why you really went to Sparrow Hill yesterday morning."

I look over at Knepper. She's watching me, two fingers touching her chin, like I'm a painting she's trying to decipher. Burke taps the table. *Look at me.*

"We've got three locations"—Burke starts to tick them off on his fingers—"Bailey's vehicle, the barn, and the property where you found her phone. And we've got you, at two of those locations."

A flutter of panic. "Am I a suspect or something?"

"You're not a suspect. In fact, I think you're a witness. I think you know something you're not sharing with me, something you maybe don't think is important."

"I went to the barn because I heard something. A rumor."

"A rumor."

"This girl who lives on my street—this kid—she said she

saw someone covered in blood running down Sparrow Hill the night Bailey disappeared."

I've caught Burke off guard; he pauses with his coffee at his lips. Sets it back down instead of taking a sip. "That's quite a story. One that might have been helpful for us to know about."

"You'd have to know this girl, Chloe," I say. "She lies all the time for attention. Tells the other kids stories about the Red Woman. I didn't want to waste your time—I honestly thought I wouldn't find anything up there."

"The Red Woman?" Burke looks at Ellie, who clears her throat.

"It's, ah, a local legend."

"So like a ghost story?" Burke almost looks amused.

Ellie clears her throat. "The property where Kacey found the blood," she explains. "There was a house there in the thirties. A family was killed—the story is that the wife walks up and down Sparrow Road at night. Covered in blood."

Burke's forehead creases. "So this girl—Chloe—she says she saw a bloody ghost?"

I pull my sleeves down over my hands. "Like I said, she's always making stuff up."

"But you still wanted to check things out for yourself," Burke says. "It's why you went up to the barn yesterday, right? Curiosity."

"Yeah, I guess."

Burke is staring at my hands, at the way my thermal shirt-sleeves are stretched over them. I let go and set my hands on the table. "Bailey is my friend. I'm worried sick about her. I heard something weird, so I got curious."

"Okay, fair enough. Were you at the vigil last night?"

I hesitate. "No. I couldn't go."

"Really." Burke blinks, taken aback.

"I had a panic attack or something. I couldn't get dressed."

"A panic attack?"

"After I got home—from seeing the blood in the barn, everyone was badgering me, asking me stuff, and I just freaked out, I guess."

Ellie gives a sympathetic nod.

Burke scratches his temple with his pen. "So you were too nervous to attend the vigil?"

"What?" I look from Burke to Ellie. "*No*. I just—*I* helped look for Bailey in the storm on Monday. I was actually out there doing something. Sorry if I didn't think standing around holding a candle would make a difference in finding her."

I can feel it: the red splotches coming to my face. The tightness in my throat from trying not to cry. A tear slips out anyway. Ellie produces a box of tissues and clears her throat again. "Detective—I think maybe here's a good place to break for the day."

Burke's eyes are on me. "That seems like a good idea."

I'm wiping my face with one of the tissues when Ellie rests a hand on my shoulder. "I'll go call your stepmom, 'kay? Let's take a walk outta here. Get some air."

I let her put her arm around me, herd me back to the waiting area. I feel Burke watching me the whole time, and that's when I remember the pendulum from the séance, still in the pocket of my jacket.

CHAPTER TWELVE

In the parking lot, I can tell that Ashley is desperate to ask me what happened inside that interview room. A quick glance in the side mirror of the SUV shows I'm white as a sheet. At best, Burke thinks I'm some sort of rubbernecker, showing up at crime scenes.

Worst, he actually thinks I know what happened to Bailey. That I was involved somehow.

Ashley makes a right toward Main Street when we leave the sheriff's station, though, and not a left toward home.

"I've got to run into the drugstore and get Lauren something to help her sleep," Ashley explains. "You don't mind, do you?"

I'm quiet. I should tell her about the sleepwalking and Lauren wanting to stay in my room, but I'm positive of what will happen: Ashley will eventually break Lauren down, get her to admit to what we did the other night.

Ashley's fingers find mine, atop my knee, and squeeze. "Oh, hon, I'm so sorry. I'm such a horse's ass, asking you to go in there."

Friendly Drugs. She thinks I'm quiet because of the thought of going into Bailey's workplace and being reminded of her.

When your friend is missing, it's not something you need to be reminded of. Bailey's absence is my new state of mind.

We pull up to Friendly Drugs and I follow Ashley to the back of the store, to the pharmacy. Tyrell is behind the counter, wearing a white lab coat in lieu of the navy Friendly Drugs polo. He looks somewhat embarrassed by it.

"Nice coat," I say, while Ashley pokes around in the aisle. "You get a promotion?"

"I'm eighteen, so I'm allowed to work back here now." Tyrell pauses. "Have you heard anything?"

"Nah. We just left her house. Her mom's a wreck. What about you?"

Tyrell glances down the aisle. I follow his gaze. There's no one but Ashley, browsing the cold medications and sleep aids.

"I heard they're close to ruling Cliff out," Tyrell says. "His dad gave him an alibi. Said he was home and in bed before midnight."

So that's why they let him go from the station earlier. If Cliff fought with Bridget, left the party, and went home, there's no way he had time to follow Bailey, kill her, and get rid of her body. "Do you think his dad's lying for him?"

Tyrell's upper lip goes flat. He looks around the store to make sure no one's listening to us. "Don't repeat this, because I don't want him coming over here and accusing me of shit. But there's a rumor going around that Cliff's dad was at the Tap Room until closing time Saturday."

"So the alibi is bullshit."

Tyrell holds up a finger. Gestures: *Shhh*. "Like I said. It's a rumor. I don't know for sure."

Ty's voice trails off as Ashley comes up to the counter, empty-handed. "Ty. Andrew didn't tell me you were working back here. I'll have to tell Russ. He'll be so proud."

Tyrell wants to work in a hospital pharmacy someday, like my father. He got into Madison's pharmacy school, early admission. Six years of school, and he'll be a *doctor*. I envy people like him, who just know what they want to do.

"What can I help you guys with?" Tyrell asks, blush creeping into his cheeks.

"Lauren's having trouble sleeping," Ashley says. "Do you have anything stronger than Benadryl behind the counter?"

Tyrell disappears as an older technician—a woman with a smoothed blowout—comes forward. Sticks a pen in the pocket of her lab coat. "Is that Ashley Markham?"

"It is." Ashley cringes. I don't know the woman. Her name tag says *DEB*.

Apparently she knows me—or of me—because she clucks and grabs my hand, her words coming out rapid-fire. "You poor thing. You're friends with her. You must be in pieces. I barely knew her—she works up front—but it feels downright scary, her being gone."

I pull my hand back. Ashley puts a protective arm around

my shoulders. "You know, we could absolutely use your help this week," she says. "The sheriff's office is putting together a volunteer search. I'm putting together boxed lunches."

"Oh, bless your heart, Ashley Markham. You just name the place and I'll be there."

Tyrell comes up to the counter, setting down a box of NyQuil next to Deb's hand. He catches my gaze and rolls his eyes. Deb holds the scanner gun over the box of meds and gives a whole-body shudder. "You just don't think of things like this happening here."

Whenever people say that, are they forgetting about the Leeds family? "Yes." I nod in agreement while Ashley signs the book promising she won't make the NyQuil into meth. Deb is staring at me.

"I hope you've been being careful," she warns. She actually *wags her finger* at me as she bags the meds. "Right about now I'm very grateful we put Kayla in karate. Denise insists on dance still, bless her. These silly girls don't know what danger is."

Ashley grips the receipt Deb hands to her. No doubt thinking of Lauren, home alone with Mrs. Lao watching her. "Thanks, Deb. You take care."

"I heard they got some detective from the state bureau of investigation," Deb says. "Someone with actual experience."

"Well, the sheriff is doing his best." Ashley gives a tight smile. The Midwest way of saying, *Please shut the fuck up now.*

"You know, I wonder if they want him off the case because of his *connection*." Deb looks over her shoulder, which is hilarious considering the store is literally empty except for Tyrell. "Everyone is saying the Grosso boy is involved."

"I'm not sure that's wise." Ashley hikes the strap of her purse up higher on her shoulder. The Grossos may not be the most well respected in Broken Falls, but it's better to be feared than loved. No one wants to mess with them and have to drive forty minutes to the Walmart outside Pleasant Plains for ammunition. Most people who go in their stores do it with their heads down. Too afraid of looking at Jim Grosso the wrong way and getting a bullet in the ass like that boy did.

Perfect reason for the people who might have seen Jim Grosso at the Tap Room Saturday night not to come forward and say so.

"Well, sleep well." Deb gestures to the plastic bag with the NyQuil—I'd grabbed it unconsciously.

"Oh, those are for Lauren," Ashley says. "You take care, Deb."

"Oh! You know, your son has a prescription here waiting," Deb says. "Did you want to pick that up now?"

I freeze. Ashley says sure, gets out her wallet again. Completely unaware of what Andrew told me the other day: that he picked up his medication Sunday morning.

Ashley drops me off at home so I can *wind down* while she goes to the Costco in Pleasant Plains to get the boxes for the hundred lunches we're making tomorrow, to donate to the volunteer search.

Andrew is in the dining room when I get home, his physics textbook cracked open in front of him, an empty pickle jar off to the side. It sends a jolt of calm through me, a brief reprieve from how rattled I am after that interview with Detective Burke.

And then I remember the bag of meds in my hand. The ones he lied about picking up the other morning.

I sink into the chair across from him. He looks up. Shakes hair out of his eyes. "Hey."

"Hey." I set the prescription bag in front of him. "Your mom and I picked these up for you."

"Oh. Thanks."

A beat of quiet as Andrew finishes up the problem he's working on—math, physics, it all looks the same to me. I swallow. "I thought you said you picked up your prescription on Sunday morning?"

"I guess I had another one waiting."

I study the top of his head. Can't tell if he's purposely not looking at me. He could very well be telling the truth, but there's still a question mark that pings in my brain when I think of those fresh tire tracks Sunday morning.

I'm being paranoid. I'm just frazzled from the interview at the sheriff's station. As I open my mouth to tell Andrew about it, a familiar, husky voice floats down the hall. I stare at Andrew: "Chloe Strauss is here?"

Andrew rolls his eyes. "She just showed up. I kinda wanted to tell her to leave."

I unwind the scarf from my neck. "You're too nice to tell her to leave."

Luckily, I'm not. I follow the chattering into the den where Lauren and Chloe are watching TV. The sight sends a shock of annoyance through me. They're only thirteen, they're not even Bailey's friends, but seeing them chatter casually over *Say Yes to the Dress* is too much right now.

"Hey, Laur," I snap. "Don't you have chores to do before your mom gets home?"

Lauren looks at me blankly; Chloe inspires that held-hostage look in her eyes. "I did them."

Chloe mutes the TV. "I heard you're the one who found the blood in the Leeds Barn."

My heartbeat stalls. "How did you hear about that? It wasn't on the news."

Chloe shrugs. "My dad heard. He says Bailey's dead."

"It's stupid of him to spread rumors." I think of all the things people are saying about Bailey—that she OD'd on drugs, that she killed herself. What the hell do they know? "Bailey could still be alive."

Chloe lifts her chin. "She's not. I know what happened to her."

Lauren's shoulders tense up. I stare back at Chloe. She even looks like a little rat: pointy nose, mousy blond hair with a gray sheen to it. "What the hell are you talking about?"

"You guys made the Red Woman angry," Chloe says. "When you summoned her spirit to the barn. She killed Bailey for revenge."

In a split second I have Chloe's arm in my grasp, yanking her off the floor. She's yelling, and Lauren is yelling, and Andrew runs into the den. "Kacey! What is wrong with you?"

"There's something wrong with her." The feel of my nails digging crescent moons into Chloe's skin is satisfying.

"Let go of her," Lauren pleads over Chloe's yelping.

I let go of Chloe. She falls back to the carpet, her eyes saucers. My voice comes out in a tremble: "She shouldn't be here. She's a lying little psychopath."

Chloe lets out a low whine: "I didn't even *do* anything—"

"Jesus." Andrew runs a hand through his hair. "Chloe, c'mon. I'll walk you home."

Chloe stands up, sidestepping me like a cowering puppy. When they reach the hall, I hear Andrew admonish her: "You can't just show up here without calling first. It's rude."

I'm shaking, Andrew's words zipping around in my head. *What is wrong with you?* Lauren sits on the floor, shrinking into herself. Her eyes are on the door, but she doesn't move to get up.

"Laur—"

"Just go away, Kacey. You mess up everything."

I turn and cross the hall to my room without looking back at her. If I do, she'll see how much what she just said wrecked me.

Lauren hates me. I hurt her friend—the only friend she thinks she has left—so she must hate me. Chloe isn't going to want to come back here now. Maybe Chloe will even tell all the kids at school that Lauren Markham's stepsister is a psycho who tried to hurt her.

I never wanted siblings. My mom had always been so inaccessible, so erratic with her affection, that I couldn't imagine having to share her with someone else.

When the social worker told me that my father had a daughter and a stepson who lived with him, I thought I would be sick. They'd hate me, I was sure of it—I imagined being relegated to an extra bed in the attic. Real-life Cinderella shit.

So I tried to avoid everyone. But Andrew wouldn't let things be.

It was a Saturday morning when he came into the living room where I was watching Animal Planet. I turned it off, like I'd been caught watching porn—even though Ashley told me to treat the house as my own.

"Are you doing anything this morning?" Andrew asked.

I shrugged. "I don't now. Why?"

"I have to drive Lauren to the dance school in Pleasant Plains." He tugged on his knit cap. "There's a Waffle Hut across the street, so I always just wait there until she'd done instead of driving back . . . and now that I'm saying it out loud, I'm realizing how sad it is that I eat by myself every Saturday. So please come."

"Waffle Hut," I said. "I already ate."

"No one is ever too full for waffles. Meet us in the car if you want to come."

I thought about it for a beat. The alternative was sitting around doing nothing, possibly until my dad woke up. Then we'd be alone, and I wasn't ready for that.

I tugged my boots on. Threw on my jacket and scuttled outside, where Andrew's car was warming up. Lauren was in the front seat; through the glass, I saw them bickering. When I climbed into the backseat, she clammed up.

"Thanks for letting me come," I said.

Lauren nodded and took out her phone. She was silent for the entire fifteen-minute ride to the dance studio, even when Andrew tried to get her to talk about why she made the trek to Pleasant Plains every Saturday. She was a teacher's helper for a baby ballet class.

"How old are they?" Andrew prodded, when we were finally in the parking lot.

"Little," Lauren snapped. "You know that." She leapt from the car and hurried into the studio, pink dance bag slapping against the back of her leotard.

"She hates me," I said.

"Nah, she always says she'd rather have a sister," he'd said. "At least on the days she wants me to drown in hellfire."

Andrew paused, holding the door to the Waffle Hut open for me. "She's shy. Once she warms up, you won't get her to stop talking and you'll miss the quiet. Counter or booth?"

"I don't care," I said. Andrew picked the booth. As the waitress brought us menus, I felt a stab of homesickness. I thought of my mother and me, in our usual booth at the diner next to her bank. The tables were grimy and the plastic seats would stick to your thighs, but they had the best silver dollar pancakes. Always with strawberry syrup.

After the waitress took our order I slid the sugar shaker in front of me. Played with the top flap, eyeing Andrew. "Did you and Lauren even know about me?"

Andrew slid the shaker out of my hands and poured a tiny pyramid of sugar onto his spoon. "I did."

My throat felt tight. Andrew's gaze flicked to mine. "They thought it was for the best—Lauren wanted a sister so badly, and it would have been too hard to explain to her why we didn't even know you."

"And why was that, exactly? I just want the version you got."

Andrew hesitates. "Your mom wouldn't let your dad see you."

Our food came out—we'd both ordered waffles: his with fresh strawberries, mine with a scoop of ice cream. I wasn't hungry anymore. Maybe it was hearing someone confirm that my mom had lied to me my entire life.

I watched as Andrew administered an even sprinkle of sugar on each strawberry. I wondered if he did the same thing every week.

"My mom and I—my life before was really screwed up," I said. "The last thing I want is to screw someone else's family up."

He looked up at me and said, simply, "I don't think you could ever do that."

After that, before I started working at Milk & Sugar in the summer, I went with Andrew to drop Lauren off every week until dance ended for the year. My sister thawed, started to pout that she couldn't join our Saturday-morning waffle jaunt, like Andrew and I were attending a club meeting.

Really, we just talked. And one morning, when he caught me playing with the scar on my lip, he didn't look away.

"How'd that happen?"

I sipped my coffee. Set the cup on the saucer with a clink. "I bit through it when my mom pushed me into a wall."

He didn't react. "I'm really sorry."

"Don't be. I pushed her back." I looked out the window to the parking lot; the hostess was standing behind a Buick, helping the elderly woman behind the wheel back out of her spot. "It's why we can't live together. I'm just as bad as she is."

"You're really not," Andrew said, after a beat. "I mean, she was the mom. It should have been her job to keep you safe."

I picked up my cup. Set it back down. "Yeah. Maybe."

I hadn't told anyone the truth before, not even Dawn. But

that's the problem with letting someone slowly chip away at your walls—when you let too much of yourself out, there's no way to get it back.

I have got to keep my shit together. The last thing I need is for Detective Dickhead to find out that I assaulted an eighth grader. By now, Chloe has probably told anyone who'll listen what I did to her.

I wait until Andrew leaves with Chloe to tiptoe back into the den. No Lauren. I head upstairs, past my dad's room and the sound of waves rising and swelling. His noisemaker, so he can sleep through our bullshit during the day. Ashley jokes that he wouldn't wake up if Led Zeppelin reunited and started performing at his bedside.

I knock on Lauren's door; instead of snapping at me to go away, she lets out a delicate "What?"

I inch my way in. She's on her laptop. I think of scrolling through her browser history and swallow back guilt. "I'm sorry," I say. "Chloe just really pissed me off."

"It's okay." Lauren looks up from the computer. "She pisses me off too, sometimes. She said Bailey was killed in the barn in a satanic ritual."

"I don't think Bailey was killed in the barn," I say. "There wasn't a lot of blood."

Just a streak to mimic the one found in the barn the night the Leeds family was murdered. I think of what Jade said earlier: someone wanted the police to find the phone on Cliff Grosso's lawn. Whoever left it there earlier could have easily made the streak of blood to throw the searchers off more—make sure they look in the wrong place.

I sit on my sister's bed, inches from her desk chair. "Lauren, I told you not to tell anyone what we did in the barn."

Lauren's face pinches. "Chloe is my only friend."

"I'm your friend. Andrew's your friend." I sigh. "Chloe has issues. I think she really believes that stuff."

"The blood." Lauren's voice is a hush. "Was it really in the same spot?"

"It doesn't mean anything. It could just be someone playing a sick prank."

Lauren pulls her knees up to her chin. After a beat: "I'm scared."

"Of what?"

She looks out the window, the one that looks out over our road, Sparrow Hill visible in the distance. "That I'm never going to see you again."

What a bizarre thing to say. Does she think that whatever happened to Bailey is going to happen to me too? I shake the thought out of my head.

"That's not going to happen." But all I feel is a wash of anxiety, imagining Ashley's reaction if she finds out I'm responsible for Lauren's freak-outs.

That's what I should really be worried about—getting sent away from the Markhams for my bad behavior. But when I close my eyes, I see the halls of juvie as Crazy Missy described them. Girls going after each other like animals for misplaced glances.

I see Detective Burke, and the way he looked at me: like he'd found the missing piece of a puzzle.

CHAPTER THIRTEEN

Thursday morning brings no news. The volunteer search is tomorrow; tonight we will assemble the hundred cardboard boxes on the dining room table and fill them with sandwiches and chips for the volunteers.

I wanted to sign up for the search, but all volunteers had to be eighteen or older and pass a background check. Jade called me last night, in the throes of a fit.

"I'm going to be eighteen in two weeks," she moaned. "I feel so useless I could puke."

While my father is still sleeping, I write a note that I'm going to Jade's and leave it on the kitchen counter, even though before she left for the café, Ashley told us to stay home.

I begged her to let me work so I wouldn't have to sit around the house all day, but she insisted I stay home and get a head start on all the reading my teachers have been assigning via email while the burst pipe and damage to the classrooms are being fixed.

I can't sit around all day waiting for news about Bailey's case. But I'm not really going to Jade's, either.

It's too cold to walk, but I don't want Andrew to know where I'm going. Somewhere between the Chloe thing and Lauren's creepy warning, I decided not to tell him about the séance in the barn, or the roof collapsing, or the blood smear.

I don't know what I want to hear right now, but I don't want Andrew telling me it's impossible for there to be a connection between Bailey's disappearance and everything else that happened on Sparrow Kill.

The bus to Pleasant Plains stops a quarter mile from Sparrow Road. When I get to the station, I am the only one there. A poster with Bailey's face on it stares back at me. We didn't hang this one on Monday.

Monday feels like a lifetime ago. In a few days it will be Monday again, and school will reopen. Will everyone be talking about the burst pipe—will Bailey be old news, since she'll have been missing for over a week? I can picture her face, screwed up at the idea of everyone carrying on as normal when we don't even know if she's alive or dead.

The steel bench at the station may as well be an ice block. I opt to stand until the bus pulls up to the curb.

I unfold the dollar bills in my glove and hand them to the driver. Frost puffs out of his mouth from the door being open. "How are ya?"

I nod an *okay* and take the seat five back from him, in case he's feeling chatty. There is only one other person on the bus; a homeless man I've seen outside the Tex Mex in Pleasant Plains.

Lauren asked, last year, why he would be on the streets in the cold when there's a homeless shelter not far away. I think of leaving the warm bed in my mother's apartment for the parking lot of the 7-Eleven in Rochester.

There's no easy way to tell a kid that sometimes the outside is safer than the inside.

Enchantment Crystals actually has a customer. I hang by the bookshelves while the creepy woman from Monday rings up a bearded guy, chatting him up about how the book he's buying really *is* the definitive guide on how to use chakras. I thumb through a book about maledictions and curses as the guy leaves, toting a brown bag with purple tissue paper sticking out.

There was something about the way the woman was looking at Bailey's *Missing* poster the other day—it almost looked like she recognized her. It's a long shot, I know. But if there was a chance she was here, I want to know why.

"Shopping for you or someone else?" The woman is watching me. She said the same thing last time I was here, but her voice is less expectant this time. Less saleswoman-y.

I can't find my words. The woman's face softens.

"Where's your friend?" she asks.

Gone, I think, before realizing she's talking about Jade. "She doesn't know I'm here."

"I've been following your other friend's case," the woman says. "The missing girl. It's very sad."

I don't know what to say. *Thank you* doesn't sound appropriate. "Did she—Bailey—did she look familiar to you?"

The woman steps out from behind the counter. She's wearing a paisley skirt that skims the floor. "Her hair. It's gorgeous. I remember seeing a girl with hair like that in here. Made me look twice."

My heartbeat quickens. "When was this? What did she want?"

"I don't know," the woman says. "I had to do a reading in the back room. When I returned, she was gone."

Something in me deflates. I don't know what I was expecting to hear—that Bailey had gotten her fortune read? That this woman somehow holds the key to finding out what happened to her?

"I'm Amber," the woman says, nodding to the book of curses still in my hands. "Makes a good gag gift, but not much else."

I expected her to have a more exotic name, like Rhiannon or Raquel. I replace the book on the shelf. "Why do you sell this stuff if you don't believe in it?"

Amber smiles. Her purple lipstick bleeds over one corner of her mouth. I want to wipe it away. "I have to stock things that people want, even if I don't personally subscribe to that set of beliefs."

"But you really believe you can contact the dead?"

The pressure in my head reaches a crescendo; I sneeze.

"How about I put on some tea," Amber says, "and we can chat?"

. . .

We're in Amber's back room, where she does her readings. The tea smells like strawberries and I watched her make it, but I still don't touch it when she puts the mug in front of me. The woman gives me the creeps—I saw her flip the sign on the door to *BE BACK IN FIFTEEN MINUTES* before she led me into the reading room.

I'm telling her about last Friday night in the Leeds Barn.

"I know the roof must have collapsed from the wind . . . but at the very moment as we were holding a séance? It was creepy." I wedge my hands between my thighs.

Amber nods. Doesn't look at me like I'm batshit. "The energy in that barn—there are probably many spirits waiting to come through, after what happened there."

I lick my lips. "I know this sounds so stupid—but is it possible my friend Bailey went missing because of what we did? The séance."

"You had a strong brown aura around you the other day." Amber refills her tea. Glances at me over the handle of the pot. "Brown can mean deception."

"So you're saying I'm lying about all this?"

"Not necessarily. It could mean someone is deceiving you. Someone you know is responsible for her disappearance."

It's not exactly a stretch to believe Bailey knew her killer—after all, Cliff was the last person to see her alive. Still, my stomach drops. "You said I knew where Bailey was, and I wasn't saying. I think . . . it's because deep down, I know she was murdered. And I didn't want to say that in front of Jade."

Amber studies me. "Did you come here to see if I can pull

any clues to what happened to her? Because nothing is one hundred percent accurate."

I hesitate, then nod. Of course it's not going to be accurate—it's going to be mostly bullshit—but I can't help thinking of the way Amber pinned down how Jade was feeling, that day we came to hang Bailey's poster. *You think that if you were with her the other night, she wouldn't have disappeared.*

Amber was right. Jade *was* beating herself up over leaving Bailey alone. How could she possibly have known that?

"A reading with a full set of cards is forty dollars," Amber says.

I have twenty-five bucks in my wristlet. I want to cry.

Amber's face softens. "But if you would like insight as to your friend's situation, there's no charge."

I feel myself thaw a bit toward Amber. "Why would you do that?"

"I contacted the police offering my services. They politely declined." Amber smiles. "I understand why."

Because this is all crap and a waste of the bus fare it took me to get here.

"But why not try to make money off me?" I ask. "No offense, but isn't that why you do this?"

Amber gets up; I think I've offended her and she's about to ask me to leave. Instead, she shuffles around the credenza by the reading room door. She returns holding three cards.

"I already pulled your friend's cards. Her past, present, and future." Amber sets down three worn cards. I can't tell what any of them are. I point to the first one, which kind of looks like people falling off a giant penis.

"What does it mean?"

"That's the Tower. I pulled it seeking answers about Bailey's past." Amber takes a sip from her tea. "The Tower means there was a sudden change in Bailey's life. Chaos. Something that made her question who she was."

I rack my brain. Cathy had said Bailey asked for help, a therapist. "How far back in this past are you talking about? Like, did this sudden change happen before she went missing?"

"That, I couldn't tell you. But her present card was interesting. It's the Seven of Swords."

I stare at Amber blankly. She points to a card with a man dressed like a clown, absconding into the night with swords in his arms.

"This card suggests betrayal, sneakiness," she says. "Deception."

"That doesn't tell us anything new," I say. "Obviously whoever took her deceived her somehow."

"Not necessarily." Amber puts a lacquered fingernail to her lip. "Taken together with the Tower, I'd have to say that whoever deceived your friend knew her well."

I feel sick. *It all means nothing. It's all bullshit.* "What about her future card?"

Amber flips over the third card. "This could potentially tell us where to find Bailey. As you can see, the Empress is in a field."

My mouth goes dry. I'm not looking at the background, or picturing Bailey lying in a field. I can't tear my eyes from the woman on the card. *The Empress.*

She's wearing a white nightgown, spotted with red roses that almost look like blood.

Amber is screwing with me. She picked that last card on purpose because I told her I suspect Bailey's disappearance is tied to the Red Woman. She's sick—coming here was sick.

"I need to go," I mumble. The blood rushes from my head, and when I stand, my knees nearly buckle. I feel like I've been poisoned, but I didn't even touch the tea Amber made.

"Wait!" Amber calls out to me as I push my way through the curtain dividing off the back room. "Sweetheart. You forgot your wallet."

I turn. Amber is behind me, a pitying look on her face, hand extended with my wristlet in it. Beyond her, there's a glass case that catches my attention.

I pause. In the glass case, on display, is the pendulum. The one Bailey brought to the barn. But it can't be, because that pendulum is still buried beneath the underwear in my nightstand.

I come to a full stop, aware that Amber is following me. I point to the pendulum. "Where did you get that?"

"It's a new style, one hundred percent angelite," Amber says, ready to unlock the case. "It just came out this year."

My toes curl. "No—my friend has the same exact one. She said it was her mom's. That it's vintage."

Amber laughs. "The manufacturer bills it as a vintage style, but between you and me, it was made in China."

I can't tear my eyes away from the display case. That shade of teal—the design on the chain—it's the *same one.*

"Would you like to see it?" Amber asks.

I shake my head. "Is that the only one you carry?"

162

"It's the only one left," she says. "My associate sold the other one not long ago, I believe."

A funny taste comes to my tongue. "When did she sell it?"

"Hold on," Amber says. "I'll get the sale log."

The back of my neck is clammy and cold. The blood is returning to my head. Amber dips behind the counter and emerges with a marbled notebook. She thumbs back a few pages before pausing. "Ah! Two weeks ago."

"Does it say anything about who bought it?"

"No, just that it was a cash transaction. I could call my associate and see if she remembers, if you'd like?"

There's no point. I know it was Bailey—it's the same exact pendulum she'd said she found in her mother's old things.

So she lied about where she got it. Just like she lied about why she was leaving the party.

There's only one thing I'm sure of anymore, and it's that Bailey Hammond, alive or dead, is a liar.

And I want to know what else she lied about.

Junior Year
June

Have you ever had a secret so big it would destroy you if it got out? Spoiler alert: I do. And it's so bad I almost don't want to write it here, even though not even my nosy-ass mom could find my hiding spot for this notebook. (Spoiler alert: a nifty slit cut in the underside of my mattress.)

My secret is that I have a problem, and it's a boy. Not Cliff Grosso, although he's a royal thorn in my ass, telling everyone we did things in Tyrell's house that we didn't. This boy is different. He's the nicest person I've ever met. The type of nice where if you even *think* about making fun of someone, this boy's face pops into your mind and starts judging you. He's funny without being mean, something the other boys in Broken Falls can never achieve with their lesbian jokes and bad impersonations of Mrs. Gonzalo, the vice principal. Everyone calls her Gonzo because of her nose, and that's always made me sad.

This boy's beautiful in a way that is absolutely devastating, with a smile that makes you feel like you're the only person he sees.

I've loved him since the moment I laid eyes on him.

The problem: the boy does not love me back. How do I know he's not into me? Because if a guy is into you, he'll fucking

TELL you. Even if he doesn't form the words with his lips—*I'm into you!*—he'll find other ways. For example, if he knows you work at the local drugstore, he'll find an excuse to pick up his prescription during one of your shifts and not send his mom to do it. If he runs into you and you casually mention you're going to his best friend's party, he'll show up at the goddamn party because he knows you'll be there.

That's only a small sample of things he would do if he *were* into me.

But the fact that I love this boy isn't my nasty secret. In fact, some people know how I feel. Val Diamond knows, because I've been in love with him for the better part of my life. In eighth grade, Val and I even came up with a grand plan to make him fall in love with *me*—I'd enter the spring talent show and sing Joni Mitchell's "A Case of You" while locking eyes with him in the front row. He didn't even show up for the performance.

Obviously Jade knows how I feel about him, because Jade is my person and I don't hide shit from her. But she doesn't know how bad it is. That my feelings for him are like a chronic illness, flaring up at the worst times. And I've got it bad again— so bad it's infected my brain and I think I may *actually* be going crazy.

So, you want to know the crazy part. The shit that's too shameful for print. Well, here it goes.

Last night: in my brother's room next door, where my dad is relegated to every night, he was snoring, the vibrations were coming through the wall and keeping me awake, and I started to itch all over. So I did something I haven't done in ages, something I used to do when I couldn't sleep. (No, not THAT, gutter mind.) I grabbed my keys and I snuck out, and I went for a drive. It had been months since I'd done it; I never even told Jade about all the other times, because she'd say I have issues. And I wouldn't even be able to argue with her because she's right; what I do is so completely fucked up and here's why:

I went to his house. HIS HOME.

I parked across the street and turned my headlights off and just *watched* the house like I did all those other times before I swore to myself that I was sick, I had to stop. You know what the worst part of *pining* for someone is? Not knowing what they do, who they really are when no one else is around. People show such a small slice of their real selves to the rest of the world; home is the only place where you can act like your real self, where you really *are*. I want to know who he really is; I want to know what he sounds like when he gets pissed at his little sister. I want to know what he wears to bed and what his sheets smell like. I want to know how his hair looks when it sticks up in the morning or what his breath smells like and what kind of shit he watches on YouTube when no one else is around. I wanted to scream it, text it to someone. *I want him so bad!*

But poor me, he doesn't want me. Maybe I'm still Hammy Hammond to him. Maybe he sees into my soul when he looks at me and sees *my* true self, the one I hide away to everyone but this stupid journal. Maybe he sees the craziness that compelled me to drive to his house in the middle of the night like some creepy stalker.

He will never love a Nothing girl like me. He likes girls like Meg Constanzo, his ex-girlfriend. Meg, who is the holy grail of cute AND hot, even when she's sweaty from her lacrosse and tennis games. Meg, who posts a picture of a waffle and gets over a hundred likes. Everyone calls her *fatty* because she's obsessed with food, even though she's barely one hundred pounds. Because what's funnier than a twig who can stuff her face? There's not a guy in school who would not want to date her. Unlike Bridget Gibson, who is a dick to the lowest members of the high school caste system, Meg is nice to everyone. *Everyone* loves her.

I fucking hate her.

Before you start thinking I'm a traitor to the female gender or something, it's important that you know I've tried not to hate Meg. Who can hate her when she's so fucking nice? But I can, because I have been conditioned like a puppy to hate people who have things that I don't. One of my most vivid childhood memories is running home from the Diamonds' house and telling my mother they were getting a pool. *Well,* good old Cathy snapped, *that's a little showy.* I have fought against my instincts, even tried to get Meg to notice me and be my friend. But why would she notice a Nothing girl, just like *he* doesn't notice a Nothing girl?

How am I supposed to like the girl who has everything when she had the only thing I've *ever* wanted: him?

Have you ever wanted something so badly you thought it just might kill you?

CHAPTER FOURTEEN

It's snowing lightly Friday morning. There are rumblings the search will be canceled until one of the organizers posts on Facebook. *THE SEARCH FOR BAILEY IS ON!!! DRESS WARMLY AND IN BRIGHT COLORS.*

Ashley and Andrew are signed up for the search, while my dad is staying home with Lauren. The search is supposed to end at five; Ashley lets me borrow Andrew's car for the day so I don't have to wake my dad up for a ride later when we close at three.

I rarely drive. Ashley taught me last summer, so I could get my license, but I don't have my own car. And the roads here make me nervous. They're packed with snow, and deer are likely to jump out at any moment.

I leave earlier than necessary and take the whole drive at twenty miles per hour. Andrew's car feels tiny in comparison to Ashley's SUV, rattling over every bump in the road. The snow comes down in steady flakes.

I open the café with my key and get several pots of coffee going. Rob is five minutes late, as usual, but we're hardly busy when I flip the sign on the door to *OPEN*. The people who do come in are wearing *FIND BAILEY* buttons.

"Where did you get those?" I ask Meredith, Tom Cornwell's adult daughter. Her son is in Lauren's grade.

Meredith looks embarrassed for me. "The Diamonds had them made for the search volunteers."

"Oh."

When I bring Meredith her usual cinnamon latte, she uses her free hand to unpin the button. Hands it to me. "You should have it."

Once she leaves, I pin the button above my right boob. I imagine what Jade would say about it. *How is a fucking button supposed to help find her?*

Unease settles over me. Jade must know by now that I'm avoiding her. And I can't even come up with a good reason why. Maybe it's the way she looked at me when I told her what I said to Ellie Knepper about Bailey wanting to run away. Maybe I'm still guilty about missing Bailey's vigil. Or maybe it's because I have something else to hide from her now—the fact that I went to the spiritualist shop and spoke to Amber. Jade will just find a way to make me feel humiliated about it, or worse. I think of the look in her eye when she confronted me about

169

telling Ellie Knepper that Bailey may have run away. She'd stared at me as if she were seeing something that wasn't there before—something untrustworthy.

It means I can't tell Jade about the pendulum. Not yet—not until I find out why Bailey lied about where she got it. Otherwise, Jade might think I'm trying to make our missing friend look like a liar to get the heat off me.

My head goes hollow as I think of the way Amber looked at me: *It could mean someone close to you isn't being truthful.*

Jade had promised me she wouldn't tell Burke about the barn, or Lauren sneaking out with us. But I'm not Jade's best friend: Bailey is. And Jade will do anything to bring Bailey home.

Even if it means telling the police everything.

Even if it means making me look like a liar to Detective Burke.

Around eleven, a Camry with a Broken Falls High Dance Team sticker on the back window pulls up outside the front of the café. I recognize it as Val Diamond's car and freeze in place. Outside the front window, I spot Bridget Gibson and Val approaching the door.

I turn around, hurry behind the front counter. Bend down and make a big deal of finding the bleach-soaked rag we keep by the pastry case for spills.

When Bridget and Val approach the front, I shake off a tremble. I don't know why; girls like them have just always inspired that reaction in me. Like despite their perfect smiles and sugary-sweet voices, I should be afraid of them.

"Hi, Kacey," Val says, not meeting my eyes. "Can we have two vanilla lattes?"

I nod, suddenly voiceless, as I accept the five-dollar bill in Val's palm and make change. Bridget is hanging behind Val, immersed in her phone. They take one of the empty tables as I get the latte machine going.

Once the mugs are filled and steaming, I make my way to their table and find my voice. "Is there anything else I can get you?"

Bridget looks up at me. Says nothing, as if I don't exist. Her nose is red, as if she's been crying. She has always reminded me of an animated Disney princess—overexaggerated green eyes, honey-blond hair, and freckles.

But here's the thing about Bridget: she's actually kind of terrifying. Rumor has it she made a middle school boyfriend cry when he forgot to decorate her locker for her birthday. Her peons love her; they call her Gibby, their go-to girl to throw down when someone is an asshole to them.

I've always steered clear of her. Didn't want to get on her bad side.

Now, I just don't care. I look Bridget in the eye. "Let me know if there's anything else you need."

As I turn to head back to the counter, Bridget calls out: "Kacey."

My name sounds strange coming out of her mouth. Desperate, almost. I turn around.

"Someone went to the police and said they saw Bailey's car outside Cliff's house last week," she says.

I stop and turn around. It feels like the floor is shifting beneath me. "Bailey went to Cliff's *house*?"

Bridget's voice is icy. "Did you know?"

My hands go into the back pockets of my jeans. "Know what?"

"That he was hooking up with Bailey behind my back."

So this is why they're here. They think I have some sort of gossip; that I can confirm an affair between Bailey and Cliff.

She didn't tell me shit, I want to say. *Go talk to Jade.*

But that would be throwing fuel on a fire. I steal a glance at the counter; Rob is still in the kitchen, listening to AC/DC and being generally oblivious to what goes on up front. I take the third chair at Bridget and Val's table. "How do you know that they were hooking up?"

Bridget looks at me as if I'm dumber than the stray muffin crumb on the table. "Why else would she be at his house?"

"I don't know," I say. "I thought he hated her."

"Apparently not," Bridget says.

My thoughts swirl. *Did Jade know? Jade would have said something*—"It doesn't make any sense. Bay never told me."

Val pipes up, her voice quiet as a mouse's. "She probably didn't want you and Jade to know."

"Whatever, I broke up with him," Bridget announces. "So it's officially no longer my problem."

"How can you say that?" I ask, my eyes finding Val's, as if I'm waiting for her to jump in and agree with me. But she looks down at her latte. "Even if you hate her, shouldn't you be at least horrified that Cliff may have—"

"He didn't kill her," Bridget snaps. "Don't even say that. He was home all night after the party."

"You really still believe him?" I ask. "After he never told you Bailey was at his house?"

Bridget's eyes go glassy. "I know he wouldn't hook up with that skank unless she threw herself at him."

"Bridget," Val says softly.

"Whatever." Bridget's eyes flick to me. "Cliff isn't even the one Bailey really wanted. You should know that."

My hands go cold. "What are you talking about?"

Val looks nervous. Bridget flicks her hair over her shoulder. "If you don't know that she was only friends with you to get to Andrew, then I feel sorry for you."

Almost Senior Year
July

I'm floating. Forget all the emo shit I said in my last entry. I'm *floating* because I think I was wrong about everything.

If a guy likes you, he'll just tell you.

But what if he's also the shy, sensitive type who guards his feelings? Especially after the last girl he opened himself up to broke him into a million pieces. Fucking Meg Constanzo, who dumped him sophomore year with no explanation. I've been waiting to be the one to put him back together. I know it's supposed to be me. If it's not, then every romantic comedy ever lied to me. I'm the dutiful childhood friend, the one who always gets looked over until one day he opens his eyes and sees, *Of course! It's her!*

It just sounds like bullshit, doesn't it? But that doesn't mean there's no truth to it. Because I think it might *finally* be my turn. I think Andrew Kang *finally* sees me.

But I'm getting ahead of myself. To start at the beginning: Yesterday the Markhams threw a birthday barbecue for Lauren. Kacey called the other night while I was at Jade's and asked if we wanted to come and keep her company, since she was scared about meeting the rest of her father's family. *Her* family.

"Well, obviously you want to go," Jade said, looking at me

while covering the speaker with her thumb. "McSketch will be there."

Jade doesn't like Andrew, and I keep telling her she doesn't have to hate him just because he doesn't like me back. She insists that's not why—she says she doesn't like him because he's *uppity*. Says he thinks he's too good for Broken Falls, never shows up at parties to make a point about how straightedge and *good* he is.

I never told her about the pills I see Ashley picking up from Friendly Drugs every month. The ones with Andrew's name on them. The ones that say *Do not mix with alcohol*. I looked up what they're for, and they're antidepressants.

Anyone else might wonder what a guy like Andrew Kang has to be depressed about; he's got the perfect family, he's smart, and he's a shoo-in for whatever college he wants to go to, so he has a one-way ticket out of Broken Falls. But I think I get it; I see a sort of restlessness in his eyes that I recognize in myself.

I feel it when I see the same customers at Friendly Drugs every day over the summer. I feel it when my mom makes Frito casserole for dinner even though we just had it a couple days ago and I realize God, it's another Tuesday already.

I feel it every night when I hear my dad laughing until he chokes at his seven p.m. sitcom reruns. He must have seen every episode five times by now, but he still cracks up like he's never heard the jokes. That's what this whole town reminds me of sometimes. People who are laughing at a joke that has long passed.

Sometimes I imagine running away with Andrew Kang. I picture him whispering in my ear, *Let's just go,* and then we'd get into his car and his fingers would find mine over the cup holder and it would be just the two of us again like it was when we were kids.

Anyway. I shook Jade off my phone and told Kacey we'd definitely be at Lauren's birthday party.

Mrs. Markham was at the back gate when we arrived, tying a giant pink balloon in the shape of the number 13 to the fence. It was exactly the type of thing I'd find humiliating at thirteen, and I felt a wave of pity for Lauren.

"Girls." Mrs. Markham finished knotting off the ribbon and beamed at us. "You are too sweet for coming. Let me introduce you to Aunt Jess and Uncle Ken."

Jade jabbed my ribs with her elbow. "This is a family party," she hissed in my ear.

I gave her a look like, *So?* I tugged at the hem of my jean shorts as Ashley turned around. "Lauren has been having some trouble with her friends at school," she said, her voice low. "I'm just—Kacey is so lucky to have friends like you girls."

I smiled. "We're lucky to have her." I was suddenly aware of the small box in my hand—a ring in the shape of a wave Jade had helped me pick out from the silversmith in Pleasant Plains. I held out the box to Ashley.

"Oh, that was so sweet of you," Ashley said, taking it. "Let me show you where the gifts are." When she turned her back again, Jade muttered *This is so fucking awkward* in my ear.

Ashley led us toward a picnic table covered in a blue cloth with a shimmery piece of netting over it. Next to a pile of gifts was one of those tiered trees of cupcakes. Each had a different sea creature molded out of fondant: starfish, oysters, clown fish, even an octopus with round candy tentacles.

"Those are awesome," I said. "Where'd you have them made?"

Ashley lit up. "You'll never believe it, but Kacey made them."

Jade ran a finger along one of the pearls, perfectly shaped from fondant and dusted with that shimmery edible powder. I smacked her hand away.

"She's really talented," Jade said, but I could hear the layer of frost in her voice.

"I know!" Ashley beamed. "Mr. White recommended her for AP art. The board has to approve it, since she doesn't have the prereqs, but we have our fingers crossed."

"Fingers crossed," Jade deadpanned. I wanted to elbow her. I wasn't in the mood for hearing about how it wasn't fair that Kacey could just slide into AP art when Jade had to work her ass off for it. If there's one thing I'll never get Jade to understand, it's that things are just easy for some people. They just fall into a Cinderella-fairy-tale ending like Kacey did.

Not that I'm bitter or anything. But I know Jade is; even if she won't say it, I know she resents that the Markhams and my family have enough money to send Kacey and me to college. Meanwhile, Jade's dad hasn't saved a penny for her and has such horrible credit he can't even cosign a loan for Jade.

"Where are Kacey and Andrew?" I asked.

"I don't know." Ashley frowned; something at the gate had caught her attention. More guests—the creepy little girl from down the street, Chloe Strauss, and her parents. "Excuse me a minute," Ashley said, wandering off.

"Don't be a bitch," I whispered to Jade at the exact moment Lauren spotted us from across the yard. She dropped her hands to her sides shyly and made her way over to us. She gave me a huge hug, then turned to Jade. "Thank you for coming."

"Where's Kacey?" I asked, at the same time I saw them through the bay window in the kitchen. Andrew was leaned back against the counter, and Kacey was standing next to him, almost intimately. They were talking. In their own private world. My stomach dropped to my toes.

Lauren was babbling. "Aren't they so cool?"

"Huh?" My eyes snapped back to Lauren.

"The cupcakes," Jade muttered. We were still standing over the table with the desserts and the gifts. The box in my hand felt pathetic. The ring felt cheap and stupid compared to the cupcakes Kacey had no doubt spent hours making.

"Yeah, they're awesome." I knocked my shoulder into Lauren's. "Happy birthday, girl."

"Thanks. Wanna find Kacey? She said we could all play volleyball."

Jade and I followed Lauren around the giant net set up several feet from the fence. The Markhams have always had the nicest backyard of anyone I know—a pool, a koi fountain, and a sprawling deck with a hot tub. Jade snickered once that they're like the Brady Bunch. *I bet they're secretly fucked up,* she'd whispered. I told her all families are fucked up, but at least they get a pool out of it.

Kacey and Andrew barely heard us enter the kitchen from the side door. "Whatcha talking about?" Jade said, a little too loudly.

"Nothing," Kacey said, putting distance between her and Andrew. "College stuff."

"Can we play volleyball?" Lauren asked.

"Sure, Monkey." Kacey flicked the end of Lauren's ponytail. "We just have to finish up the iced tea."

"I've got it," Andrew said. His voice was like bells in my stomach. "You guys play. I'll catch up."

"Oh! We should do sisters versus *practically* sisters," Lauren said.

Jade muttered, *Hope you're ready to get your butt kicked,* and Lauren giggled. I hung behind as she, Kacey, and Jade filed out the side door.

I saw my chance then. "I've got to use the bathroom," I said. "I'll be out in a sec."

But by the time I'd shut myself in the bathroom next to the kitchen, I'd lost my nerve. I sat on the toilet and inhaled. *Hey, Andrew. We never hang out anymore.* It was so simple. I would not be a goddamn wimp. We were in diapers together, practically. In preschool, we played army with those little plastic bears meant for learning how to count, back when my mom still worked and shared carpooling with Andrew's mom.

I flushed the empty toilet and washed my hands. Stepped out into the kitchen, where Andrew was adding a mountain of mix to a glass pitcher of iced tea.

His mouth parted with surprise when he saw me. He smiled. "You caught me. I like it extra sweet."

I folded my arms across my chest, forcing myself to be cool. "I didn't mean to be such a creeper."

"Nah, you weren't. It's just weird seeing you in here again."
His smile turned sad. "The last time you were here was my seventh birthday. Remember those teal overalls you used to wear?
They were made out of that fuzzy stuff—"

"Corduroy. I can't believe you remember that." I tried to hold back the smile blooming on my lips. *Be fucking cool.*

"I remember everything."

So do I. "That was the party when your stepdad dressed up as Darth Vader, and we hit the piñata with light sabers."

Andrew laughed. I hadn't heard him laugh since sophomore year. Since the whole thing with Meg Constanzo dumping him, he'd been broody. Different. But lately, I caught him smiling again. *You made him laugh.*

"We used to have so much fun," he said. "I miss that."

"I do too." Sadness mingled with the butterflies in my stomach. *I miss it too. But we can still get it back.*

Andrew's eyes twinkled. "Remember how ticklish you were?"

"I still am," I laughed, and then he came at me from the side and used two fingers to tickle the space above my hip. My heart leapt into my throat. *Don't ever stop touching me.*

I squealed and grabbed his fingers. He was laughing, and I was laughing, and God, the look on his face. I'll be replaying it in my mind forever, like a scene from a favorite movie. I'll feel his fingers grazing my side like a warm glow in my stomach forever.

Then his mom called to him from the open window, asking where the iced tea was. I followed him outside, our *moment* interrupted. When Jade asked me why I was wearing a shit-eating grin, I just shook my head and took my position by the volley-ball net.

I'm closer than I've ever been.

Something is finally going to happen between us. I can feel it.

CHAPTER FIFTEEN

When Bridget and Val leave the café, I ask Rob to watch the front counter so I can lock myself in the bathroom.

She was only friends with you to get to Andrew.

I lower the toilet seat and sit, hugging my knees to my chest. Bridget is wrong; Bailey and I are friends because I sat next to her that first day in local history. She asked me to be her partner because I was *there*. We're friends because of fate, not because of *Andrew*.

Fucking Andrew. I'm not stupid; I know that every girl in our grade has been in love with him at some point. But I'd always assumed that Jade and Bailey were immune to his charms. Jade is constantly making fun of him, calling him McSketch, pointing out how he wears basket shorts even in the freezing cold. *He's so weird.* Bailey would even sometimes join in.

But then a flash of a memory comes on strong, like a migraine. Meg Constanzo.

Meg is one of the girls that other girls like to hate—she plays a sport every season. Her wardrobe is entirely J. Crew and her ponytail is unnaturally bouncy. But when she smiles at you, it's impossible to hate her, because she just looks like she really means it.

Bailey hated her anyway. We were hanging out in the parking lot after school last spring, waiting for Jade to finish uploading her photographs to the Mac in Mr. White's room. Bailey and I leaned against the chain link separating us from the fields, soaking up the last bit of sun before her four p.m. shift at Friendly Drugs.

The gym doors opened at the side of the building, and the lacrosse girls jogged past us. Meg was at their helm, already a captain even though she was only a junior. She smiled and waved at us. *Hey, guys.* That was the entire transaction.

When the lacrosse girls were gone, Bailey said, "God, I fucking hate her."

I watched them run onto the field, sticks held high, their laughter echoing up to the parking lot. "Meg? Why? She's nice."

"It's so fake," Bailey said. "No one is that nice."

It took months for Andrew to open up to me about what happened the previous fall, why he missed so much soccer practice and got kicked off the team.

"I was dating this girl for like six months," he'd said, over teaching me how to play Risk. "When she broke up with me, she wouldn't tell me why. And I guess I sort of just shut down."

Color had crept into his cheeks when he said it, like I would judge him for something. Judge him for the pills I'd seen Ashley pick up for him from Friendly Drugs.

But I understood; after a particularly bad fight with my mom, I wouldn't want to leave my room for days. My bed was my only comfort from the feeling that started with being unable to face one person and ended with being unable to face the world.

Andrew told me the girl's name with a shrug. Meg Constanzo. From what I knew about her, she was exactly the type of girl that it made sense for Andrew to date.

But I didn't put the pieces together that day in the parking lot when Meg said *hey* to Bailey and me. *God, I fucking hate her.* I'd written it off as Bailey feeling bitchy for no reason. A flash of a moment, so quick you could blink and miss it.

Now I'm left wondering: what else have I missed?

Moments after Bridget and Val leave, my phone buzzes in my back pocket with a text from Jade: *what did bitch 1 and bitch 2 want??*

I swallow, shaking off the eerie feeling of being watched. Jade works at Tim's Taqueria down the street; no doubt she saw Val's Camry parked outside the café when she arrived at work for her eleven-thirty shift.

I can't shake Bridget's words from my head. Could it be true that Bailey was only using me to get to Andrew? Jade's not stupid; she must have known how Bailey felt about Andrew. Jade was the best friend, and I was the extra friend. There are things you tell your best friend that you don't tell the extra one.

I wonder if they did it on purpose: not telling me that Bailey was into my brother.

I delete the text from Jade and head back to the sink, praying that she won't come over here when she realizes I saw the message and chose not to respond. Jade's boss, the eponymous Tim, is a hardass and only lets her have short breaks.

The thought is comforting. I don't want to see Jade right now. I don't know how to make what we have work; not only do we not know how we fit together when we don't have Bailey as our connective tissue, but Jade is suspicious of me.

I need time to figure out how to handle her. Get her back on my side. And I'm not going to do that by entertaining rumors over coffee with the two girls Bailey hated more than anyone.

I'm washing dishes when the bell over the front door tinkles. I crane my neck to look over the counter in time to see the two men coming in. One white, one black. Both in work pants and heavy parkas. From the highway snow removal company, maybe.

I've never seen them in here before, but then again, Pete's Dinette is closed today so all of the workers could join the search for Bailey. These men are probably regulars there; they stare at the menu over my head, puzzled by words like *organic* and *seven-grain* before settling on two coffees and a stack of buttered toast.

I yell for Rob to throw the toast in before I start on the coffees. The men take the table closest to the counter—the one covered in sugar left from an overzealous toddler this morning. I was so distracted by Val and Bridget I forgot to clean it up.

One of the men—the white guy—leans back in his chair so vigorously it groans. "You see any of the searchers on your way up?"

I keep one eye on them as I start a fresh pot of coffee.

"Nah, I heard most of 'em got sent to Pleasant Plains," the black guy replies.

"Makes sense. Seems like if she were in Broken Falls, someone would've found her by now. They asked everyone with land to search it good."

My hand trembles around the handle of the pot. I think about interrupting—*You sure you want that coffee black?*—just to get closer and hear their conversation better.

The white guy takes a napkin from the holder in the center of the table and tears at one of the corners. "You hear? Jim Grosso was the only one who wouldn't consent to a voluntary search of his property."

I freeze. The black guy whistles. "He's got that big shed and everything."

"Isn't his boy involved with the Hammond girl somehow? At least, that's what people are saying."

The bell in the kitchen dings; Rob passes me a plate of buttered toast. My back turned to the men, I keep one hand on the coffeepot, cursing the crescendo of the gurgle the fresh drip makes. I step away from the machine so I can hear the men better.

"I heard Sheriff Bill's got his eye on one of the girl's friends," one of the men says.

I whip around, forgetting my hand on the coffeepot. It slips from my grasp and shatters on the floor. Hot coffee continues to pour out of the machine, splashing the thighs of my jeans. I ignore the way the wet spots are scalding my legs and react stupidly, trying to pick up the pieces of the shattered glass from the pot.

"Whoa, whoa!" Rob runs out of the kitchen, brandishing a rag. "Don't touch."

But it's too late—there's a slice down my thumb, like a paper cut, but deeper. The men are staring at me; I can feel it. Rob wraps the rag around my finger, and I swear he can hear my heart trying to leap out of my chest.

"Can you get them two black coffees?" I choke out. Then I make a run for the kitchen.

I hear Rob apologize to the men as I stick my finger under cold water in the back sink. *Sheriff Bill's got his eye on one of the girl's friends.* They were talking about *me,* and they hadn't even realized it.

Cold sweat springs to my face. I stand over the sink, watching my blood circle the bottom of the sink, staining bits of egg stuck in the drain. *People think I did this. People actually think I could have killed Bailey.*

And why wouldn't they? I'm the outsider who waltzed into Broken Falls a year ago with no explanation. Russ Markham's bastard child, the girl with purple hair and a sketchy past. The media is saying Bailey knew her attacker; everyone knows no one *from* Broken Falls is capable of murder.

But there *is* one other person. Someone who actually had a reason to want to hurt Bailey. And for whatever reason, the police believe the bullshit alibi his dad gave him.

I don't. And I need something, anything to prove that Cliff Grosso is the one who is hiding the truth about that night.

When Rob comes back into the kitchen, he pushes his bandana up his forehead and takes my finger gently. "There's Band-Aids in Ashley's office. Go get one and I'll watch the front."

"I've got to go," I blurt. "I'll be gone an hour, max. You can handle things on your own until then, right?"

"Kiddo, I handle this place on my own all the time." Rob blinks at me with bloodshot, pot-addled eyes. "What's going on?"

"There's just something important I need to do."

Rob glances at the closed door to Ashley's office, where she usually is. Fielding calls from distributors. Working on our paychecks and schedules. "Maybe I should call Ash."

"Please. Don't do that. She doesn't have her phone with her, anyway. The volunteers aren't allowed to carry them because people might take pictures or whatever."

Rob just looks at me.

"An hour." I hold my hands up. "I swear."

Rob rubs his stubbly chin. Sighs. "Okay. I'm calling you if you're not back by then."

I'm sitting in Andrew's car, engine running. My phone is ice-cold in my injured hand as I look up the number for Grosso's butcher shop.

Someone picks up on the second ring. The voice is raspy, male. "'Lo?"

"Is this Jim?" I ask.

"Speaking. What can I do you for?"

Hanging up would be too suspicious. "I'd like to place an order. A big one."

Jim Grosso sighs. "Hold for me a minute, okay?"

I keep my voice even, chipper. "Sure thing."

When the line clicks, I end the call. I turn on the radio and wait five minutes before I call Grosso's Hunting and Game. I immediately get a gruff male voice on the phone that sounds like Cliff.

I hang up.

I breathe hot air into my gloves and start the wipers on Andrew's car. They whisk away the fattening snowflakes landing on the windshield. If the snow keeps up, they'll have to end the search early. Panic needles me; I shake my head. I have to do this.

I punch a vague address into my phone GPS—Cypress Circle—because I don't know Cliff's exact address. The directions lead me down the same back roads Jade and I took the other morning.

When I arrive, the Grossos' cabin is dark; no smoke billows from the chimney this time. I park far from the house, midway between their property and the nearest neighbor. *What the hell am I doing?* With shaky hands, I pull the beanie I left on Andrew's passenger seat over my ears and step out of the car.

I keep toward the edge of the Grossos' property, hoping the trees and falling snow will obscure me from any prying eyes. The snow packed on the driveway crunches under my feet, despite my efforts to make my footsteps delicate. I glance in the garage; there's a snowblower, an ATV, but no Jeep Wrangler papered with NRA bumper stickers. Just like I thought, Cliff isn't home.

Snowflakes catch on my eyelashes as I creep around the side of the house. *Footprints.* The Grossos will come home and see my footprints. It's too late now. I hope it snows harder to cover my tracks and keep plugging away toward the shed.

I freeze. There's a rustling in the woods, the snapping of twigs. I crane my neck to see better; a fawn stares back at me, a statue except for its jaw working a mouthful of deer feed. I slowly show my hands and it stops chewing. In a flash of brown, it jolts away into the woods.

Overhead, a woodpecker pauses from its tapping. I let out the breath I was holding and continue up to the shed, breathing in through my nose. There's no rotten smell this time, no stink of blood. The frost paralyzes my nasal cavity, but I can detect pine needles and rust.

I'm brushing my hand over the padlock as a voice sounds around the other side of the shed.

"Don't move or you're dead. I mean it."

All the blood in my body drains to my toes as I see Cliff Grosso coming at me, a crossbow on his shoulder, the tip of the arrow pointed at my heart.

CHAPTER SIXTEEN

The words tumble out of my mouth: "I'm sorry. I'm sorry. Don't kill me."

"What the fuck do you think you're doing?" Cliff tilts the bow twenty degrees downward. Still close enough to send the arrow flying into a less vital part of me.

"I don't know." My inner thigh is wet; I must have peed a little when I saw the crossbow. "What were you doing in the shed?"

"Fueling up the snowblower. What are *you* doing on my property?"

I can't stop my knees from shaking. "It was nothing—just let me leave. I swear to God I'll never come back."

Cliff's upper lip twitches. "You're not going anywhere until I call the police so they can find whatever you left back here for them to find."

"What? I didn't leave anything. I swear to God."

"Just like you didn't leave Bailey's phone?" Cliff rubs his upper lip. Nervous. He thinks I planted Bailey's phone on his property.

"I swear I didn't do it," I say. "Please let me go."

"Nah. I don't think so. Because someone's fuckin' framing me," Cliff says. "And I think it's you."

He lifts the crossbow; I yelp again, but he's just switching arms. He digs a cell phone out of his pocket and dials. I sneak a glimpse at the screen—he's calling his father, not 911, which almost makes me piss myself all over again.

My heartbeat thrums in my ears, drowning out what Cliff mutters into the phone. I'm going to pass out. When he ends the call, Cliff turns to me: "My dad's calling the sheriff. He says not to let you leave."

My teeth are chattering. The pounding in my ears dissolves to white noise. "I need to sit. Can I at least—can we go inside?"

Cliff grabs me by the arm. Pulls me with him around the shed, then pushes me inside the open door at the other end. He must have been in the house the whole time, watching me through the window.

Crossbow still cocked on his shoulder, Cliff moves to a stack of lawn chairs. He grabs one off the top with his free hand and drops it in front of me. "So, sit if you want."

I sink into the chair and dip my head between my knees. When I come back up, Cliff is staring at me. "You're one strange bitch, you know that?"

I lick my lips. They've gone numb. "Why do you think I planted Bailey's phone?"

Cliff shrugs. "I heard you know where she is, and you're trying to make sure everyone's looking at me."

"Who's saying that?" I demand. "That I know where she is?"

"People. Around." Cliff shrugs. "Everyone knows you keep magically finding evidence."

"I didn't find the bloody sweatshirt." Something about the way that crossbow is pointed at me is making me bold. He's not going to shoot me: not with Sheriff Moser on his way here. "Speaking of, you're not missing a sweatshirt, are you?"

Cliff snorts. Shakes his head. "Yeah, cops showed me a picture of the sweatshirt. Not mine." Cliff stares at me. I notice for the first time how far apart his eyes are. I will never understand the bewitching effect he has over girls like Bridget, who could do so much better.

"You didn't answer me," he says. "Why the hell are you here?"

The lawn chair is ice-cold beneath my butt. "I came here looking for Bailey."

"You think I'm keeping Bailey in my *shed*?" Cliff blinks at me. "You really must be out of your skull. She's dead, haven't you heard?"

"You seem pretty confident about that."

"Whatever. I feel bad about it and all, but it's time to face facts. And I'm so sick of people trying to pin this shit on me because of what happened last year."

I keep my eye on the crossbow, my teeth chattering. "Maybe they think losing a scholarship is big enough of a deal to kill someone."

"Yeah, maybe. But I already told the cops I let it go. I didn't give a shit about Bay anymore."

"Then why wouldn't you let the cops search your backyard?"

"Whatever. My dad is a private person." Cliff shifts his crossbow to his other shoulder again. "Besides, my Jeep is at the crime lab right now. I let them search it because I got nothing to hide."

So stupid. I hadn't even considered the possibility that Cliff would turn his Jeep over. I'm fumbling; I can't take my eyes off the crossbow. I'm sure he's not going to use it—it's all about control with him—but it's still nerve-racking to have it in my face. I decide that whatever happens when Jim Grosso gets here, I can't leave without answers.

"Bailey was here, wasn't she? A week ago," I say.

Cliff's expression darkens. "How do you know about that?"

"Bridget told me."

Cliff's shoulders rise. "Don't talk to me about Bridge."

I would be perfectly content not to talk to Cliff Grosso about anything, but grilling him is a distraction from how completely fucked I'll be once his father gets here.

"Just tell me why Bailey was here," I say. "If you weren't hooking up with her, what did she want from you?"

Cliff's shoulder muscle twitches under the weight of the bow. He won't answer me; if it was sex Bailey wanted from him, why not admit it? Cliff Grosso is not known for his modesty. Before he started dating Bridget, when someone was saying his name, it was usually accompanied with the name of whatever girl he bragged about sleeping with most recently.

And besides, Bridget already broke up with him. It's not like he has anything left to lose. So why the stubborn silence?

Why does he look *scared*?

Outside, someone shouts Cliff's name. His eyes flick to the shed door. "In here!"

Cliff hangs up the crossbow on the rack next to a bunch of gardening tools. Sheriff Moser, the hood of his parka pulled over his leathery forehead, is standing in the doorway. He looks back and forth between us. "Well, what in Sam Hill is going on here?"

Half an hour later, I'm still sitting on a couch in the Grossos' living room. Sheriff Moser is standing in the doorway to the kitchen, and Jim Grosso is standing off to the side. Jim is even more frightening than Cliff; he was a linebacker too, back in the day. It's not hard to imagine his enormous arm muscles slamming a cleaver through a slab of meat.

Cliff is on an armchair catty-corner to me, and everyone seems generally unconcerned that he was pointing a crossbow at me thirty minutes ago.

There's a commotion outside the front door; through the living room window, I spot the back of my father's head, his hair rumpled from sleeping. The deputy posted outside the Grossos' house the same loudmouth who blurted the news about blood being in Bailey's car—raises his voice to match my father's. Sheriff Moser's gaze darts back and forth between the door and me, as if he's weighing whether it's a good idea to leave me alone with the Grossos.

"Uh, you all wait right here." Moser steps outside. "Jim, why don't you come with me and we'll sort this out."

When his father is gone, Cliff folds his arms across his chest and stares me down. I avoid his eyes, trying not to think about what will happen if his father presses charges for trespassing. What the sheriff will do to me for showing up somewhere I don't belong for the second time this week.

Some muttering outside. Moser steps back in the house, waves me over to him. I feel like a criminal, even though Cliff is the one who rear-ended Ellie Knepper when he was drunk.

"Alrighty. Jim here has agreed not to press charges for trespassing as long as you stay away from his house and his son."

"His son—like I'm stalking him or something?" I ask.

"I think I've got it from here, Bill," my father says sharply. "Kacey and I are going to go home now, if that's all right."

Moser tips his hat. "You take care, you hear? All this just makes me want to go home and be with my daughter."

My father nods and guides me with a hand on my back to Andrew's car, which is waiting several hundred yards from the house.

When he speaks, his voice is sharp. The sort of sharp that's usually reserved for Lauren when she's acting like a brat. "Follow me home. Straight home."

And that's all he says. He never has much to say to me, anyway.

Ashley and Andrew get home from the search not long after my father and I get home. The search was supposed to run until five, but the weather made it too dangerous for people to be walking up and down the winding roads between Broken Falls and Pleasant Plains.

When I saw Ashley's SUV pull into the driveway, I ran into my room like the coward that I am. Which is where I'm hiding when the arguing in the kitchen starts. I can't help myself; I crack open my door so I can hear.

Ashley's voice carries down the hall: "What the hell was she doing there?"

My dad's response is measured, even. "I don't know, Ash. No one tells me anything that's going on around here."

"Maybe if you were home, ever!"

The sound of a fist hitting a hard surface makes me jump. "I was home all day with Lauren!"

"I asked you to check on Kacey at the café," Ashley says. "Make sure everything was all right.

"I didn't know she required twenty-four-hour supervision." His voice is almost inaudible compared to Ashley's.

"There are a lot of things you don't know about your daughter, Russ."

I don't know what my father's response would have been, because the sound of the phone ringing interrupts him.

"Hello?" There's a pause that goes on for days. A *Thank you, we'll be there as soon as possible,* end call. I know it's the sheriff's office by the polite panic in Ashley's voice.

"They want to talk to her," she says.

"Again? They *just* talked to her!"

"I don't know, Russ. Do you blame them after what happened today?"

I grab my coat and head down the hall, my heartbeat drowning out the sound of their bickering. When I step into the kitchen, both of them turn and stare at me like they've never seen me before.

"Ready when you are," I say, then add, "to go to the sheriff's station."

Ashley and my dad look mortified. They know I must have heard everything, but it doesn't bother me.

For some reason, I want them to know I heard every word.

Ashley brings me to the station so my father can get some sleep before his night shift. This time, there's no negotiating Ashley being in the room for the interview. She plunks down on the chair in the corner, one protective eye on me as Ellie Knepper puts a hand to my lower back and guides me to the table.

"Detective Burke will be right in. Can I get you folks anything? Coffee? Water?"

"Maybe some water," Ashley says. As Ellie disappears, Ashley points up at the camera in the corner of the room. A light pulses twice.

"Just be honest." Ashley's voice is clipped. Like I haven't been honest up until now.

My chest constricts. What does she think I'm hiding?

There's the fact that I snuck out Friday night, but that hardly feels relevant right now. I'm in way deeper shit.

I'm sweating by the time Ellie returns with two bottles of water. I want to twist the top off and shotgun the whole thing greedily, but Burke is with Ellie, and I don't want him to see that I'm nervous.

"Thanks for coming in." Burke slides into the seat opposite

mine. Moser drags a chair across the room to join us at the table. Burke cringes at the metal legs scraping against linoleum.

"You understand why you're here, don't you, Kacey?"

I lick a raw spot on my upper lip. "The Grossos are pressing charges after all?"

"No," Burke says. "Sheriff Moser is handling that matter. I want to talk more about Bailey."

My stomach goes into free fall. *Sheriff Bill's got his eye on one of the girl's friends*. I want to ask if I'm a person of interest, but I can't bring myself to do it with Ashley sitting in the corner.

But Ashley must sense the change in atmosphere, because she pipes up. "Does Kacey need an attorney?"

Burke looks over at Ashley. "That is entirely up to you two. I still think Kacey is a witness, and not a suspect. I just need her help convincing me."

"No lawyers," I say. "I'll tell you what you want to know."

Burke sets down a photo on the table in front of me. It's the blood smear on the wall in the barn. "I want to talk about this. We matched the blood type to what we found on some other evidence."

The sweatshirt. Probably, her car. My throat goes dry. "Is it hers? Her blood type?"

Burke's chin quirks.

"Oh God." I shift in my seat. The blood is rushing from my head; I have to rest my head in my hands. Ellie Knepper gives my back an awkward pat.

"The tread marks from your boots," Burke continues. "We found matching ones all over the barn." He gives a final-sounding crack of his knuckle, like it's the period at the end of his sentence. "It doesn't match the story that you went up to the barn, stepped through the door, saw the blood, and turned around."

He's got me—there is literally no way to lie myself out of this without making it seem like I'm the one who made that blood smear.

"The other morning wasn't your first time in the barn, was it, Kacey?" Burke says.

My mind goes blank. I can't think about Jade, and how we agreed not to mention being in the barn. I can't think about Ashley, and how pissed she'll be that I snuck out and dragged Lauren along.

There's literally no way out of this mess but to tell the truth and hope that Burke believes it.

"Okay," I say. "We were there Friday night. Before Bailey went missing."

Burke leans forward on his forearms. "Who's we?"

I swallow. Tamp down the urge to look at Ashley. I only have one option if I'm going to keep any semblance of peace at home. I've already lost one of my best friends. I can't lose my family too.

"Bailey, Jade, and I," I say.

"Just the three of you?"

"Yes. It was just the three of us."

"Okay. What were you three doing up there?" Maybe I'm imagining it, but he emphasizes the word *three,* as if to let me know he thinks my story is bullshit.

I have to force the words out: "We held a séance."

Burke blinks at me. "A séance?"

Ellie leans in to him: "Like communicating with the dead."

Annoyance flits across Burke's face. "I know what a séance is." Still, he's staring at me like I'm making the whole thing up.

"It was Bailey's idea," I say. "I know—it was stupid. She wanted to try to summon the Red Woman. Jade and I aren't into that stuff, but you'd have to know Bailey. If you don't go along with her plans, she gets really—pissy."

"Did Bailey get like that often?" Burke blinks at me. "*Pissy?* I'm just trying to get a better sense of what she's like."

Possessive. "She would get mad at me if I didn't do stuff like sneak out with her and Jade. If I said no, she'd just show up at my house anyway."

I can practically feel Ashley cringing behind me. Her obedient stepchild, leaving through her bedroom window to do God knows what.

Burke taps his forefinger to his chin. "But she didn't just show up at your house the night of the party?"

I shake my head. "I told you. I didn't want to go."

"That's not what Jade Becker says. She says you seemed upset on Sunday that Bailey never texted you about picking you up and bringing you to the party."

Fucking Jade. All she did was tell the truth, but it feels like a knife in my back. Of course Jade would tell the truth—she'd do anything to get Bailey back safe.

Burke studies me. "You realize that contradicts your earlier story that you decided not to go to the party on your own, and went to bed?"

Don't you fucking cry. "I didn't really want to go to the party. So when Bailey didn't text me, I was relieved, I guess."

"And you're sure she didn't just show up at your house

201

anyway? While you were sleeping." Burke adds the last part as if it's for my benefit. As if he doesn't really buy that I was asleep.

Panic corners me. "My stepmom told you I was home all night." I turn in my chair to face Ashley, who nods. But there's something else in her expression.

Distrust.

"I don't get why you're doing this to me." A tear leaks out of my eye when I look at Burke again. As I wipe it away, Ellie Knepper materializes over my shoulder with a box of tissues. "I don't *know* anything. Shouldn't you be talking to Cliff Grosso? Someone saw Bailey at his house just last week—people are saying his dad is lying for him about where he was Saturday night—"

"Cliff Grosso is not a person of interest at this time." Burke cuts me off.

I clamp down my mouth before opening it again. "Why? Because he was dating the sheriff's great-niece? Because his family owns half the businesses in town?"

Burke smiles. "I can assure you there's no law enforcement conspiracy regarding the Grosso family. The investigation is simply taking us in a different direction."

"In *my* direction." My hand forms a fist under the table. "That's total bullshit."

"Kacey." Ashley's voice is like the crack of a whip.

Burke removes a photo from the folder in front of him and sets it on the table between us. It's a grainy image, probably from a security camera. I recognize the gas station at the corner of Mills Pond Road and Sparrow Road.

Passing by is a blue Honda Civic. It's too dark to see the driver's face, but there's a clear shot of the license plate. GRR. It's the same license plate I looked for a thousand times in the BFH parking lot in a sea of blue Honda Civics while I waited for her after school.

It's Bailey's car. The time stamp in the corner reads 11:31 p.m.

I do the math in my head: Bailey left the party at a quarter after eleven. Prairie Circle and Kevin Sullivan's house is about a ten-minute drive from our house.

"Notice this?" Burke taps Bailey's right headlight. "Her blinker is on. Like she's headed down Sparrow Hill."

"You think she left the party to meet me?" I shake my head. "No. She could have been going to Sparrow Hill—back to the barn—"

"And why would she do that?" Burke watches me, expectant. I have no answers for him. Only pieces of information that grind to a paste in my brain. *Had* she been coming for me, and something stopped her?

Ashley pipes up. "How much longer will this take, Detective? I'd really like to get Kacey home. It's been a long day for all of us."

"Of course. Just one more thing for now." Burke thumbs through another file folder filled with sheets of paper. "Can you verify your cell phone number for me?"

"Are those Bailey's phone records?" I don't mean to blurt it.

Burke's eyebrows meet in the middle. "They are. She liked to text quite a bit. We haven't gotten the content of those messages yet, since they were deleted, but it's only a matter of time. The crime lab has ways of recovering them."

203

Relief settles over my shoulders. Because those phone records will show that Bailey and I had no contact at all on Saturday. As I recite my number, I think, *This is it. He'll see I never called or texted her. He'll see I couldn't have gotten her to leave that party.*

Burke repeats my number back to me, thumbing through the pages in the folder. "So if I'm not mistaken, the last time you texted Bailey before she went missing was Friday night."

"Right." I nod. "Like I said, we snuck out. She texted to tell me she and Jade were coming to pick me up."

"Right." Burke smiles. "Then I guess we have nothing more to discuss at the moment."

I exhale for what feels like the first time in hours as Ellie escorts Ashley and me from the interview room to the front doors. Outside, the snowfall is picking up. I want to shout it into the sky: *The phone records will set me free.*

So why was Burke holding them to his chest like they were a winning hand of cards?

CHAPTER SEVENTEEN

Ashley doesn't speak to me as we sign out of the sheriff's station. I keep my eyes on the powdery snow beneath my feet in the parking lot. Study the tread tracks from the boots that screwed me over.

"I think it's best if you don't work on Saturdays until all of this is sorted," Ashley says once we're shut in the car. She's livid, I can tell. But she's still trying to make a punishment seem like she's doing me a favor.

"I'm sorry I snuck out. They didn't give me a choice—they just showed up—"

Ashley cuts me off: "Leann Strauss was at the search today." There's something simmering under her voice. It makes my insides shrivel up.

Ashley pinches the area between her eyes. "She said Chloe

has been saying that you're witches. She knew about the—whatever it is you guys did in the barn last Friday night."

I squeeze my eyes shut. The world is swimming.

"Lauren was with you, wasn't she?" Ashley's voice is straight-up terrifying. "That's why she won't sleep, or eat."

I want to tell her that it was just a stupid séance, a dumb game—that nothing really happened—but it'll only make Ashley angrier with me. She already watched one of her children fall apart. Who knows how long Lauren will take to recover from what happened in the barn?

"She caught me sneaking out," I whisper. "She wanted to come."

"She's a child! A child who would do absolutely anything for validation from her older sister."

A tear squeaks out of my eye, hot and angry. "I didn't know you resented me that much."

"Don't be manipulative. You've done nothing but hide things from me since Bailey went missing," Ashley says. She sounds on the verge of tears too. "Is there anything else you need to tell me?"

"No."

"I didn't think so."

I feel my temper flaring. My mother would be screaming at me, and Ashley's calmness is only a reminder that she's not my mother and never will be.

Ashley doesn't broadcast that she cut my hours; instead, she tells everyone over dinner that *something has come up* at the café and she'll be working more, so basically we need to keep our shit together while she's gone.

And Mrs. Lao will be here each day my dad isn't home or sleeping. So basically, every day.

"That's so not fair," Lauren says. "We're old enough not to need a babysitter."

"Eat your pizza," Ashley snaps.

I turn to Andrew when everyone seems distracted. "Did you find anything at the search today?"

But Ashley has the hearing of a bat. She sets down her water glass, hard enough to rattle ours. "Not at the table."

I don't even get a chance to think about how to respond, because the doorbell rings. My fork drops from my fingers. Ashley cringes, and Andrew's face falls; nothing good follows the sound of the doorbell lately. Even Lauren stops pushing the food around on her plate and freezes.

My dad is the one to stand up. Ashley doesn't bother barking at us to keep eating as he crosses through to the foyer and unlocks the front door.

Sheriff Moser's voice carries through to the table, settling over us like frost. "Good evening, sir. Hope I didn't interrupt dinner."

"We are eating, actually. What is this about?"

"We're following up on some things regarding the Bailey Hammond case." Ellie's voice now.

"You already talked to my daughter earlier," my dad says. "I think that's enough for one day."

Moser's voice is apologetic. "No disrespect intended, Mr. Markham. But we're here to talk to your son."

CHAPTER EIGHTEEN

"It's just a few routine questions," Moser says. "We're going through everyone who knew Bailey at this point."

Ashley puts down her napkin. *"Knew?"*

Moser goes red in the face. Ellie Knepper gives him a look like he's the stupidest man she's ever laid eyes on.

"You can follow us back to the station if you'd like," she says, glancing at Andrew. "It shouldn't take more than an hour."

"Why can't you talk to him here?" My father asks.

Andrew stands up. "It's fine. I'm eighteen. They're just routine questions, right?"

He looks at Ellie Knepper for affirmation, but Moser pipes in: "You bet. We'll have you home before *Jeopardy!*"

"Andrew—" Ashley starts to get up, but Andrew is already

putting on his jacket. "Mom. I'm eighteen. You really shouldn't leave Lauren and Kacey alone. Russ has to work, remember?"

My father goes red in the face to match Moser's. And then Andrew is gone, stepping out the front door and chatting with Moser about Badgers basketball like this is a perfectly normal Friday evening.

But I know better: nothing will ever be normal again.

Andrew isn't home in an hour, or two for that matter. I hear his car pull in at nine, nearly two hours after Moser and Knepper showed up at our doorstep, and I hear his footsteps head straight for his room.

At a quarter to eleven, when I hear Ashley's bedroom door shut, I text Andrew: *you up?*

He types back: *yeah.*

Me: *what did the police want to talk to you about?*

Him: *I'm coming down. Den?*

I'm up and out of my room in an instant. I slip into the den, leaving the light off. The remnants of today's fire still glow in the hearth.

I grab the poker and stoke the fire, waiting for the delicate sound of footsteps. Andrew slips into the room, rubbing his eyes. I can't bring myself to pounce on him about Burke just yet; he looks like shit.

I sit down on the hearth, leaving room for him to sit next to me. "How was the search?"

"Pointless," he says.

I wait for him to go on.

209

Andrew rubs his eyes again. "I didn't want to find her—I know we were supposed to want to find her, but—"

He didn't want to find her body.

"Every time we saw something out of place, we were supposed to flag it. I saw this black trash bag." He props his elbows on his knees and leans forward, his face in his hands.

I put a hand to Andrew's back. Feel his sharp inhale. He sits up straight. "I don't think they have any idea what they're doing. They wasted so much time by not looking for her right away. They say if a missing person isn't found in the first forty-eight hours . . ." Andrew covers his face again, his voice trailing off.

I mentally complete his thought. *Then the odds are that they won't be found alive.* I pull my knees to my chest. "Who did you talk to at the station? Moser?"

Andrew shakes his head. "Some uptight guy. Detective Burke?"

I force myself to say the words: "What did they want to talk to you about? Me?"

Andrew's hesitation confirms it. I nod. I am strangely calm for someone whose world is crashing down on her.

"Hey," I ask. "Did you go somewhere Saturday night?"

Andrew pops a knuckle. "Where would I go?"

"You lied about picking up your prescription."

Andrew lowers his head. Massages his eyelids. "I just drove around."

"Saturday night. The night Bailey went missing. You just *drove around*." I'm furious—Ashley might suspect that I wasn't home in bed like I said I was that night, and meanwhile, Andrew was the one who snuck out.

"Look, I know how it sounds, but you have to trust me," he says. "I told the police about it."

"Where did you go? When did you sneak out? I didn't even hear you."

Andrew looks at me like he's in pain. "Kace, just let it go."

Anger flares in me. "No, I won't let it go. That detective thinks I had something to do with Bailey going missing and meanwhile you're just *driving around*—"

Footsteps overhead. The stairs creak. Moments later, Ashley appears in the den doorway. Andrew stands, like he was on his way out, but it comes off suspicious as hell.

Ashley looks from Andrew to me. "What are you doing? Is everything okay?"

"Yeah," Andrew says. Hands in his shorts pockets. "Everything's good."

Ashley searches her son's face. "I heard you get up—"

"We were just talking," I say. Even though it's the truth, it sounds like a lie rolling off my tongue. Ashley looks at me. There's something in the way that she regards me that wasn't there before.

"I couldn't sleep," Andrew says, as if that's a perfectly reasonable explanation for having a clandestine meeting in the den in the middle of the night.

"Well, try to." Ashley frowns. "You're both overtired."

She's looking at us as if she sees something she can't unsee.

CHAPTER NINETEEN

I wake up in the morning to a text from Ashley saying that my dad decided to take an overtime shift, so Mrs. Lao is coming to "keep an eye on things" while Ashley's at the café. I don't have the energy to be annoyed that I'm seventeen and have a babysitter for the day. There's something ominous lurking under the text, almost as if Ashley's trying to tell me that I need to be watched.

I don't bother getting out of bed at all. It feels nice. Maybe I'll do this every day. The thought of school on Monday, of the homework I meant to do last weekend and never got around to, makes me feel ill. When Mrs. Lao comes over at nine and tries to make me get up, I tell her I have cramps.

"I have licorice root at my house," she says. "I'll get it and make you tea."

"No, thanks," I say. "You really don't have to be here. I can watch Lauren."

"Not leaving girls alone." Mrs. Lao shakes her head. I don't have the heart to point out that I'm twice her size. I at least convince her the tea isn't necessary, but she refuses to leave, so I guess we both lose.

I force myself out of bed. Pop my head into the den. Lauren is curled on her side, Jerome at her feet. He picks up his head to growl at me. I hiss at him to shut up and he freezes, lets out a huff of air, and rests his head back on Lauren's bare foot. She's passed out. In the living room, Mrs. Lao has a morning talk show blasting, a perky woman extolling the virtues of a ten-speed blender.

There's a voice in my ear.

"Kacey?" Mrs. Lao.

A ragged, annoyed sigh of relief slips out of me. She's behind me, snuck up on me. She looks me up and down. "Jade is here."

Shit. No doubt here to rip me a new one for ignoring all of her calls and texts. "Where is she?"

"I made her stay outside," Mrs. Lao says. I brush past her and make my way downstairs and to the mudroom. Pull my boots on. From the window, I see Jade's dad's truck idling at the curb, her behind the wheel.

My bones ache with distrust. All I want to do is get rid of Jade as quickly as possible. When she sees me coming down the driveway, she reaches over and opens the passenger door.

I climb in, jaw set. The leather seat is freezing beneath my pajama pants.

Jade still hasn't done her eyeliner. I wonder if it's a mourning ritual, and she won't put it on again until Bailey is home, one way or another. She looks me in the eye with disgust. "Are you *trying* to get yourself killed or arrested?"

"Why are you here, Jade?" The acid in my voice makes Jade suck in her cheeks.

"What's your problem?" she asks.

"That detective made me come in again for questioning yesterday. Someone told him that I was supposed to go to the party, but that Bailey ditched me. That I was *upset.*"

Jade's eyebrows furrow. "Jesus, Kace. I had to. That guy—he's relentless. I would have admitted to having a bag of coke in my pocket if it got me out of that room."

I don't say anything. I can't bring myself to tell her that Burke knows we were in the barn Friday night now too.

"Anyway, what does it matter?" Jade asks. "You didn't have anything to do with this."

I'm quiet. Jade leans over, forces me to look at her. *"Kacey."*

"Burke seems to think I did. Even Cliff freaking Grosso thinks I was involved."

Jade stares at me. "Why did you even go to his house?"

"I wasn't thinking. I thought I'd find something. I don't know." I'm on the verge of tears. *I just want someone to believe that it wasn't me.*

I swallow to clear my throat. "Did you know that Bailey was at Cliff's house last week?"

Jade sits up straighter. "What?"

"Someone saw her car outside," I say.

"And how many blue Civics are there in Broken Falls? It could have been someone else."

"Why are you so desperate to believe that Bailey told you *everything* she did?"

Jade's cheeks turn ruddy. "Why are you doing this? She could be dead. Your priorities are a little screwed up right now."

My knee is jiggling. She's right, but the nagging voice in my head says Bailey might be dead because of the things she didn't tell us.

"She didn't like me," I finally say.

"And who told you that? *Bridget?*" Jade plops back in her seat. "That's ridiculous. Bailey was the one who asked *you* to hang out."

To get to my brother.

I let out a frosty breath. "Did you know she was into Andrew?" I ask.

Jade frowns. "Of course I did."

"How come you guys never said anything?"

"Honestly?" Jade peers at me. "She told me not to."

"Why? I wasn't going to blab to him or anything."

"Don't sound all insulted." Jade lowers her mirror to check her eyeliner. Realizes it's not there. A sigh bubbles between her lips. "She never told anyone how she felt about him. Not even me. I just figured it out."

"But why all the secrecy? It's not like Andrew would be mean about it. Maybe he even liked her back."

Jade tilts her head to look at me. "Kace, come on. You know he saw her like she was still the kid from his preschool class."

"I just don't get why she was so intense about hiding it," I say.

215

"Because she was intense about anything that could possibly hurt her," Jade says. "If she found out for sure that Andrew wasn't into her, it would destroy her."

For some reason, I think about the tire tracks by Andrew's car Sunday morning. The lie about picking up his prescription. A clump of snow falls from a branch overhead and lands on Jade's windshield, jolting me in my seat.

Jade's the one to finally speak again. "Did you tell Andrew what we did in the barn?"

"No. Why?"

"Because whoever made that blood streak—Burke says they were smart. It distracted the police for a couple days. Kept the search in Broken Falls when Bailey's obviously not here."

My stomach sours. "What are you saying?"

"The cops were asking a lot of questions about him." Jade looks out the window. "Wanted to know if he and Bailey were close."

I do a one-eighty in my seat so I'm facing her. "Jade. You can't possibly think Andrew did this. They *weren't* close—he would have no reason to want her *dead*."

Jade's quiet for a beat, then says, "I saw the gas station picture. Bailey was headed this way that night."

"She could have been headed for the barn."

"Will you stop with the stupid barn? It was just a distraction, they're saying. Just like leaving the phone on Cliff's property so the police would think he was involved." Jade eyes me. "Kind of sounds like something someone smart would do, doesn't it?"

Tears sting my eyes. "He's my brother. You're not going to convince me he had something to do with this."

Jade looks at me with pity. "He's not even your real brother."

I'm already grasping the door handle. "I don't want to talk to you anymore."

I sound pathetic, like a child, and I'm crying like one by the time I'm halfway up the driveway.

"Kacey," Jade calls out the window. "If you're covering for him, I'll never forgive you."

And then she peels away, and I'm alone.

In the living room, Mrs. Lao has returned to her talk show. I sneak back into the den, past Lauren, still curled up with Jerome.

The family computer is in here. I open the top drawer, saying a silent prayer of thanks for Ashley's affinity for organization. There is a sheet of paper with passwords for all of the family accounts—online banking, the Netflix subscription. Everything is here.

Why do the police seem to think Andrew knows something? He and Bailey were friends as kids, but they barely talked anymore. And Ellie Knepper wasn't even interested in Andrew that first day she came to talk to me at the house.

If Burke is interested now, he must have a new reason.

Something like those phone records he was holding Friday.

With shaking hands, I type in the web address for our cell phone provider and input the username and password when prompted. It's all numbers—a combination of Andrew's and Lauren's birthdays.

I click through to Andrew's number, pulling up his log of recent calls. There aren't many outgoing ones; Andrew isn't a big phone talker. He's a face-to-face person.

I run a finger down the screen, stopping when I see the first three digits of Bailey's phone number.

Andrew called her twice, at 11:15 p.m., the night she disappeared.

Almost Senior Year
August

I'm going crazy. I must be seeing things. It's the only explanation for what happened today.

Let me back up. Today was senior service day, the day every
one of us dreads and not one of us can get out of. (Alicia Rivera
tried, saying her juvenile arthritis meant she couldn't stand in
the sun all day; I am sure she regrets it, since Mrs. Gonzalo
made her spend the day at the Broken Falls nursing home playing bingo with Q-tip heads.)

Our assignment was to "beautify" some shitty-ass park outside Pleasant Plains; our entire class had to meet at school to get
on the buses at six this morning. Jade ambled out of her front
door right on schedule—I had to call her twice to make sure she
was up, because Mrs. Gonzalo wouldn't say what would happen
to those who missed the bus.

Jade bitched and moaned the whole ride to school, using my
rearview mirror to apply liner to her puffy eyes. "She can't stop
people from graduating."

I didn't want to call her bluff. Aside from my first choice,
Bloomington, I've already started applications to schools in
five different states. B-student schools in Americana that I will

219

probably get into, ones that have Division Two football teams and dorm buildings with water damage. I can't fucking wait.

We pulled into the parking lot at the same time as Andrew and Kacey; the sun was rising hot in the sky already. Kacey had her hair pulled back in the red bandana she wears to work. She fiddled with it as she shifted, aligning herself with Jade and me.

My stomach flipped as Andrew gave us a wave and bounced to catch up with Tyrell. I couldn't help myself: "What, he's too good for us?"

Kacey's mouth opened with surprise. Jade elbowed me. We fell a couple paces behind Kacey, and she muttered in my ear: "If you're trying to hide how you feel about him, you're doing a shitty job."

A foul mood came over me like a noxious gas. I was frustrated; since Lauren's birthday, we hadn't hung out with Andrew at all. Every time Jade and I went over to Kacey's, Andrew was either at Tyrell's or his summer internship at the historical society. The moment we had in his kitchen feels like it was years ago. Like a fever dream that never happened at all.

A crowd had pooled in front of the sign-in table. People muttering, bitching.

"Even our buses are assigned?" Bridget Gibson, Queen Complainer. Mrs. Gonzalo, jarring in her jeans and T-shirt, shooed Bridget and Val away from the table. Val frowned. "Can we switch with someone?"

As we signed in, I spotted the problem; Bridget was on bus 1, and Val was on bus 2—with Kacey and me.

"What the fuck," Jade muttered under her breath. "It's like they did this on purpose."

"The assignments are random, Miss Becker!" Mrs. Gonzalo flitted by; if she heard Jade curse, she didn't think it was worth the effort to stop and chastise her. Mrs. Gonzalo joined the teachers herding people onto the buses.

Kacey and I paired off and headed for our bus; Mr. White was sitting in the front seat, chatting with Ms. Stefani, the new art teacher, because everyone knows they're fucking.

"Hey, Mr. W," I said coyly. "Did you draw a short straw?"

"What makes you say that?" He grinned. "There's no other way I'd like to spend my Saturday."

Kacey and I settled into an empty pair of seats; she took the aisle. As we talked about whatever—the heat, the college application essay she was reading for me—I kept one eye on the bus door.

Outside my window, Andrew fist-bumped Tyrell; they split off, Tyrell heading for Jade's bus, Andrew for ours. My heart dipped into my stomach.

"Bay?" Kacey was looking at me, those freaky eyes of hers patient and focused.

"Yeah?"

"I asked if you emailed it to me yet."

My common app essay. "Oh, no. I'll do it right now."

I pulled out my phone, keenly aware of Andrew's presence on the bus; he walked past us, nudging Kacey's shoulder with his, on purpose. She smirked, pink creeping into her cheeks. I forced a swallow and finished up sending her the essay.

"Hey," I said. "So I'm going to check out Madison the last weekend in October. You should come."

"Madison the school?"

"Yes, doofus, the school." I don't want to go to school in Wisconsin, never have, but my parents are making me visit Wonder Brother's school. *Ben* loves *it there*. Ben also loves grimy sports bars and Kanye West and boobs.

Kacey's eyes were on the ring around her thumb; she gave it a twist. "I would never get into Madison."

"I probably won't get in either. Just come. It'll be fun."

"I don't know if I could get off work. But I'll ask."

The bus door shuttered, and the engine coughed to life. Mrs. Gonzalo whistled—once to get our attention, another time to get us to shut the hell up—and began reading off our group assignments for the park.

"Group A: Bailey Hammond, Valerie Diamond, Eliot Butler, and Thomas Alonzo."

My stomach clenched. *Fucking Val.* I pictured her cringing in her seat at the back of the bus. I was so distracted I almost missed Mrs. Gonzalo rattling off the next group: ". . . Andrew Kang, and Kacey Young."

My skin felt hot; the heat made its way to my head, muddling my brain. *Andrew and Kacey. Kacey and Andrew.* When we hopped off the bus, one by one, drifting into our groups, I couldn't tear my eyes off them.

Our group's assignment was pulling weeds; Kacey's group and another one were tasked with painting the gazebo at the center of the park.

Val and I worked in silence; I knew she wouldn't say anything. She never does. She just looks at me like some wounded bird, like she's the one who was wronged.

Meanwhile, the painting group was having a hell of a time.

222

That was when I saw it: Andrew, brush in hand. Coming at Kacey, flicking the tip across her nose. She shrieked. Laughing. I felt like I'd been sucker-punched. If I had balls, they would have shriveled up into my stomach.

I turned my attention back to the weeds. Val was watching me; I knew she saw it too, how gross Andrew and Kacey were being.

So I said: "Are you supposed to flirt with your stepsibling?"

Her voice was small. "You think they're flirting?"

I leaned back on my butt. Brushed dirt off my kneecaps. "Look at the way she looks at him."

Val lifted her eyes, hands still tearing at the root of the dandelion. She didn't say anything for a beat. Then: "Wow."

A thrill rippled through me. The sun was hot on my back. I absorbed the full weight of what I'd done. I'd passed the seed of suspicion to someone else; soon it'll spread as quickly as a virus. *Kacey Young wants to fuck her stepbrother.*

Because Val can't keep her mouth shut. She's never been able to.

Later, before we got back on the bus, Jade met up with me while Kacey was using the porta-potty. "Why were you talking to Val?"

I opted for total deflection. "Do you think there's something weird going on between Kacey and Andrew?"

Jade's mouth formed a line. "Seriously?"

I told her what I'd seen. Reminded her of that night we ran into Andrew and Kacey and Lauren at Culver's, and how Kacey had looked at us like we'd interrupted something. I thought of all the excuses not to chill at her house—*My dad is sleeping. My sister will want to hang out with us*—and felt heat come to my face.

She's trying to keep Andrew to herself.

I studied Jade's expressionless face. "What are you thinking?" I asked.

"I think . . . you're kind of fixated on her."

I didn't know what to say; it's moments like that when I think Jade knows about my night drives to Andrew's house. I've thought about telling her, on those rare nights where her dad was working a double and we tapped into the stash of weed in his sock drawer. Just blurt it out in a smoky haze: *I go to his house. I never get close enough to see him; I just like knowing he's there.*

But I never say anything. Because there are things that are just too fucked up to tell even your best friend.

CHAPTER TWENTY

Andrew lied to me. The police didn't want to talk to him about *me*—they know he called Bailey right before she left the party.

I stare at the screen. The phone calls are only twenty seconds each. Barely enough for a real conversation.

But short enough to decide to meet somewhere.

But *why*? Bailey and Andrew rarely ever spoke; I didn't even know Andrew had her phone number. I'd thought the only thing they even had in common anymore was me. Those days in the pictures hanging in the hallway—Andrew and Bailey, trick-or-treating as the red and pink Power Rangers—they're long gone. There was no rift between them, no cataclysmic event: they just grew up and grew apart.

At least, that's what I thought.

I have to confront Andrew. Ream him out for not telling me about the phone calls. Demand to know where he went Saturday night and why he gave me a bullshit excuse about picking up his prescription when I asked. My steps are purposeful, angry, as I head upstairs and bang on the door of his room. I don't care if Mrs. Lao can hear.

There's no answer.

"Andrew," I hiss. I give it five seconds before opening the door.

His room is empty; I look out the window overlooking the driveway. His car is gone, too. I turn to go, and my gaze lands on his phone, waiting on his nightstand. Wherever he went, he forgot it.

Fuck it. I cross the room and grab it, slide my finger across the screen. Andrew's passcode is his birthday, easy.

I scroll through his calls until I reach last Saturday night. *Bailey, Bailey. Where's Bailey?*

But there's no record of him ever calling her. Though, how easy is it to just delete a call from your phone. Like it never happened at all.

When I get downstairs, Mrs. Lao is still entranced by the blender demonstration on TV.

"Where's Andrew?" I ask over the grinding blasting from our surround-sound system.

Mrs. Lao mutes the television. "Tyrell's. Studying for physics test."

I'm rooted to my spot. There's a tight feeling, low in my stomach.

Because there's no way Andrew has another physics test already—we just took midterms two weeks ago.

On Sunday morning, it's not snowing, so Broken Falls and Pleasant Plains law enforcement are joining together to do a massive ground search for Bailey. At least, that's what the news says. The weather is still barely above freezing; I think of all those police officers in their heavy parkas, heat warmers shoved into their gloves, and let my body give in to a shiver.

I have been waiting since yesterday to get Andrew alone to confront him about the phone calls and the lie about where he was yesterday, but Ashley has been watching over us like a hawk, keeping vigil in the den to make sure I don't leave my room in the middle of the night.

But my grounding is suspended: for today, at least. Sunday is the busiest day of the week at the café and the usual register girl called out sick, so Ashley begrudgingly admits that she needs me to come in and help out.

Paula Schulz, who works here when she's not calling PTA meetings and ferrying her kids to dance and soccer, and I share register and coffee-filling duties for the morning throng of regulars. When they file out, Paula ducks into the kitchen without a word to me.

An unsettled feeling comes over me. I busy myself wiping down the coffee bar with a wet rag, trying to hear Paula and Rob's conversation in the kitchen. Or at least, I hear Paula talking *at* Rob:

—surprised people are coming in, considering—

My heart crawls into my throat. I bag Tom Cornwell's left-over toast for him and he leaves, and then I corner Paula as she's coming out of the bathroom.

"So, what's up?" I ask her. "We haven't worked together in a while."

Usually this is enough to invite an avalanche of gossip; Paula knows what's going on at the high school even before I do. Who's failing AP French. Which couple of the week is breaking up.

Paula doesn't look at me. "Nothing really. You mind if I take my cigarette break now?"

I nod, my throat tight. "Sure. It's pretty dead."

Too dead for a Sunday. When Ashley comes out of her office at the end of the day to count out the registers, she frowns at the number on the receipt. "It's bitter out," she says. "Everyone is probably staying home."

I think of Paula's dismissal of me and have to sit down. It's not the cold keeping people away from Milk & Sugar.

It's me.

At the end of the day, we sit in the SUV in silence until Ashley finally speaks.

"I'm having Lauren see Andrew's therapist next weekend."

I use my teeth to scrape away a flake of dead skin from my lips. "I'm sorry."

"No. I wanted to tell you it's not your fault." Ashley sounds like she's going to cry. "It's been a rough couple of years for all of us. With Andrew's issues, and your father not being around—I don't think some stupid sleepover trick in a barn is making Lauren this way."

I think back to what Jade said at Bailey's the other day. How my moving in couldn't have been easy for Lauren. "It's my fault. Out of nowhere she had to start sharing you and my dad with some messed-up girl."

"Do not say that." Ashley takes my ice-cold hand in hers. "I wouldn't trade you moving in for anything. It's just—I thought I'd have a couple more years before I had to parent a teenage girl. I thought I'd have *help*."

Meaning, my father hasn't done shit to parent me since I've moved in.

"Andrew was two when I met your father," Ashley says. "We had only been engaged a few weeks when he found out about you. I didn't think I could do it. I wanted to call everything off.

"He convinced me that nothing would change, that Andrew and I and our family would come first. He fought for me, and I stayed, because I was young and I had a fatherless toddler and I wanted someone to fight for me." Ashley wiped her eyes. "It wasn't until we had Lauren that I realized *you* should have come first."

I won't let myself cry.

"And then I met you, and I just knew you *belonged* with us. You're not who you think you are, Kacey. There's good inside you."

I start to cry.

Ashley squeezes my hand. "If you know anything, *anything* at all about what happened to Bailey, please tell me. I promise I'll still love you, no matter what."

A fissure splits down my middle. All of the shit with Burke and the rumors finally got to her. She thinks I killed Bailey, or at least know who did.

Andrew called her. He left the house. I think he was involved. The words are on the tip of my tongue. I don't owe Andrew anything, but it still feels like an unforgivable betrayal even to consider that he had something to do with Bailey's disappearance.

So I keep my mouth shut, thinking how that's the truly inconvenient thing about having a family: even when you don't owe them anything, you feel like you owe them fucking everything.

Monday morning. Getting dressed for school feels like prepping for my own execution. Jade hasn't called or texted me since our argument on Saturday, and this place is so damn small that everyone probably knows we're sort of fighting by now.

I stuff myself into jeans and a fleece pullover. I haven't showered since Saturday and I couldn't give less of a fuck.

As I stand over the bathroom sink, dabbing concealer over the blemish on my chin, I hear Andrew and Ashley arguing in the kitchen. She wants to drive us to school, but Andrew insists she's being ridiculous. She'll have to pick Andrew up from track practice and rush back to the house to get Lauren and bring her to her five-thirty dance class.

Ashley relents. She watches us from the kitchen window while Andrew backs out of the driveway. The opening chords of a Tom Petty song thrum under the classic rock station's DJ's complaints about another cold Monday morning. I wait until Andrew swings out of the cul-de-sac before I turn the radio off.

"Why didn't you tell me you called Bailey the night she went missing?"

I expect some bullshit excuse to tumble from his lips, but he sighs. I smell his toothpaste. "How do you know about that?"

I logged in to your phone bill because I don't know if I could trust you anymore. The irony is too much right now. "I just heard, okay? Why did you do it?"

Andrew keeps one hand on the wheel. Uses the other to wipe a piece of crust from his eye. "The cops brought me in to ask why I called her, and I said they must have been butt dials while I was driving."

"I didn't know you even had her number."

"She was my friend too. I've had it for ages." Andrew scratches the back of his neck.

I tilt my head to the window and shut my eyes. I think of how the calls to Bailey were deleted on his actual phone. I'm not ready to admit that I snooped through it while he wasn't home. I don't want to add *gross invasion of privacy* to my list of recent crimes. "A butt dial. That's really the best you can do?"

"The best I can do? What's that supposed to mean?"

"That I'm supposed to believe your phone just *happened* to call Bailey while you were out driving around the same time she went missing?" The cold crawls up my neck to the part my scarf doesn't reach. "I hope you at least came up with a better story for the police."

"Hold up. You think I had something to do with this?" Andrew finally sounds angry. "You're not serious, right?"

I loop a piece of scarf around my finger. "I'm just thinking of how it must look to the police."

"Well, don't. Because I had no reason to hurt Bailey, and I can't believe I even have to say that to you."

I swallow. "Were you really at Tyrell's yesterday?"

"What the hell—of course I was."

"Then why did you lie to Mrs. Lao about going there to study? There's no way you have a test today when midterms were two weeks ago."

"Because I didn't think she'd let me leave otherwise. Not with the way my mom has been going black ops on us." Andrew shakes his head. "This is all so messed up. You're interrogating me worse than that detective did."

We both sit, simmering, for the rest of the ride to school. Andrew turns the radio back on. His jaw is red and splotchy. I imagine the thoughts cycling through his head—whether he's thinking of ways to keep up with all of his lies, or if he really is telling the truth and is pissed at me for not believing him.

I think of Jade telling me she'll never forgive me if she finds out I'm covering for Andrew. Is that why Burke is laying into us? Because he thinks Andrew killed Bailey and I'm lying for him?

When Andrew pulls into his usual spot in the school parking lot, neither of us moves to get out.

"Kace," he says. "You realize how ridiculous this all is, right? I had nothing to do with whatever happened to Bailey."

My feet tingle—I can't breathe in this car, but I don't think I'll be able to breathe in that goddamn school either—

"Did anything ever happen between the two of you?" I blurt.

Andrew blinks those dark lashes of his twice. *Those lashes could make a girl go crazy,* I think.

"Me and *Bailey*?" He looks surprised.

I pull my scarf up to my chin. "She wanted it to happen."

"Yeah, well it didn't." Andrew cuts the engine. "Even if I did, that's a big fucking leap to murder."

Andrew said the word *fucking*. Andrew doesn't curse—not at his parents, not at Lauren, not with his friends, and definitely not at me. All I can manage in response is "We're going to be late."

Andrew makes a disgusted noise. "I can't believe you'd *ever* think that of me. That really sucks, Kacey."

"I just—I saw the security footage of her turning onto our road. You have to admit it looks like you called her to meet up with you—"

"I *didn't* . . ." Andrew's eyes go wide. Pleading. "I thought you knew who I was."

It's the biggest cliché, but I think: *I don't know who anyone is anymore.*

We're definitely going to be late for homeroom now. I watch the throng of stragglers hustling from the parking lot to the side entrance, even though it doesn't make a difference. You get marked down regardless if you're one minute late or ten.

"I guess I'll see you after school," Andrew says.

"I guess."

I unbuckle my seat belt, catching one of the girls looking up at me as she passes the Mazda. Val Diamond, a bouquet of purple carnations in one hand.

Her gaze lingers on me—and Andrew—a beat too long. I climb out of the car and she turns her head, scurries toward the building like she never saw us at all.

. . .

Fuck this place.

It starts with the scene in the wing where the seniors' lockers are. Someone has draped the *BRING BAILEY HOME* banner from the vigil across the hall. Val's purple carnations poke out of the holes on Bailey's locker. People hang around in front of it, waiting to tape messages to the outside and gawk.

I don't see Jade anywhere.

After the bell rings in homeroom, the vice principal, Gonzo, clears her throat over the loudspeaker. Her voice is harried, almost as if someone is behind her, whispering the words in her ear, as she tells us that she knows there's a lot of *uncertainty* and *unease* but this is a school day and we need to carry on like everything's normal.

I sweep the hallways for Jade again after homeroom. As a result, I'm late to art, which is all the way downstairs.

Mr. White doesn't say anything, just looks at me with this sad look on his face, as I make my way to my table. Jade's seat is empty, as I knew it would be. When I reach my seat, Meghan Constanzo nudges the girl sitting next to her, who has her back to me. Mike Lin averts his eyes as I sit, and everyone gets quiet in a way that makes it totally obvious they were talking about me.

Mr. White lowers the volume on his radio. His dreadlocks are tied back today. AP studio art is for seniors only; he makes a little speech telling us that we have the period to work on sketching out our 3D projects and he's here for us if we need to talk.

When he raises the radio volume, we all stand to get our sketchbooks from the shelf by the window. We're supposed to leave them at the end of every class so Mr. White can look through our drawings and plans.

I fall to the back of the line so I don't have to make eye contact with anyone. When I have my book in hand, I look out the window. A figure with a hood pulled over his head is making his way across the soccer field, hugging the edge of the wooded area along the parking lot. I recognize the hoodie and the backpack as Tyrell's.

I shove my sketchbook into my shoulder bag and go to Mr. White's desk instead of my own. He looks up at me. Warm chocolate eyes. "You okay, kid?"

"Can I have the pass?"

Mr. White frowns. "I'm supposed to limit them today."

"Please." My foot jiggles a bit. "I need a minute in the bathroom."

He discreetly hands me the hall pass, a clunky plastic thing with a sign-out sheet that no one uses. While Mr. White is distracted by Meghan asking for his thoughts on her sketch, I hold the pass to my chest and grab my bag.

The hallway is quiet, a testament to the canceled arts and music classes in the wake of last year's budget cuts. I dig out my phone and text Tyrell: *Wait up.*

The side doors resist as I push my way through them. Squint at the glare of the sun bouncing off the snow on the soccer field. Several feet away, Tyrell stops, puts a hand to his pocket. Must have felt my text come through.

I run to catch up with him because I know where he's

headed—the overflow lot behind the soccer field, the place where you're screwed into parking if you're late in the morning, and then you wind up being doubly late because of the long walk to the school. I doubt he forgot something in his car; more likely, he's ditching class.

Tyrell turns at the sound of my footsteps. "Hey. What are you doing?"

"Same as you," I pant.

We pick up our pace, not wanting to be spotted by a security guard looking out the second-floor walkway.

Tyrell is quiet; the sound of our feet crunching the snow fills the silence.

"A little early to be ditching," I say. "Why'd you show up at all?"

He shakes his head. "All this shit—those people who didn't even know Bay taking pictures of her locker—I tried, but I just can't do it. I can't be here."

"Where are you gonna go?" Tyrell's mom works from home. Runs a business for women who host gourmet kitchen supply parties.

"I dunno." We're at his car, a silver sedan.

I swallow. "Do you want to go to Waffle Hut? I need to talk to you about something."

Tyrell looks back at the school, as if adding me to the mix makes ditching a doubly bad idea. He unlocks the passenger-side door and opens it for me.

I get in. It's not like I have anywhere else to go.

. . .

We're in a booth at the back of the Waffle Hut; our server looked us up and down before seating us and taking our orders. Probably torn between the moral obligation to ask why we're not in school and the promise of a tip on a slow morning. My coffee is blissfully hot between my frozen hands; I'm holding it tightly, thawing my fingers. Tyrell sips from a sweaty glass of ice water.

He's the one who finally says something. "Is this about Andrew?"

I think of the way he and Andrew answer the phone. Always trying to top each other's ridiculous nicknames. *Hey, Johnny Rocket. What's up, Shoeless Joe Jackson.* Guys act like they're afraid their dicks will fall off if they use the term *best friend*. But not Andrew and Tyrell—they're shameless in their love for each other.

"Did he say something to you?" I ask. "About why the cops talked to him the other night?"

Tyrell's eyes flick from the rim of his glass to me, nervous.

I lean forward—my impulse is to whisper, even though we're not in Broken Falls anymore. "I saw the phone records," I finally say. "Andrew called her before she left the party. Twice. He was the last person she talked to."

"*Andrew* was?" Tyrell's eyes snap open and he looks back up at me. "Nah, that doesn't sound right."

I wipe a line of condensation from my water glass with the tip of my finger. "I know. But it looks like Bay left to meet up with him. It looks *really* bad."

Tyrell lets out a low sigh. Rubs his eyes. "Shit."

I find myself wedging my knife through the prongs of my fork. Picking it up like it's a gun, the way Andrew always used to do when we came here while Lauren was at dance. I instantly put it down. "I'm just trying to understand all this."

I don't mention the tire tracks by Andrew's car last Sunday morning, or the way he lied about how they got there. Even though it's Tyrell, it would feel like a betrayal. Anything that comes out of my mouth now has the chance of making its way to Detective Burke.

"Understand what?" Tyrell asks. "You think Andrew actually had something to do with this?"

Our server brings over our orders: a stack of toast for me, scrambled eggs for Tyrell. When he leaves us, I can barely look at the food. Tyrell is still watching me. Waiting.

"I don't think he hurt Bailey," I finally say. "But if he had a reason to—if he was pissed at her about something—I'd want to know what it was. Since that detective is up my ass and everything."

"You're asking me if *I* think Andrew had a problem with Bailey." Tyrell sets down his fork. It's not a question; it's an accusation.

I fold my hands and press them into my stomach. I want a do-over. I want to rewind to the time when I thought Andrew wasn't capable of this. I want to still believe he's the guy who gags when the liquid stuff comes out of the ketchup bottle and there's no way he could go through with getting blood on his hands.

"Kacey." Tyrell's voice is hard. "You know Andrew—he didn't do this."

"Yeah." I look down. I don't want him to see what I'm thinking as he squirts ketchup on his eggs. Because all I can see is the blood smear in the barn, and all I can think about is how smart whoever took Bailey would have to be to have made it and thrown off the whole search for her.

"Shit." Tyrell pats his back pocket. I can tell that his phone must be buzzing there by the look on his face. Pure dread. I set down my toast as Tyrell slides his phone out and looks at the screen.

"It's my mom," he says. "We're fucked."

The school must have called her. I should be freaking out, terrified about what Ashley will do to me for cutting, but the last few moments are playing in my head on loop.

Tyrell had acknowledged that I was asking if Andrew had a reason to hurt Bailey, but he'd never answered.

Senior Year
October

I fucked up. I went too far, and I almost ruined everything. Actually, maybe I did ruin everything. That remains to be seen, because this weekend was a complete and utter shitshow.

Kacey, Jade, and I were supposed to hang out. We hang out every weekend—we're KaceyAndJadeAndBailey. I have even been willing to forgive the shameless flirting with Andrew on service day. I didn't text her for an entire day afterward, which made her so pathetically needy. So many texts, demanding answers.

Are you okay?

Did I do something??

After twenty-four hours, I responded back: *Of course not. Let's chill.*

Kacey's like an abused puppy. The more you ignore her, the more she wants you. I find it endearing, because I like being wanted.

But now I know for sure that the bitch can't be trusted.

It all happened Saturday night. I'd been texting Kacey throughout the day: *what are we doing tonight?* She never responded, so when I picked Jade up from the taqueria after her shift ended at nine, we called her. She must have hit the *fuck you* button, because it went right to voice mail. I scrolled through to her house number.

Jade sat up straight as a meerkat. "What the hell are you doing?"

"Getting more information, obviously."

Lauren picked up on the third ring. I switched to speaker-phone and Jade leaned in.

"Hey, babe," I said. "Where's your sister?"

"Madison," Lauren said. "She and Andrew are visiting the school."

"Oh really. They went alone?" I stared at Jade, as if to say, *Told you, bitch.*

"Nah, my mom's with them."

"Is your dad home?"

"Yeah, he's sleeping. He worked half a day."

Gotta love younger kids—they'll give you all the information in the world if they think you'll keep talking to them. I pictured Lauren growing up into one of those girls who would hand you their social security number and bank account information if it meant you'd include them in something.

"Then sneak out," I said. "Chill with me and Jade."

A hard elbow to my ribs. Jade mouthed, *Have you lost your fucking mind?*

"Um." Lauren's voice was small. "How?"

Hadn't this child ever watched any sort of teen movie ever? "Just arrange your pillows under your bed like you're sleeping, close your door, and leave," I said. "But be quiet about it. We'll be there in ten minutes."

I expected her to say no, but instead all she said was "But what are we going to do?"

"We'll figure something out," I told her. "That's the fun part."

I hung up, and Jade burst into laughter. "We're not actually hanging out with a fucking eighth grader."

I looked away so Jade couldn't read my face. I didn't want her to sniff out what I was thinking. *If we can't have Kacey, we'll take the Mini-Markham.* "We are. And maybe she'll actually grow up to be interesting."

"This is so about Kacey," Jade said. "You're trying to fuck with her through Lauren."

"What do you care?"

Jade smirked. "I hope you know what you're doing."

That makes two of us. I flipped my lights off as I pulled over on Sparrow Road, behind the Markhams' house. Lauren slipped out the back door. Her black North Face was zipped up to her chin, and she was wearing leggings stuffed in Uggs.

She was breathless when she climbed into my backseat.

Jade held up her phone. "Tyrell texted me that he's having people over."

In the rearview mirror, I saw Lauren's eyes light up. It was a terrible idea, even though I had seen girls Lauren's age—Keelie March, Brendan March's big-titted little sister—at Sully's parties. I leaned into Jade and hissed: "We're not bringing her to Tyrell's. He'll narc on us to Andrew."

Lauren frowned, and Jade rolled her eyes. "Let's just go to Taco Bell."

"Wait." An idea wheedled its way into my brain. "Ben's visiting his friend who goes to Milwaukee," I said. "I'll call him and see if anything's going on."

"Milwaukee the college?" Lauren squeaked.

Jade stared at me like I was smoking crack. "That's an hour and a half from here."

"It's only nine o'clock. Stop being lame, both of you."

Where are you, I texted Ben. *I'm coming to Milwaukee.*

Now?? Jesus, Bay.

Come on. I'm bored.

I could hear my brother sighing. Then the ellipsis popped up in the text box. He was taking a long time with his response.

Party at Billy's frat later. Kappa Tau house. What are you gonna tell mom?

Sleeping at jade's, duh.

When we got to Milwaukee, Jade started to bitch that Lauren would never pass for a college freshman. I looked the kid up and down. She's tall for her age, so I figured if she kept the jacket on no one would notice her flat chest. I got my eyeliner out of my purse and did a little magic.

I looked over at Jade, who was fiddling with her Warby Parker frames. Her allergies have been so bad she hasn't worn her contacts in weeks.

"Give Lauren your glasses," I told Jade, who said, "What the fuck?"

"They'll make her look older."

"I'd like to be able to *see* the shitshow that's about to unfold, thanks."

"It's not like you're blind without them." I slipped the frames off Jade's face. "It's like I gave you beer goggles and you didn't even have to suck down a Natty."

"That's a type of beer, right?" Lauren was adjusting the glasses on her face. Jade just stared at her for a beat, then looked at me. "Your brother is going to shit himself when he sees this."

I pushed that thought out of my head and locked the car. Most likely, Wonder Brother wouldn't even recognize little Lauren Markham—he hasn't seen her in years.

As we climbed the steps to the frat house, I could practically feel Lauren quaking behind me. The guy at the door was a weasel-faced kid with a decent body. Probably a pledge. Badly in need of Proactiv. I was prepared to drop Ben's name, but the guy just yawned and told us it was five bucks each. I pulled the bills out of my purse while Jade muttered about how the house looked like a crack den.

"Relax." I shoved her beer cup at her as we fell into line for the keg. "I'll stay sober and drive. Just please get wasted so I don't have to hear your bitching."

I was feeling particularly nasty, probably still roiling at the thought of Kacey and Andrew in Madison together. See, the more comfortable I am with someone, the less I'm afraid of acting like a total monster. But Jade actually looked hurt, so I draped an arm over her shoulder as an olive branch.

"I just hope you know what you're doing," she muttered, while I nudged Lauren to let the sad sack (another pledge) manning the keg fill her cup.

We had to shoulder our way to the flip cup table and planted

244

ourselves at the end of the line. Lauren looked terrified of the cup in her hand. I put a finger at the base and tipped it toward her mouth. She giggled, foam sticking to her upper lip, some of the beer missing her mouth and sloshing on the floor.

"You're at a frat party," I said. "I bet What'shername who's been giving you shit has never been to a frat party."

"Keelie March," Lauren corrected me. "She brought vodka to the cast party for *Oklahoma!* and they all got drunk."

That was when I locked eyes with a guy in a Kappa tee. He and his friends descended on us like sharks. Asked if we went to UW.

"Just visiting," I said. "I think I want to go here next year."

Frat boy buddy offered me a tour of his freshman dorm. I said maybe I'd take him up on that. Jade rolled her eyes. An overwhelming urge to hit her seized me. Any time I talked about college, she did that. Acted like I was being painfully basic. She just doesn't *get it*—that shitty frat house filled with fives and sixes, it may be beneath us, but at the same time it's not. I'm not beneath playing the game if I can get the fuck out of Broken Falls.

Sometimes I think Jade thinks the only way we're getting out is by *Thelma and Louise*-ing it. I wanted to grab her, tell her that movie wasn't real. *This* is our alternative to staying in Broken Falls forever.

I didn't get the chance to pull her aside and ask her what her problem was, because the guy in the Kappa shirt had mentioned that there were people blazing upstairs, and Jade was gone like a dog after a squirrel. Lauren and I waited for our turn at the flip cup table.

"That looks hard," she said. "I think I should just watch you."

"You've got this," I told her sweetly. "Your brother is amazing at this game."

"My brother goes to parties?" Lauren asked. Her face was scrunched up like I'd talked about her parents having sex.

"He used to," I said. "When we were freshmen."

"Now he's such a nerd. Every time we go to Pleasant Plains we have to stop at that game store where those guys play Magic: The Gathering and it's *so embarrassing*."

"Seems like he and Kacey are pretty close," I pressed.

A spark of something in her eyes. Jealousy, maybe. "We both are. I mean, she's our sister."

"She's *your* sister. He's like, not her real brother." I raised an eyebrow, like I'd just thought of it. "Do they hang out alone a lot?"

Lauren craned her neck to get a look at the flip cup table. Only half listening to me. "I mean, maybe? They're always arguing and laughing about dumb stuff, and when I ask what they're talking about they won't tell me."

There was a curling in my gut. The thought made my blood boil, but I couldn't grill Lauren any longer because two spots opened up at the flip cup table. She was so bad it would have been funny if it weren't for the intense girls on our team giving her razor glares every time she fucked us up. Two games later, we got kicked off.

"That was *fun*. And *hard*." Lauren was giggly, on the verge of sloppy. I should have known a couple beers would be all it took. I couldn't bring the kid home like that, and I was over the stupid party anyway. My phone said we'd been there for an hour and I still hadn't seen Ben.

"I'm going to get Jade," I said. "Wait right here."

Rookie mistake, obviously, but hauling her ass up and down the stairs was more trouble than it was worth. I plucked Jade out of the house's loft, blitzed out of her mind. I'd underestimated Kappa; the dudes obviously got the good shit.

When we got back downstairs, Lauren was right where I left her in the corner. Except she had company, Kappa tee guy's friend, the one who offered me a tour of his dorm. He leaned in, mashed his lips on Lauren's. I could see her giggling and turning her head from the stairs.

"What the fuck?" I was on them in seconds, yanking the guy off her by the back of his polo. "She's *thirteen*."

The guy gaped at me, eyes bloodshot, didn't even get a chance to respond because of a booming voice behind me, saying my name.

Ben. So pissed off.

He didn't say a word to me until we were back at my car, despite Jade and Lauren giggling and saving each other from face-planting on the cracks in the sidewalk.

"Have you been drinking?" He looked me up and down. I shook my head, too tired to snipe back at him that he said I could come.

"Get home." His voice vibrated with anger. "Get *her* home."

He nodded toward Lauren, who was tearing dandelions from the ground, blowing the seeds at Jade, who stuck out her tongue to catch them.

"This is seriously fucked up," he whispered at me. "I just— there's seriously something wrong with you if you think this is okay."

I made Jade sit in the backseat the whole ride home because she was high as shit and pissing me off. Lauren puked on the floor in the front seat, and I started to cry, exhausted and thinking about standing outside with a hose at one a.m. when we got home. Jade was like, "Chill, that's what all-weather mats are for," and Lauren laughed and I told them both to shut the hell up.

There's seriously something wrong with you.

I'm starting to think he's right.

At school on Monday, we waited for Kacey by her locker. I asked her as casually as I could what she did over the weekend.

"I had to finish my common app essay," she said, pulling her hair up into a messy bun.

Jade stared her up and down. "All weekend?"

Kacey dropped her arms, giving up on the bun. "Yeah, and I hung out with Lauren. Ashley was away."

You fucking liar. You fucking terrible *liar.* Her lies brought a slick of sweat to my palms. Jade just kept smirking; she put the heel of her boot on the locker adjacent Kacey's and leaned back. Kacey glanced over at us, blinked. Like she was surprised we were still there.

"What did you guys do?" she asked.

Jade's smirk stretched into a grin. "Bay's brother got us into a frat party."

"Where?" Kacey looked at me, her eyes suddenly big. I could practically see the blood stopping in her veins.

"Eau Claire," I said, and the first bell rang. Kacey dropped her gaze back to her portfolio. Had she looked relieved to hear we hadn't been in Madison too? I'd missed it.

"It was a real shitshow." Jade hiked the strap of her tote bag up over her shoulder. Her eyes met mine: I wanted to mouth, *What the hell do you think you're doing?* She wouldn't tell Kacey what we'd done, how we brought Lauren to the Kappa Tau house, how she'd puked in my car—

Then Jade reached out and pinched my wrist, said, "See you at lunch," and flashed me a wolflike grin. I knew what she was doing, that it was all a game to her. I'd been the one who *convinced* her it was all a game. It was my idea to drive to Kacey's house, prove that she was lying about being home, and drag her little sister out to party.

My tongue tasted sour as I watched Kacey and Jade walk off to first period—art—together. I jogged to catch up with them. "J! Let me see your math homework quick."

Jade stopped and turned, blinked at me. "I'm gonna be late."

I shrugged—*Like you care*—while Kacey scuttled off to class, dutiful little thing she is. I'll bet she just wants to suck Mr. White's dick. Jade let out a heavy sigh when she was gone. "What, Bay?"

"You can't mess with her like that. If she finds out what we did, we're in deep shit."

"You mean she'll stop talking to us?" Jade said. "Why do you care, if you hate her so much?"

I'd said a lot of things about Kacey, but I'd never said I hated her. Do I hate her? I don't even know anymore. Sure, she consumes most of my thoughts, and I've considered how satisfying it would be to punch her in that stupid fucking face of hers, but it's not like I want to be rid of her. In fact, the thought is down-right distressing. Because if I lose her, I'll lose Andrew too.

"I just don't want to get in trouble," I said. "I couldn't give a shit what Kacey will think."

Jade laughed. She actually *laughed*, like the idea of me not caring what Kacey thinks was hysterical. "Bay, you're so frig-ging fixated on her, you're not even thinking straight."

For the first time in five years, I didn't know what to say to Jade. But somehow I came up with the most pathetic thing ever: "You don't like her either."

Jade gave me a wry little smile. "Isn't that what you wanted?"

I'm in study hall now, and I'm still sick over the conversa-tion. It's never been like that between Jade and me before—so much *subtext*. I can't lose Jade. Jade is my person, the only per-son I really like in this town. We take care of each other—we need each other.

I would sooner die than lose Jade.

CHAPTER TWENTY-ONE

By some miracle, my own phone doesn't start to ring until we've paid for breakfast and we're hurrying out to the parking lot. I wince before accepting the call.

"Where the hell are you?" Ashley barks.

I cringe. "With Tyrell. We're on our way back to school."

"On your way *back* to school," she repeats. "Do you know that your father wanted to call the police when he said the school called and you walked out? If the security camera hadn't shown you driving off with Tyrell, I would have."

A tear leaks out, stinging my wind-burned cheek. "I'm sorry."

"Is there something you need to tell me, Kacey?"

I can't. She's going to find out about Andrew's phone calls to Bailey anyway; I doubt Burke is done with Andrew yet, and there's no way Ashley will let Andrew talk to him alone anymore.

"Go back to school," Ashley says. "I swear if you don't, I'll call the sheriff myself."

And then for the first time ever, she hangs up on me.

Next to me, Tyrell sucks in a breath and lets out a low-pitched *shiiiiiit*. "My gas light went on. We gotta stop and fill up."

"Seriously?"

"We're already in deep shit. Five more minutes won't make a difference."

He pulls up to the pump at the Fill N' Go and climbs out of the car. I tilt my head to the window as a guy in a Badgers hoodie comes out of the gas station cashier.

Bailey's brother, Ben. My mouth goes dry as his eyes connect with mine. He looks so much like Bailey it's spooky: freckles dotting his nose, big hazel eyes. I hold up a hand as Ben walks over to Tyrell's car.

I open the door and climb out. Ben's eyes are red. "Hey, Kace," he says. "Shouldn't you be in school?"

I shove my hands in the pockets of my fleece. "It . . . I just didn't want to be there."

Ben's eyes flick to Tyrell. He gives him a grim nod. Turns back to me. "I hear you. I just got my leave of absence approved so I could come home and be with my parents."

"I'm so sorry," I say, for a lack of anything better.

"I should have been here. I should have come right home, to help look for her. Now it's probably too late."

Tears leak from Ben's eyes. His shoulders drop. There is something so ugly and painful about seeing a big man crying.

"Sorry." Ben wipes his eyes with the sleeve of his hoodie. "The whole drive back here, I kept thinking about how I failed her."

"There's nothing you could have done," I say. "And you're here now."

"I should have told my parents how reckless she was acting. She was out of control. Bringing your sister to that frat party—"

The insides of my ears go cottony. *My sister. Frat party.* I must have heard him wrong.

I stare back at Ben. "What?"

Ben sucks teary snot back into his nostrils. "Oh, shit. I thought you knew—"

"Bailey brought Lauren to a frat party?" I can't control the rage seeping into my voice. I'm so loud that Tyrell looks over. "Was Jade there too?"

Ben nods. "When I saw them I made them go straight home. I should have called my dad—made him come get her."

I swallow. "When was this?"

"Second, maybe first weekend of October? It was Milwaukee's homecoming."

A click, pieces sliding into place in my brain. They took my sister to a frat party while I was away at Madison, visiting schools with Andrew and Ashley.

Tyrell clears his throat. Rests his arm on top of his car. "Kace, you ready to go?"

"Yeah." I turn back to Ben. Swallow my rage. "Thanks for telling me. About Lauren."

He nods. "Take care of yourself, okay? And stay in touch."

It takes all my restraint not to punch Tyrell's dashboard when I climb back in the car. Ben thinks it's too late for Bailey, that she's dead, and for the first time, I hope she is.

Because if she makes it back to Broken Falls alive, I'm not so sure that I won't kill her myself.

I never intended to lie to Bailey and Jade about where I was that weekend. But I hadn't planned on going to Madison with Ashley and Andrew, either.

It was the night of parent-teacher conferences when I came home from Bailey's house and saw the brochure for Madison Art Institute on the dining room table.

"Mr. White gave that to me," Ashley said over my shoulder, beaming with pride. "He thinks you could get in. He even said he'd write your recommendation."

My lips tingled; I put a hand to my mouth. I knew Mr. White liked my work, but art school?

"I thought we could visit this weekend," Ashley said, rubbing my shoulder. "We're already going to be in the area so Andrew can look at Madison. It'll be fun."

Instead of excitement, I felt a flutter of panic. I'd turned down going to visit Madison with Bailey over the summer. I could practically hear her response if I told her I was going with Andrew and my stepmom instead. *It's whatever, Kacey.*

Before I could say anything to Ashley, my dad wandered into the room, a takeout container of lo mein in hand. Ashley flashed him the brochure, grinning.

"Wouldn't it be great if Andrew and Kacey both went to school in Madison?" Ashley gushed. "They could keep each other company on the weekends."

My dad peered at the brochure. "Art school? Huh."

The pride in me guttered out. He may as well have said *circus camp* for all the contempt in his voice.

Something flashed in Ashley's eyes. "What's wrong with that? She's talented enough."

"I didn't say there was anything wrong with it." My dad wouldn't look at me. "It's just I thought she was thinking something more practical, like culinary school or community college for a year or two."

Ashley set the brochure down. "Mr. White says having an art degree would give her a leg up in the culinary design world. Anyway, we're just looking."

In other words, *Please shut the fuck up now*. My dad finally looked at me. Forced out a smile. "Whatever you want."

I wanted to vomit. I tried to tell Ashley I couldn't take the weekend off, she needed me at the café, but she insisted that I was coming to Madison and we were looking at the Art Institute on Sunday and that was that.

We spent Saturday looking at Madison for Andrew, and the night in a hotel not far from the Art Institute. After dinner, Andrew insisted we play Scrabble in the hotel lobby while Ashley went back to the room. I was feeling bitchy, muttered something about not being in the mood to get my ass kicked.

"What's really bothering you?" he asked. We were in two armchairs by the hotel bar, watching a woman stir a martini in the middle of an intense argument on her phone. Andrew was trying to make me laugh by filling in the gaps, pretending to be the person on the other end.

"Nothing," I told him.

"Okay. Sure." He put his tiles in a pile. "You just thinking about how much you'll miss me when I go away to college, then?"

I didn't feel like lying. I'd spent most of my life lying about how I felt so I wouldn't make other people uncomfortable. I told him everything that had happened with my dad earlier in the week.

"I thought he'd be excited," I said. "About what Mr. White said."

"He doesn't get excited about stuff. That's just how he is."

"Not with the Packers," I answered.

"Yeah, but that's the Packers."

When I looked up, Andrew was looking at me, pity in his eyes.

I pulled my knees to my chest. "I've never asked him for anything. I don't expect him to pay for me to go to college."

"I know you don't," Andrew said. "You should let him, though. He kind of owes you."

The thought brought pressure to my eyeballs. "I don't want to owe *him* anything. I already owe your mom so much, for giving me a job. And she's not even related to me."

Andrew picked at the beginnings of a hole in the knee of his jeans. "Why do you talk like that?"

"Like what?"

"Like you're, I don't know. Not really our family."

"I didn't mean it like that," I said. "It's just. I don't know."

"No," Andrew said. "I kind of get it. Before you moved in with us, I felt the same way."

We were both quiet. We didn't need to talk about the dad he doesn't remember, or the strange looks people gave us in public—*that guy must be adopted*. We just sat there, arranging our Scrabble tiles, knowing that even if the feeling went away when we were tucked back in our beds at home, for that moment, we didn't have to feel alone.

I was midway through making the word *swimming* when my phone buzzed. I had a text from Bailey: *Where are you, girl? Let's do something*.

It was stupid to lie, to tell her I was home working on my common app essay. Andrew, Ashley, and I would be home by early afternoon the next day, and she and Jade would never know the difference.

I really thought it would be that easy—just for one night, to have something to myself. A conversation by the fire with the only person I'd ever really been able to open up to completely. I was tired of feeling like every move I made had to be accounted for and approved by my friends.

But Bailey had caught me after all. And when she couldn't have me, she'd taken Lauren in my place.

Gonzo and a security guard are waiting for Tyrell and me at the front steps, like we're fugitives about to turn ourselves in. Ashley must have called and told the school we were coming back.

There's really no point; the day is practically over.

Gonzo stirs when she sees us. I have to stop myself from

holding up my hands and saying, *I'll come quietly, Officer*. None of this is funny, but it's also so pathetic it's hilarious. If you're going to cut school, you don't show up at all. Ditching halfway through the day was a classic rookie mistake. It's like I can't even fuck up properly anymore.

Meanwhile, my friends managed to sneak my sister out to a party in Milwaukee and keep it a secret from me for months. I imagine blurting this out to Gonzo, like it's some sort of defense for my behavior. *Did you know that Bailey Hammond brought a thirteen-year-old child to a college party?*

Gonzo brings Tyrell in for questioning first. I sit outside her office in the chair of shame, tears streaming down my cheeks. I'm not embarrassed; I'm enraged, and crying seems like the least self-destructive reaction right now.

I feel so goddamn stupid. I think of Jade's face when she saw Lauren the night of the barn, the way she looked at Bailey and said, *She'll tell*. They weren't afraid that Lauren would rat on us for sneaking out—they were afraid she would tell *me* about the frat party if they didn't let her come to the barn.

From across the room, Gonzo's secretary makes a sympathetic face at me. "You want a tissue, hon?"

"No, thanks."

"Ya know, your mom was really worried about you." She gives her desk a reassuring pat, realizing she's too far from me to be of any comfort. "I'll bet Mrs. G will go easy on you. Maybe just detention and not a suspension."

I close my eyes, bite my tongue, because she really is trying to make me feel better.

Some murmuring behind Gonzo's door. Tyrell walks out. Glances at me and mouths *detention,* and shrugs. Gonzo raps her red-lacquered nails on the door frame, and I get up.

I keep my eyes on the window behind her as we sit and she starts her spiel about how very concerned she and my parents are about me. Gonzo and I have never even spoken before this moment. Outside, the buses are beginning to pull up to the curb.

"When would you like to fulfill your detention?"

I meet Gonzo's eyes. They're apologetic, like she's the one who did something wrong.

"Um, today, I guess."

"Okay, then." Gonzo selects a pen from the cat-shaped mug on her desk. Starts to fill out the details of my crimes on a pink notepad. A flash of black between the buses. An SUV curves around them, finds a spot in the strip marked for visitors.

Detective Burke gets out of the driver's-side door. Shields his eyes from the sun and takes in the school.

"Kacey?" Gonzo raps her desk with her pen. "I asked if you have a way of getting home after detention."

"My brother—or I can take the bus—" I can't tear my eyes from Burke ascending the ramp outside. He disappears around the front of the building as the bell rings.

Gonzo tears the pink slip from her notepad and hands it to me. "Go straight to the basement, okay? No side excursions. They'll be expecting you."

I nod and stuff the slip in my pocket. I throw my bag over my shoulder and hurry out of Gonzo's office, but it's too late. Burke is already here, signing in with the secretary.

When he sees me, he smiles. I pretend that I didn't see him and head for detention.

He doesn't follow, which is how I know he's not here for me anyway.

Ashley is so mad she barely speaks to me when I get home except to tell me I'm officially grounded. I'm to go to school and come straight home.

But perhaps the worst punishment of all is her telling me my father wants to speak with me. He's sitting at the kitchen table, the chair across from him pulled out and waiting for me.

"I understand you're going through a really hard time right now." My dad draws in a breath. "But you are not the kind of kid who skips school."

You don't know what kind of kid I am, I want to say. *You've only known me for a year.*

The only time I really get to see my father is on Sundays, in front of the LED flat-screen he indulged in for the very purpose of watching the Packers. Even then, with all of us piled in the room together, he's usually only interested in talking to Andrew. My most noteworthy interaction with my father was the day Ashley told him one of my sculptures was being entered into the county art fair; he gave my shoulder a squeeze and said, *Well, isn't that something.*

I don't take it personally; he has nothing in common with Lauren and me—we frighten him, with our foreign interests in books he'll never read and the ever-present threat of finding a tampon in the garbage. Some men just aren't cut out to be fathers of teenage girls.

But at least Lauren has memories of a time when their relationship was different. When my father was the type of man to play Pretty Pretty Princess with his little girl and would allow a photo of him adorned in a crown and clip-on jewel earrings. When Lauren used to cry over problems he could fix, like a skinned knee or a favorite stuffed animal left behind in a restaurant booth.

I don't have any of that to look back on. I wish it only made me sad, not pissed off, but my anger and sadness have always had a codependent relationship. I don't know not to be angry at the fact that who I am now isn't good enough; that I'm not a little girl.

Because that's what no one wants to talk about. That at some point, every little girl grows up and gets ruined.

"Okay," I tell him. "It won't happen again."

My dad's lips form a relieved smile, and it hits me: the words that just came out of his mouth are Ashley's. It's the same thing she said to me the other day: *You are not the kind of girl who sneaks out.* All of this was staged so we could have a deep father-daughter moment.

He picks up his plate, and I have to swallow back the bulb of anger stuck in my throat. "How can you do that? Pretend I'm— you have no idea what kind of life I had before you took me."

My father turns. Looks at me as if he's never seen me before. "What?"

"I was a *bad kid*. I cut school all the time. And when my mom and I fought, I went crazy."

"Stop that," he says. "You're not crazy."

"But you think she's crazy. That's why you left her."

"Kacey, you know your mother probably better than anyone does." His eyes are pleading. "She has a lot of problems. I wasn't equipped to deal with them, so I left. I didn't ever mean to leave you, too. But she didn't want me to be in your life."

"But did she really say you couldn't see me? Or was it just an easy way out for you?"

My father cups his chin. Sad puppy-dog eyes.

I want to hit him. "Do you have any idea how messed up I am?" I say.

My father gapes. He's looking at me like a stranger. I wonder if he's thinking it: *Is my daughter fucked up enough to kill her best friend?*

The lock in the front door turns. Andrew steps into the kitchen. Hearing the door, Ashley comes in from the living room. No doubt she was listening in on my father and me this whole time.

She looks Andrew up and down. "You said you'd be home from the track meet an hour ago. I've been calling you."

"I didn't go to the track meet."

"Then where the hell were you?" Ashley looks from him to me, like I had something to do with this. I think of Detective Burke's appearance at the school this afternoon and my chest tightens.

"I was at the sheriff's station," Andrew says. "They wanted to talk to me again."

Ashley turns to me, slowly. "Kacey. Please go to your room."

. . .

The argument lasts half an hour. I can't hear most of it, but the parts I catch are bad. My dad: *It doesn't matter if you're eighteen. We should have been there.*

Ashley: *Do they think you had something to do with this?*

Andrew: *Of course not—just routine questions—*

Ashley: *About what? Kacey? That detective—has it in for her—*

Andrew: *They're talking to everyone—not just Kacey and me—*

Andrew doesn't tell them about the phone records. He's lying—so he doesn't worry them, maybe.

Which means that whatever went down in that interrogation room today made Andrew think there's finally something to worry about.

Later, I have to brush my teeth upstairs, because Andrew is soaking in the bathtub across from my room while Lauren showers upstairs. When I come back to my room, I see my phone blinking and pick it up.

There's a text from Andrew.

Meet me in the bathroom. Not really in the tub. There's something I have to tell you.

CHAPTER TWENTY-TWO

Andrew is sitting on the bathroom rug when I open the door, so I sit down on the toilet seat and pull my knees up to my chest. The water's running into the bathtub, and it's loud enough to drown out our conversation.

"I didn't just drive around the night Bay went missing," he says. "Around ten, when my mom went to sleep, I drove to your dad's hospital."

I hug my knees tighter. "Why?"

"I wanted to see if he was really working."

My arms fall from my knees. "What? Why wouldn't he be working?"

"Because I thought he was lying about all the double shifts." Andrew puts his face in his hands. "Two weeks ago, my mom left her cell phone on the table when you guys left for the café.

She got a call from an unknown number, so I figured I'd pick up and tell whoever it was to call the café instead."

I don't know where this story is going, but I don't like it. I lick my lips. "Who was it?"

"Some woman named Beth Schrader. I didn't recognize the name as one of her friends, so I Googled it." Andrew looks up at me, bleary-eyed. "She's a divorce attorney in Madison."

Divorce. The word lands like a punch to the kidney.

"Why didn't you tell me?" I ask. Even if Andrew wanted to keep this a secret from Lauren, he could have told *me.*

Andrew's eyes glisten. "I confronted my mom about it. She made me promise not to tell you or Lauren. I'm so sorry, Kace."

I'm shaking. A million thoughts zip through my head: where will I go? Everything I was so afraid of—Ashley getting pissed at me, being sent back to New York, having to live with my mom again—it was all set into motion before I even stepped a foot in that barn.

But of course it all makes sense—Ashley's constant anger at my dad's work hours. Her little speech to me in the car the other day: *I wanted someone to fight for me.*

How badly had I wanted my perfect new life to work out that I was willing to overlook things that were right in front of my face?

A thought breaks through the cloud cover in my brain: *I can't lose them.* Ashley will no doubt get custody of Andrew, and Lauren, and the house—

"I'll never see you or Lauren," I blurt. "I can't live with my dad alone. I barely know him—I'll have to go back to my mom."

"Don't say that. I think she's waiting until we go to school—

and if we both go to school in Madison we'll see each other all the time."

If I even get into school in Madison. If not, who knows what will happen to me? I can't think about that right now. "Why does she want to leave him? Is it because of me?"

"Of course not. She wouldn't get into it with me, so I thought maybe he was—"

"Having an affair."

"I thought. But I saw his car in the parking lot—and I felt like an asshole and came home."

I inhale. Exhale. "Did you tell the police all this?"

"Of course I did. But no one saw me at the hospital. No one can confirm I was there. It looks like I'm full of shit about where I went that night."

My voice comes out hollow. "This is bad. The phone calls were bad enough . . . but you sneaking out. It's bad."

Andrew holds his head in his hands. "Can you stop saying that? I know it's bad. What are the goddamn chances my phone picked *her* to butt-dial that night?"

I draw in a breath. "Swear to me you never hooked up with her."

"I swear to *God*."

Swear to me it was just a butt dial. Swear to me you really drove to the hospital Saturday night. Swear to me you didn't meet up with Bailey.

But I stay quiet. Somewhere in the back of my mind, the doubt lingers.

"*Kacey.*" Andrew looks at me with wild eyes. "You can't be

thinking that I did this. I had *no* reason to want to hurt Bailey, let alone kill her."

I can't tell him what he wants to hear: that I know him, and he's not capable of hurting anyone—never mind a girl who's been his friend his entire life. I want to believe so badly that Andrew's not lying, and it really was just a butt dial. I want to believe he's not a liar.

But everything I've believed so far has been wrong.

So I say the only thing I can think of: "You'd better find a way to convince Burke of that."

I wake up feeling like I'm dying. Cramps—real, actual period cramps, not invented ones to get Mrs. Lao off my back—at four a.m. I wind up curled on my side on the bathroom floor. After an hour, Ashley comes down to check on me. I wonder if she went to bed at all last night, or if she stayed up and listened to my every movement.

She presses a cool hand to my forehead. Removes it and sits down next to the toilet. "Did you get any sleep at all?"

I shake my head.

"Stay home today." She disappears, and I think that's it. Minutes later I hear the beep of the microwave; Ashley returns with a hot beanbag that smells like lavender. She hands it to me and I press it into my abdomen.

Staying at home isn't that simple. Ashley stays with me, and even though she swears Paula can manage the café on her own, I feel like shit about it. I fall asleep on the living room couch for a couple hours; when I wake up again, my textbooks and shoulder bag are on the coffee table.

I'm so behind on my work, even though it brings a fresh pang to my gut to admit it. I'm basically a prisoner—Ashley sits at the kitchen island on her laptop so she has a view of the living room—and without any new developments online about Bailey's case, I really have no other choice but to get started.

I dig out the prompt for my essay due tomorrow; getting down three hundred of the seven-hundred-and-fifty-word minimum is more painful than my uterus imploding. I'm so mired in it that I jump when the doorbell rings around two-thirty.

Ashley leaps up to answer it. I hear Val Diamond's pleasant, parent-approved voice: *Just bringing Kacey some work she missed.*

"That's so thoughtful," Ashley says. "Why don't you come in for a hot chocolate?"

I pad into the kitchen, where Val stands awkwardly by the kitchen island, peeling off her gloves. The bizarreness of the scene settles over me: Val Diamond is in my house. Val Diamond, who barely looks at me during Spanish class, brought me my homework.

Ashley starts setting up the kettle on the stove. "Wasn't that sweet of Val to bring you your homework?" Ashley says. Her smile is tight, though, as she looks me up and down. "Are you feeling better?"

"Not really," I say. "Do we still have that extra-strength Tylenol?"

I know it's upstairs, in her bathroom, where all the medication is. Ashley nods. "Keep an eye on the kettle?"

Val's gaze skitters over me as Ashley ducks out of the kitchen. "I really did bring your Spanish homework."

"Thanks." I sit. Val takes the stool across the island from me. She's actually doing this—staying for hot chocolate.

After a beat of silence, she opens her mouth. "The other day, at the café. I'm sorry Bridget was so rude."

"Is that why you're really here? To say *sorry* for her?" I feel my eyebrows knit together. Bridget being nasty is a day-to-day occurrence and hardly a reason for showing up at my house.

Val's mouth forms a line. "I just . . . can't imagine this being easy for you. I know how Bailey can be."

She's dancing around something; I wonder what Val knows. If it's something bad enough that she felt the need to come here and tell me.

"Look," I say. "I know that Bailey did some . . . terrible stuff behind my back." I can't bring myself to say the words: *She brought my little sister to a* frat. Not when I don't even know how to confront Lauren about the party.

A rattling sound upstairs, as if Ashley couldn't find the Tylenol and dumped the entire contents of the medicine chest.

"It wasn't just you," Val says. "She did the same kind of stuff to me in middle school. We were really close. Like, we had matching outfits when we were little. Then one day she just stopped talking to me and I started hearing people say she was calling me a two-faced bitch."

Val's eyes are glassy. I wonder how long she's been waiting to tell this to someone who would believe her. Val is popular, Val's best friend is Bridget Gibson—of course you'd look at her and Bailey and assume that Val was the one doing the dropping.

"I'm really sorry," I say, and I mean it. "I'm sorry I always ignored you just because she did."

A tear snakes down Val's cheek. She wipes it away. "I'm not even mad at her anymore, that's the sad thing. I don't even believe she wanted to drop me."

"What do you mean?"

"Bailey had so many friends before she met Jade. When Jade moved here, Bay just started *discarding* them, one by one. I always thought that Jade had something to do with it. Like, if Bailey was hearing rumors about me talking shit about her, Jade was probably the one who started them."

The kettle starts to whistle on the stove, and I jump up and remove it from the heat. As I turn back around, I catch Val wiping a tear from her cheek.

I hand Val a napkin. She blows her nose. "Sorry. I'm being ridiculous," she says. "It's just, I just think you should be careful. About who you trust."

"You mean Jade."

Val starts tearing the dry edge of the napkin into strips. And that's how I know: she didn't come here to give me some vague warning. She heard something: something she's afraid to tell me.

"Val. What are people saying?"

Val looks up. "I— Nothing specific. Just . . . rumors."

My patience is unspooling. "What kind?"

"About you and Andrew."

The cramp deep in my belly twists at the suggestion in her voice. I don't need her to elaborate. "He's my stepbrother. Who the fuck would say something like that?"

Val looks at me from below her lashes. They're clumping

270

together, her mascara wet from her earlier tears. "This summer—at senior service day? Bailey kind of said something to me."

Of course it was Bailey. I feel like a dumbass for even asking. "I didn't know you guys were talking again."

"We weren't," Val says. "But when we were pulling weeds, we both saw you and Andrew painting the gazebo." Her face goes red. A flicker of a memory—the way Andrew had swiped paint on my nose with his brush. It makes my toes curl.

Val's face is apologetic. "Bailey looked at me and was like, 'Are you supposed to flirt with your stepsister?'"

I nod, stupidly, like a broken bobble head. "Thanks for telling me, I guess."

Val's lips pinch together. "I thought she was just jealous. And then today, I heard people saying you two . . . you know."

I'm thankful I'm sitting. Is that what Tyrell was holding back from me the other day   that he'd heard the rumors about Andrew and me? Because accusations like that—me sleeping with my *stepbrother*—it would be enough to make either one of us want to kill Bailey.

It finally hits me, how stupid it was to leave things off with Jade the way I did. I should have known she'd turn on me—she started turning on me the moment Ellie Knepper told her that I suggested Bailey might have run away.

The floor above us trembles, and Ashley comes into the kitchen, breathless. "There's only one Tylenol left. You want me to run out and get more?"

I shake my head. When Ashley's back is turned, Val touches my hand and whispers, "Just be careful, okay? Jade scares me. Both of them scare me."

Senior Year
November

I hate Kacey Young so much that I'm scaring myself. I hate her big freaky eyes that scream *Love me!* I hate the effect she has on people—that mix of pity and admiration. She's the girl who needs saving. The one the guy scoops up at the end of every shitty movie, kissing her tears away and making her *whole again.*

It's alarming how easy it is to hide how much I hate her. It's weird—the more I hate her, the more I want to be around her. We hang out after school almost every day, sometimes alone when Jade is working, and I act like nothing is wrong, that I don't soothe myself to sleep by imagining pushing her off a bridge.

I've Googled her thousands of times, trying to find the part of her she keeps locked away from us. I found something—an old blog that's registered to the same email address she uses now—but it's private. I've tried hundreds of different password combinations—I've even tried to teach myself rudimentary hacking. That's how badly I want to crack Kacey's head open like a nut. Scoop out all the thoughts inside and dissect them one by one.

Jade hates her too—it's almost all we talk about now when

Kacey's not around. All it took was Kacey flaunting that application to Madison Art Institute one day at lunch for Jade's face to turn sour. It doesn't matter that Jade never cared about the fact that she couldn't afford going to a fancy college before; it's the fact that *Kacey* gets to live out a dream that should have been Jade's.

I know what it feels like: like something's been stolen from you, even if the thing never belonged to you.

I really think Andrew and I would have had a chance if Kacey hadn't waltzed into our lives. Andrew *saw* me for once—the only problem is *she* was standing in the way, right between us. *Look at me! Poor girl abandoned by Daddy, here to wreck shit.*

I know something is going on between them. It's not innocent flirting anymore. I *saw it.*

I've been to the Markhams' house every night this week. I told my parents I picked up the closing shift at Friendly Drugs, even though they hate me leaving work when it gets dark. Instead, I hang out at Jade's from four to eight-thirty, making mac and cheese and lazing on her bed on our phones. She hasn't asked why I've been spending so much time at her house; I figure if she does I'll say my mom and I haven't been getting along.

I'm on Sparrow Road by nine, ready for my drive-by. For the first few nights I didn't see anything—maybe the flicker of a light in the den, or Kacey's lamp on in her bedroom.

But last night. Last night I saw something that made me sick.

All of the lights were on in the den; I could see Andrew and Kacey on the couch, lounging at opposite ends. Their feet touched in the middle. They were just *laughing,* at what, I'll never know. But it doesn't matter. If you could see the way he was looking at her. All I could think was, *No one has ever looked at me like that.*

I have my answer now to *Where does Andrew Kang go when he's gone?* To her. He loves her. I know it.

I fucking hate Kacey Young. I hate her so much I wish she were dead. I hate her so much I want to be the one to do it.

I know they say that hate can destroy a person. But I've never felt so alive.

CHAPTER TWENTY-THREE

have to talk to Lauren—hear it from her that what Ben said about the party is true—but I can't get her alone until after dinner, when Ashley goes upstairs to call her sister. Lauren is already changed for her evening ballet class—black leotard, pink tights, and a gauzy skirt. She's tucked into the corner of the living room couch, bent miserably over her phone. I wonder if this will all be worth it in ten years—why Ashley doesn't just let her quit dance if it makes her so unhappy.

Lauren's fingers stop moving across the screen of her phone when I plop down next to her. I nod to her skirt. "Ballet tonight?"

"Pointe. Miss Longo says if I can't get up by the spring I should take lyrical instead next year."

I glance down at Lauren's legs. Her thighs and calves are

muscular, strong. She's been struggling with pointe all year, though: coming home from class in tears because Miss Longo picks on her. I wonder if her wobbliness has anything to do with how Emma and Keelie March are in her class, probably always watching. Rooting for her to fall.

How long has Lauren been depressed for? Could it have started after the fucking *frat party* my friends dragged her to?

I squeeze Lauren's knee. "Are you okay? You're scaring me. You're not yourself."

Lauren's mouth forms a stubborn line. I keep pressing. "Laur, did something bad happen? Something you don't want to talk about?"

"No. What are you even talking about?" Her nose bunches up. "You sound like Mom."

"I know that Bailey and Jade took you to a party in Milwaukee."

Lauren freezes. The contents of my stomach churn; I think of my sister around a bunch of lecherous frat boys, accepting a drink from Bailey and Jade all while they cackled about how fucking funny and clever they were, bringing a kid to a college party.

A niggling voice in my head reminds me I was only a year older than Lauren the first time I let a boy put his hand up my shirt. But Lauren isn't me; she's too trusting. She still lives in her Rapunzel tower with her stuffed sea creatures.

"Lauren. Did anyone at the party do anything to you— something you didn't want—"

"What?" she almost yells. "Gross! No."

She finally looks me in the eye. She's telling the truth. "Are you going to tell?"

I gnaw the inside of my lip. "No. But that was really, stupid, Laur."

"Bailey didn't say where we were going. She just told me to sneak out and hang out with them."

I feel like a pile of garbage. I wasn't there for her. I wasn't there to protect her that night, or the night in the barn. "They—they're not your friends. You're too young to be hanging out with them."

Lauren casts her eyes down.

"I know you feel alone, but you're not. Screw Emma and Keelie. You'll make new friends. And in the meantime, you have me. You have Andrew."

"Is it true?" Lauren whispers. "That you and Andrew had scx?"

My stomach falls and vomit threatens in my throat. "Who the *hell* said that?"

"Austin Schultz," Lauren says. "He asked me if it was true."

"Paula's kid?" My heartbeat picks up. Paula Schulz who works at Milk & Sugar—she has a boy who's Lauren's age.

I think of the way Paula wouldn't look at me the other day, and my insides shrivel up. How long have the rumors been circulating?

"Is it true?" Lauren's voice is so small.

"No. Lauren, of course it's not true. Did Austin say who told him that?"

Lauren shakes her head. "But it's not . . . he's not the first person who said something to me."

I'll bet I know who it was. "Bailey?"

"Kind of?" Lauren gnaws at a hangnail. "At that party—she

277

kept asking about you and Andrew doing stuff alone. It's like she thought I was dumb and didn't understand why she was asking."

But Bailey is gone—dead, everyone says—so there's only one person left who could have told the student body that I fucked my stepbrother.

I finally gather the nerve to call Jade. After one ring it clicks and I hear her voice: *Hey, I'm either sleeping or I don't feel like dealing with you. Leave a message.* . . .

There's that suction-cup feeling in my stomach again. Jade ignored my call, and she doesn't care that I know she ignored my call.

It's a huge fuck-you.

So I think of a response that is both equal and pathetic: I block Jade on every social media account I have and flop into bed, not caring that I've just declared war.

I'm washing my face before school in the morning when I smell smoke.

Something is burning in the kitchen. I run down the hall and round the corner in time to see Lauren poking inside the toaster with a wooden spoon. I shoo her out of the way and fish out the charred remains of an English muffin.

"I was upstairs," Lauren explains.

"Where's your mom?" I ask.

"She had to take Andrew to the sheriff's station for another interview."

I use two fingers to dump the burned muffin into the trash, tamping down the urge to puke all over it. They want to question Andrew more. Of course they want to question Andrew more—he's the last person who called Bailey.

I think of what Lauren told me last night—what people are saying about Andrew and me—and my knees go numb.

"Why didn't your mom get me up to tell me?" I ask Lauren.

"She wanted to let you sleep." Lauren is still in her pajamas. "I have to wake Dad up to drive us to school."

You are thirteen, I want to shout in her face. *You should be able to make yourself breakfast and put yourself on the bus.*

I steel myself. I'm horrible. Ashley just wants her daughter to get to school safely. It's not that unreasonable, now that girls are disappearing around here. It's unreasonable for me to think that every kid is supposed to grow up the way I did, like a roaming dog.

"Is Andrew in trouble?"

I don't have the heart to lie to her and say everything is fine. "I don't know, Monkey. I'll make you another muffin. Go wake Dad up."

Lauren flees the kitchen without looking back at me. She's tossed the bread knife into the sink, into a soapy bowl caked with last night's spaghetti sauce. I don't have time to wash it.

Ashley has another set of knives—one that only she had been allowed to use, until I proved I could dice onions without chopping my fingers off. It's a stainless steel professional set

279

and probably cost a thousand bucks. And I'm using one of them to cut an English muffin.

I slide the knife case box out from the overhead cabinet and open it, running my finger across the handles in search of the bread knife. I linger for a beat over the space where the chef's knife should be.

Should be.

I push aside the mess of dishes in the sink, racking my brain for the last time I saw Ashley use the chef's knife. She hasn't cooked all week, except to make that casserole for the Hammonds—and I washed the dishes that morning.

Heart in my throat, I pull out the dishwasher rack, even though everyone knows better than to leave Ashley's beloved stainless knives in there with the other grime-covered utensils. The chef's knife would have been washed and put away whenever it was used.

I sink to the floor, the knob of the lower cabinet digging into my back. It doesn't mean anything.

Six-inch chef's knives don't just disappear. Just like people don't just disappear.

I cover my mouth with my hands. I replay my conversations with Andrew. Pick them apart for any indication he was bullshitting me the entire time.

His night drive. The phone calls. He'd explained them away so easily.

How the hell is he going to explain the knife missing from our house?

I wiggle my phone out of my jeans pocket and call Andrew, even though I know he can't answer. I let it ring all the way through, just so I can hear his voice-mail message. *Say this is all wrong. Say you didn't take that knife.*

Say you didn't know the rumors about us. Say you would never hurt Bailey even if you knew she started them.

The pounding of footsteps on the stairs. I scramble to my feet, realizing I've forgotten to make Lauren another English muffin.

I realize why Ashley wanted my dad to drive me to school when I arrive.

Everyone already knows why Andrew isn't with me.

The sea of bodies in the hall seems to part for me. There are no whispers or pointed stares, but their thoughts are displayed clear on their faces.

Andrew Kang is not a killer. Andrew Kang is the nicest guy in school.

Did she really have sex with her stepbrother?

Did they really kill Bailey together?

Do you think he's covering for her?

My rage returns tenfold when I show up at Jade's locker and she's not there like she is every morning. She must have realized by now that I blocked her, and she doesn't even have the guts to face me and ask why.

Jade isn't in first-period art, but it's not unusual for her to stroll in a few periods late. By Spanish third period, my anxiety is spiking. On the way into Mrs. Callahan's room, I stop by Val's desk.

"Hey." She looks up at me. A weak smile before shifting her gaze to see who's watching.

She doesn't want to be seen talking to me.

"Um, have you seen Jade today?"

"Yeah, I think she was in second period." Val scratches the back of her neck, one eye on Bridget, who is at the desk next to her.

"Did you see her in homeroom?" I ask.

"Nah, she wasn't there. I think she came in late."

Just in time for second period, so she wouldn't have to see me. By the time I get back to my desk, I'm seething. As the bell rings, I slide my phone from my pocket and send Jade a text. One I know will get her attention.

Where is your mom REALLY jade??

Everything is falling apart, and I am desperate to take someone down with me.

I get a response at the end of the period.

your locker

When the bell rings, I spring out of my seat. I'll be late for algebra if I cross to the senior wing first, but fuck it.

Jade's waiting at my locker when I get there. Before I can open my mouth, her fist comes flying at me. I duck her punch; the sound of her fist slamming into my locker makes people turn around.

"Fuck you, Kacey," she says, loud enough for everyone to hear. She turns on her heels; I grab her arm.

"I'm right, aren't I? You lied about your mom just like you lied about Andrew and me."

Jade looks down at my hand on her wrist. "Get off me."

"Just tell me why. Do you know where she is?"

Jade yanks herself out of my grasp, so violently I lurch

forward. I ignore the stinging in my wrist and swing it, back-handing Jade across the face.

Someone starts to shout about a fight. I'm shaking—I *slapped Jade*—as I turn to head down the hall, in the other direction of the art room. That's when she grabs me. Slams me into the row of lockers. Pain sears across my forehead and my brain rattles against my skull.

My forehead is raw, prickling from where it connected with the locker door. Blood. I drag my fingers down her face.

I'll kill her.

Shouting—so much shouting—someone grabs my shoulders, pins me to the lockers. Mr. White: "What is wrong with you?"

He drags me toward Gonzo's office, past the SAS guard holding Jade back. Her nose is bleeding around her rhinestone stud. Gonzo trots out of her office, barking at everyone in the hall to get to class.

They all stare at me as they scatter. Mr. White won't even look at me. I'm so incredibly fucked, but my pulse is steady. A calm settles over me, as if I've gotten something important out of the way.

My only regret is not drawing more blood.

"What on earth were you thinking?"

I stare back at Gonzo. Everyone keeps asking me that, but they don't want the real answer. "I don't know."

Gonzo stands up and paces the room. Her eyes are red. "The only reason I'm not expelling you on the spot is that the sheriff's office just called me."

"What?" I look up, the bone above my eye throbbing where it connected with someone's locker.

Gonzo looks at me, her upper lip trembling. "They're holding a press conference this afternoon. I'm canceling all after-school activities."

My stomach sinks to my feet. "Why? Did they find Bailey?"

"I don't know." Gonzo grabs a tissue from the box on her desk. "Go to the nurse and get a pack of ice for your face."

The nurse lets me lie on the cot in her office instead of going back to Gonzo's office where Jade is waiting for her father to pick her up. Thankfully, someone sees the indignity of having to face the person who just kicked your ass. I have a sweaty Ziploc bag of ice pressed to my temple.

The bell rings. At the beginning of the next period, Gonzo comes on the loudspeaker and announces that all after-school activities are canceled.

"Mrs. Gonzalo got in touch with your mom," the nurse says when she comes to refresh my ice. "She and your dad are a bit tied up right now, but one of them will pick you up as soon as they can. Can you say your ABCs for me?"

This is her way of checking that I don't have a concussion. The words *a bit tied up* pinball in my head.

With Andrew. At the police station.

When the nurse isn't looking, I slide out my phone. Fire off a bunch of texts to Andrew.

What is going on
What are they asking you

284

I even text Ashley: *Is everything okay??*

But over an hour ticks by, and they never answer. At lunchtime, a pimply freshman comes in, puking into a plastic bag. The nurse skitters out of her chair to attend to him. I hear the SAS lady who escorted the puking kid say that the office called his parents, and no one can pick him up.

While the nurse is distracted, I fish my headphones out of my bag. Plug them into my phone and pull up the local news's website. They're live streaming the press conference about Bailey in ten minutes. I roll onto my side on the cot, brush my hair over the headphones. It doesn't matter; the freshman has vomited all over the floor, and now the nurse is cleaning it up.

The press conference starts; my screen goes black as the video buffers. When it loads again, Detective Burke is standing outside the Broken Falls Sheriff's Department. Cathy, Ed, and Ben Hammond stand off to the side of the lectern. Ben is sobbing so hard that Cathy has to hold him up.

Burke clears his throat. "At dawn this morning, we were informed of reports that human remains were found on a property on the Minnesota border."

My blood turns to ice.

"It's with difficulty that I can confirm the body belongs to Bailey Hammond."

Senior Year
December

I always thought I could get away with murder. I've watched enough TV to know all of the stupid mistakes that will land you in prison for the rest of your life. (Cell records—how can people be so dumb? Or getting caught on a security camera at Walmart buying bleach and garbage bags and a shovel like no one will raise a fucking eyebrow at *that*.)

I've spent more time than I'd like to admit plotting out murders, thinking about all the ways I could cover them up and ride into the sunset while the police scratch their balls. Having an accomplice can be the key—someone to muddy things up and cause enough doubt that the law can never really pin it on either one of you. Obviously this can backfire, if you're sloppy, or if one person can't keep her mouth shut.

But I think I've got it all figured out.

First you pick your kill site. It's got to be somewhere easy to clean up, someplace where the smell of bleach will go unnoticed for weeks, or blood, if everything goes to hell and you have to get out of there pronto. Somewhere like a barn up on a hill where no one can hear her screams. You plan to lure her there under false pretenses, but it must be compelling, something you can convince her not to blab about. Because you don't want her telling anyone ahead of time where she's going or who she's going to be with. You want everyone to believe she just climbed out her window one night and disappeared forever. So you invent a bullshit story about people doing séances in said barn, summoning the spirit of the Red Woman with five candles, because you know your victim won't be able to be the girl who bitches out. And then you feel like a fucking genius, because you know she's so desperate for friends that she'll do whatever you say, she'll follow you anywhere.

Then there's the important part: method. A gun is no good, because there's the matter of obtaining a gun. You could steal your father's hunting rifle, but they can always trace the bullet if they find the body. And what if someone hears the gunshot? A knife is preferable—a big-ass hunting knife with a long handle so you don't injure yourself while you're getting your stabs in. She'll scream, but there are two of you—one to hold her down and cover her mouth, and one to do the dirty work. You hit a snag when you realize you have to be eighteen to get a hunting knife—so you enlist help from the only person in Broken Falls who has no reason to help you with anything, ever. Except he is a greedy fucker, and when you offer him double what the knife is worth to do an off-the-books transaction, he responds within hours, and you meet up and the knife feels so magical in your hands you feel like Harry fucking Potter, or Gandalf.

Then there's disposal. Once she's lured into the barn and the deed is done, you roll her body up in a tarp and drive as far as you can go and still be back before everyone wakes up in the morning and discovers she's gone. You bury her body under leaves and sticks, and maybe you'll get lucky and a fresh layer of snow will cover the whole thing by the morning. You have your clothes to think about, too. They'll be bloody, and almost impossible to truly dispose of. You have to make sure they can't trace it back to you, so you drive to the shittiest of all the Super-Marts, one that's twenty miles away where no one will recognize you, one with no security cameras. You buy men's sweatpants and hoodies to throw off the cops if they ever find the clothes where you bagged them and buried them. No one ever suspects girls, because we're sugar and spice and everything nice, right? You pay in cash at the SuperMart and nod when the cashier asks if you're buying clothes for your boyfriend. There's the issue of *her* seeing you both dressed in men's clothing, so you decide to leave the sweats in the trunk and quickly change into them when her back is turned.

And then there's the phones. You're paranoid that even if you don't make outgoing calls from your cells, they'll be able to trace where you were the night of the murder. So you leave them at home, even though you feel naked going out without them. But you text her first, say you're coming to pick her up. You know she'll wimp out like she always does, find some excuse not to come out. You say *fine* and go anyway, because if you just show up she won't be able to fight it. But the records will show that your phone was sitting on your nightstand all night, which corroborates your story that you were in bed, asleep, when she climbed out that window, never to be seen again. And as for an alibi, you and Jade have all you've ever needed.

Each other.

CHAPTER TWENTY-FOUR

It has to be a mistake.

They can't have found Bailey's body—she can't *actually* be gone.

Even though all the pieces pointed to her being dead, I don't believe Burke. They must have gotten it wrong.

Girl goes missing. Girl is found dead. I knew the story, but I still wanted it to end differently. I selfishly wanted this nightmare to be happening to some other person, in some other town like it always seems to happen.

The nurse sticks her head in and whispers: "Kacey. Your mother is here."

My mom? That's impossible—

I swing myself off the cot and hurry out the door, down to the main office.

Ashley. Of course, it's Ashley. She's waiting in one of the chairs next to the secretary's desk, her face matte with dried tears. She knows—everyone knows by now. She jumps up when she sees me. The way she looks at my face makes the bruise Jade left there pulse.

"They want to talk to you," she says, once we're in the car. "Andrew has a lawyer now. She's agreed to sit in on your interview."

I swallow. "So I'm guessing the interview isn't optional."

Ashley ignores that. "How is your head?"

"Killing me."

She doesn't say anything else to me the entire ride to the sheriff's station.

When we arrive, Ellie Knepper escorts us into an open interview room like we're VIPs. Detective Burke is waiting inside, and he doesn't waste any time.

"The lab got partial prints off the blood smear in the barn. Oddly enough, they didn't match Andrew's."

"So you think they'll match mine," I say.

"Would you be willing to submit your prints? To rule you out, of course."

I nod. "Fine. Whatever. I didn't do it."

"I want to believe you, Kacey. But whoever killed Bailey—and you've gotta understand that it's looking like that person was Andrew—they had help."

My blood chills. *Jade.* But it makes no sense.

"This was a planned effort," Burke says. "Someone killed Bailey, went all the way to the border to get rid of her body, drove over to Sparrow Hill to make that blood smear, and then dumped the bloody clothes, her phone, and her car. It's possible to pull it off alone. But I don't think that's what happened."

"It *wasn't me*. I can't help you."

Burke sets a paper down on the table. It's a copy of an Internet search history. *Leeds Massacre crime scene photos.*

"We seized your family computer today. This search was done on it," Burke says. He sets down two photos: one, a grainy printout of the bloody handprint, the other, the blood smear from the other day. "This was one hell of a distraction. Made us lose quite a bit of search time. Luckily for whoever made that handprint, you were there to find the blood just as our search was ramping up."

"You think we *planned* that? I told you I only went to the barn because Chloe Strauss said she saw the Red Woman."

"See, we talked to Chloe Strauss." Burke folds his hands together. "And we think she actually *did* see a female covered in blood around three a.m. The timing would line up—it takes three hours round trip to drive to the border. We know that Bailey left the party around eleven-thirty."

Burke pushes the paper toward me. "We were able to pull the content of those deleted texts from Bailey's phone. Why don't you check them out?"

My heart plummets to my stomach as I pull the paper toward me. At 11:15, Bailey texted Andrew.

Hey. Did you mean to call me?

Yeah. Something I need to talk to you about. talk in person?

My back sweats against my hoodie. I can only imagine what was going through Bailey's head. The boy she'd loved forever asking to meet her for a late-night confession.

I read on.

Ok. What about??

Kacey.

The blood drains from my head. I feel Ashley's eyes on me, desperate to see what I'm reading. I stare down at the paper. Five minutes after Andrew's last message, Bailey responded: *ok . . . I can be at your house in like fifteen minutes*

if that's ok

No, don't want to wake my fam up. Can you meet me at Leeds Park?

Sure.

Thanks. See ya in a bit.

And then, eighteen minutes later: *I'm here.*

Burke takes the printout back. "That's it. The last text she sent."

"I think I'm done talking to you guys," I say.

They're keeping Andrew, which means either he's cooperating with the interrogation or they have enough evidence to hold him. I don't have the heart to ask Ashley which it is; she sobs silently the entire drive home. I touch the tender spot on my forehead.

My dad is waiting for us in the living room. I can't look at him.

Ashley lets out a sob when she sees my dad. He rushes over to her, grabs her by the forearms to hold her up.

I've never felt more like an intruder.

I slip into the mudroom, straining my ears to hear them as I

292

kick off my boots. They're arguing quietly—my dad wants to go back to the station with Ashley. Ashley's response is even, tactical: *Someone needs to stay with the girls.*

"What is the lawyer saying?" my dad mutters. "Do they have enough to keep him?"

Ashley sounds defeated. "There's no use. The DNA under Bailey's fingernails was a partial match to Andrew's."

The blood in my body drains to my feet for the second time that day.

"DNA?" My father's voice is a controlled shout. "Why the hell do they have his DNA, Ashley?"

"Because he offered it to them," Ashley shouts. "He's an adult, goddamn it. I trusted him when he said it would rule him out."

I stick my head in the doorway. "Does it mean he did it?"

"No—not necessarily. It means he had contact with her before she died, though," Ashley says.

"Ashley, should you be speaking like this in front—"

"In front of who, Russ?"

"My daughter, goddamn it."

My dad pinches the area between his nose and shakes. A silent sob.

Ashley doesn't go to him. I can't, either, even though he called me his daughter.

My father wipes the area under his eyes. "I'll stay with Andrew. Get some sleep, Ash."

When we hear the click of the front door shutting, Ashley collapses onto one of the island stools.

I still feel like I owe my family fucking everything, but I can't

293

keep my mouth shut anymore. Not for Jade, who said she'd never forgive me—but for Bailey, who no matter what kind of shit she pulled behind my back, is dead and doesn't deserve to be.

"One of your knives is missing," I tell Ashley. "I noticed this morning."

She picks her head up from her hands. "What?"

"One of the nice ones. The big chef's one. I looked everywhere."

Ashley re-covers her face with her hands. "Oh God. Oh God."

There's a sharp pang in my chest. *This is real. He did this. Why did he do this?*

"I don't know what to do anymore," Ashley says, pulling me back down from my thoughts.

I don't know what else to do, so I fill Ashley's travel mug with coffee while she calls Mrs. Lao.

"Mrs. Lao says she'll keep an eye on the house," Ashley says. "Are you sure you and Lauren will be okay?"

I nod, the ache in my throat creeping down my neck. "You should be there."

When she's gone, it's quiet. I lie on the couch, letting the sobs move to my toes. Bailey is dead. Jade is a liar. Andrew is a killer.

A shadow moves over the couch behind me.

I turn to see Lauren in the doorway. She cocks her head at me. "Kacey?"

"Yeah, Monkey?"

"Is Andrew arrested?"

"Probably," I answer.

"Why?" she asks.

"They have his DNA. It matches some they found . . . on Bailey."

Lauren starts to cry, heavy, ugly sobs. I swing my legs over the side of the couch. Sit up and look at Lauren. Her face is red and splotchy. Twisted with fear.

"What if the DNA came from someone else?" Lauren sniffs. "Could they prove it?"

My head is swimming. Why would Lauren ask something like that?

Something Ashley said burrows into my brain. The DNA was a *partial* match. Meaning, there's a chance the DNA on the body wasn't Andrew's.

It was just *similar* to his DNA. I suck in a breath. *Fuck.*

"Lauren." My feet are frozen to the floor; I can't turn to meet my sister's eyes. When I force my body to face hers, her face is bunched up and red, like a newborn's. I swallow. "Lauren, why are you crying?"

"Because—Andrew—killed—Bailey—"

My thoughts swarm; I think of the texts Burke showed me.

I don't want to wake my fam up.

"No, he didn't."

I've never seen Andrew abbreviate *family* like that. It's such a small detail that Bailey wouldn't have noticed the difference. She'd never notice that she wasn't texting Andrew.

"You took Andrew's phone." As I say it out loud I know it's true. "He must have left it behind, like he's always doing—you took his phone and pretended to be him to get her to meet you."

Lauren shakes her head, her wails reaching a crescendo. "No, no, no."

"Why did you do it?" My heart is racing. My head is going to explode from trying to piece everything together. Make sense of this.

"She said I had to," Lauren cries.

I launch myself off the couch and rush over to Lauren. "Who is *she*? Jade?"

My sister stares at me. Eyes wide. "*No.* The Red Woman did."

I grab her by the wrists. "What the hell are you talking about?" Lauren wriggles away from me, letting out a primal scream.

"You don't understand. I had to do it. She *told me I had to do it.*"

"Lauren." I look her in the eyes, evenly, even though my whole body is quaking. "Did you kill Bailey?"

My sister lets out another wail. Balls her hands into fists and beats them against her head.

"Lauren, *stop.*" I get hold of one of her arms. She throws me off her; something pops under my collarbone. In the split second I take to wince and roll my shoulder, Lauren tears away from me. She's across the living room and unbolting the front door.

I run after her, holding the wall so I don't slip on the hardwood. Lauren is already running down the steps. I scream for her to stop, but my voice gets lost in the wind. Snow and ice pelt my face; I'm in my socks, still.

My toes go numb—Lauren's running around the side of the house, toward the woods. *Sparrow Hill.* If she tries to run across the street in these conditions, any drivers coming down the hill won't be able to stop in time.

"Lauren," I shriek. *"Stop."*

She halts at the edge of the road. She turns and looks at me as a car whizzes past, lifting her hair, like a veil, off her back. I kick off the snow and reach her in three steps. When I grab her, she starts to thrash and shriek again.

"Just let me die too." Her voice is guttural, as if an entity has taken possession of her body. I wrap my arms around her and squeeze. I pull her down to the ground, use my knees to pin her so she can't get away. My tears drop onto Lauren's face. "What did you do?"

She doesn't answer. She continues to shriek and sob as I dial 911 and tell them to send help to Sparrow Road as soon as possible.

CHAPTER TWENTY-FIVE

My toes are on fire. I'm on the living room couch, knees pulled to my chest. One of the EMTs keeps asking if I can wiggle my toes.

"The poor kid's in shock," Sheriff Moser says. "Get another blanket, would ya?"

When the EMT disappears, I look up at Moser. "She said—she asked me to let her die. I need to be with her."

"They're sedating her, I'm sure," Moser says. "Your parents are already on their way to the hospital. Is there someone I can call for you?"

"Um, Ashley has a sister. Andrew and Lauren's aunt." There's a fuzzy feeling in my head. Outside the bay window, lights flash red and blue, bouncing off the snow and onto the living room walls.

The EMT returns with a bulky brown blanket. Drapes it across my shoulders as Moser tells the deputy standing in the corner of the room to see about that aunt of mine.

Not mine, I want to yell. *Can't you see that I have no one?*

Moser scratches his belly and sits in the recliner so he's level with me. "I know this has been, ah, a troubling afternoon, but I need to know what happened, to make your sister, you know. Snap, this evening."

I nod. My lips are numb. The words feel garbled between them as I tell Moser about the texts, and the partial DNA match. What she said when I confronted her about everything and asked if she killed Bailey.

"She said someone told her *she had to do it,*" I say. "She said it was Josephine Leeds. The Red Woman."

Moser stops writing on his legal pad. Sets down his pen and looks at me.

"Dear Lord," he says. "This is going to be a doozy."

He questions me for another hour. No, I had no clue Lauren was involved. Yes, she had been acting strangely. No, I never thought in a million years Lauren was capable of this.

When he's finished, Moser clears his throat. "Your aunt ought to be here in a bit. Would you like me to have a deputy stay with you until she gets here?"

"I'll call my neighbor," I say, even though I know Mrs. Lao will probably come over the second she sees the police cars pull away.

After Moser and his deputy leave, I force myself upstairs. Rummage around in the bathroom for the NyQuil Ashley bought last week. Pause when I see the orange bottle with Andrew's name on it. *Ambien.*

I palm two of the sleeping pills and swallow them before I crawl back downstairs and into my bed.

When I wake, the room is dark. Someone is shaking me. I blink and look at Andrew. "What time is it?"

"After midnight. My aunt Christine is downstairs with Mrs. Lao. She picked me up from the station after they let me go."

I sit up. Rub my eyes so I can see him more clearly. His eyes are red.

"You wouldn't wake up," he says. "You scared the shit out of me."

"It's all my fault," I say. "I brought Lauren to the Leeds Barn. We made her think that shit was *real*."

I'm sobbing so hard that I start to choke. Andrew climbs into bed next to me. I put my head on his chest and he slides down so we're resting on the pillow. He lets me cry until his shirt is soaked. Until my sobs peter out into shallow breaths.

"I left my phone here that night," Andrew says quietly. "I must have left it on the kitchen counter, like I always do. Lauren saw it—she snuck it back onto my nightstand before I even got home from the hospital."

"What do you think is going to happen to her?" I whisper.

Andrew rubs an eye with the heel of his hand. "I don't know. I don't feel like this is real."

"Bailey would be alive if it weren't for me." I press a palm to my cheek. It's stiff with dried tears. I'm afraid if I make any sort of facial expression, I'll crack in half. "If I never moved here, Bailey would be alive."

"You don't know that." Andrew's voice breaks off. I wrap

my arms around him tighter. His body stiffens in a way it never has before when I've hugged him.

I lift my chin to meet his eyes. "You're mad at me. For thinking you did this."

Andrew shakes his head. "Not mad. Just sad."

I don't say it, but I think that's worse. A sob works its way up my throat. "I'm sorry. I'm so, so sorry."

Andrew's body relaxes a bit. He wraps his arms around my shoulders and squeezes. "I know."

He keeps saying it, even when the sobs take over my body again.

I know. I know.

CHAPTER TWENTY-SIX

Andrew and I have been staying at Ashley's sister's house for the past three days. The police had to come and search Lauren's room, comb through all of her things—dissect her life like a frog for signs of trouble—and Ashley thought it would be upsetting to us.

Aunt Chrissy, as I'm instructed to call her, has taken time off work to support her sister. I like her well enough. She's a padded, less bouncy version of Ashley. She talks on the phone all day and doesn't make me get out of bed. I spend most of my time online, where the news only says that police have a suspect in Bailey Hammond's disappearance in custody, but they can't name her because she's a minor.

What I do know: Lauren confessed to luring Bailey to

Leeds Park. She was going to call her from our house phone, say she needed to meet and talk about something, but she chickened out.

Until she saw Andrew's phone, left on the kitchen island. She decided to text Bailey, pretend to be Andrew.

Bailey was surprised to see her but let Lauren into her car. That was when Lauren stabbed Bailey—once in the neck, and then in the stomach.

The blood in Bailey's car corroborated Lauren's details. But she won't tell the police what she did with the knife she used.

It's a little after ten when the doorbell rings; there's murmuring in the hall, and then Christine opens the guest room door.

"Someone's here to see you," she says, like my getting visitors at her house is the most normal thing in the world.

Ellie Knepper is sitting at Christine's kitchen table. She takes me in—greasy hair, pajamas—as I sit down.

"You look well," she says, and I can't tell if she's joking.

I stare back at her.

"I saw Ashley and your dad at the hospital this morning," she says. "Lauren's improving. She's much more lucid."

"Am I supposed to be happy she's not delusional anymore? She's going to go to jail, probably for the rest of her life."

Ellie frowns. "You're getting ahead of yourself."

"She didn't do this alone," I say. "Someone her size can't move and bury a body by herself. And drive it all the way to the border? Lauren can't even drive."

Ellie shifts in her seat. "I can't discuss the details of the case with you. But it is an open investigation, and we're exploring every possibility."

"Have you talked to Jade?".

Ellie keeps on studying my face. "She insists she doesn't know anything."

"You can't trust anything she says."

"Oh, hon, I've known that since the day I met her."

Christine returns with a Disney World mug for Ellie. She smiles, showing off her bottom row of crooked teeth. When she accepts the tea, something on her finger catches the light. Sparkles.

"You're engaged," I say.

"Huh?" Ellie looks at her finger, then at me. "Oh, yeah. Still getting used to that."

I can't tear my eyes from her hand. She hadn't had the ring on a few days ago, in the interview room with Burke and Ashley.

While my family was falling apart, Ellie Knepper found the time to get engaged. It puts a funny feeling in my stomach. Not a bad one, exactly. In fact, I'm happy for her. It's the first thing I've felt other than despair since that afternoon on Sparrow Road when Lauren admitted what she'd done.

"Has Jade contacted you at all?" Ellie asks. And like that, the good feeling gutters out.

I shake my head.

Ellie frowns. "I just don't understand it. Everyone says she and Bailey were inseparable. If Jade really is involved in all this, why would she turn on her best friend?"

"There's no such thing as best friends," I say. "Everyone is only out to protect themselves."

Ellie's voice is quiet. "You don't really mean that. The world isn't as dark as it looks to you right now."

Maybe she's right.

"I have to talk to my sister," I say. "I might be able to help."

Do you believe in angels? I think I see why people buy into that shit, now. Kacey has an angel, that's for sure, and her name is Lauren Markham.

Everything was in place, the plan was foolproof—and then Lauren showed up in Kacey's room when we were supposed to pick Kacey up. Then everything was fucked. No one was supposed to see Kacey sneaking out with us.

When we were climbing up the hill, Jade whispered in my ear: "What if we got rid of both of them?"

My blood turned to ice. "That's insane."

"This is our only chance," Jade hissed. "I'll hold her down."

I knew what she was asking me to do. She wanted to go through with it—to kill Kacey while Lauren watched.

"No." I was firm. "She's just a kid."

Jade's jaw set; I wanted to turn around, say the séance was a stupid idea, and take them home. We'd been so stupid, thinking we could get away with murder. No one gets away with murder.

I think Lauren even saw the knife; I dropped my bag when we were leaving the barn. I even lost the dumb pendulum. I made the mistake of telling Jade what Lauren saw while we were on our drive back to her house once we dropped Lauren and Kacey off.

"We're so screwed," she said. "What if she says something to Kacey?"

"I don't think she will." But still, I couldn't stop the tremble working its way up my body. What if she was right—what if Lauren told Kacey *Bailey had a hunting knife in her bag* and Kacey got suspicious?

"I'll talk to her," Jade said.

"That's a horrible idea."

"Why?" Jade snapped. "Do you have a better one?"

"I just think we should forget about this. It was a really fucked-up, stupid idea."

Jade's voice was cool. "It was *your* idea."

"I was never serious. And she's not worth ruining our lives over." I couldn't look at Jade. "We would get caught. I know we would."

"And you're just realizing this?"

I knew she was pissed; it had been her idea to ask Cliff for the knife. I'd said I wanted Kacey gone, said I wished she were dead. Jade had been the one to say, *Then why not just do it ourselves?*

"Let's just forget about it," I said. "Get rid of all the stuff and never mention it again. Please."

"Whatever you say, Bay."

I dropped her off and decided to go home, even though I told my mom I was staying at Jade's. I feel sick writing that down. Something has changed between us: a huge rift. It started when I decided to go away for college. She was mad at me for leaving her behind. She got madder when I made our friendship all about Kacey, and now she's furious that I won't go through with getting rid of her. The only way I can get her back is if I go through with it, and I can't.

Here's something I've never said out loud before: Jade scares me. I really think she would have killed Kacey and Lauren both if I'd let her.

When I got home, everyone was asleep and I snuck in fine, like I did all the other times I went out for a drive and came back undetected. But I couldn't sleep; I was too freaked out by everything that happened tonight. Like it was all some sort of sign.

I wanted my mom. I found her sleeping alone in her bedroom, curled on her side. My dad banished to Ben's old room because his snoring was so bad. I crawled into bed with her like I hadn't since I was a kid and first heard of the Leeds family and worried something similar would happen to me, Ben, and my parents while I slept.

My mom stirred and turned over. Blinked and propped up on her elbow when she saw me. "Bailey? What's wrong?"

The tears started, silent and hot. I couldn't find the words. She would hate me if I told her everything I'd done: the thing with Lauren and the frat party, showing up outside Andrew's house, the plan to get rid of Kacey. They say parents are able to forgive anything, but I know my mother would never look at me the same way again if she saw what a monster I am.

She brushed away my hair from my forehead with a bony hand. "Honey, did you have a fight with Jade?"

Yes. I couldn't stop crying. *I don't want to be like this anymore. I hate myself.* "I think I need help."

"Help?" I could see the possibilities running through her head. *Pregnant.*

"Like, I need to talk to someone. A therapist."

"Okay. All right. We'll call one in the morning. Shh, sweetheart, it's okay." My mom continued to stroke my hair away from her face. "Why don't you sleep in here tonight?"

So I did. Tomorrow night, when everyone is sleeping, I'm going to burn this journal. There's too much in here that can fuck me over. There are things I said that are terrible, and there are things I want to hold on to, because the way I've poured myself onto these pages is more than I've ever been able to do with another person.

Maybe once it's done, I'll buy a new notebook. I'm thinking tomorrow, at work. There's something sexy about a blank notebook anyway. Just think of all that possibility.

CHAPTER TWENTY-SEVEN

Lauren has lost weight, and the mood stabilizers the doctors are giving her make her confused. Ashley tells me this in the car outside the hospital, she says, because she doesn't want me to be alarmed when I see my sister. I shouldn't expect her to look or act anything like herself.

Detective Burke and Ellie Knepper are meeting us at the hospital. Lauren won't know they're there—she's only allowed to have one visitor in the room at a time, anyway.

It took a few days for the police to get permission from Lauren's doctors for her to see anyone but Ashley, my dad, or the lawyer they hired. Burke doesn't share Ellie's faith that Lauren might tell me where the knife that she used to kill Bailey is, or who helped her dump the body; when he greets Ashley and me in the hospital lobby, his lip is flat. Disdainful.

"The doctor is only giving you ten minutes with her," Burke says. "You're not legally bound to share anything she tells you with us. But finding out if Jade Becker had a role in this will give the Hammonds closure."

Ashley puts her hand on my shoulder. "Kacey will do the right thing."

The doctor tells me Lauren isn't restrained anymore, but there's a call button right next to her bed if I need to use it.

My sister is all bones on the bed. Lauren's cheeks fill with color when she sees me. "Hi," she uses all her energy to say.

"Hi, Monkey," I say. I want to run out of the room, get on a Greyhound bus back to New York. "How are you feeling?"

Lauren shrugs. "The medicine makes me tired."

"Laur, I know it wasn't the Red Woman who told you to kill Bailey."

A tear slips down her cheek. "Yes, it was."

"No, it wasn't. It was Jade."

Lauren shakes her head.

"Then who was it?" I demand. "You didn't do this on your own. Everyone knows it.

"If she convinced you to do it—you might not go to jail for as long," I plead. I don't know if that's true. I don't know why she's protecting Jade.

"She said she'd kill us all," Lauren whispers.

"Jade said that? Jade threatened you?"

"No," Lauren says. "Josephine did."

I don't want to upset her and not be allowed to see my sister again. I bend down and put my arms around her. She clasps her bony arms around me, her breath hot by my ear.

When I step outside, Ashley is waiting. Her eyes are frantic as she searches my face. Behind her, Burke watches me.

"I'm sorry," I say. "She won't tell me anything."

CHAPTER TWENTY-EIGHT

Jade was careful—she'd found an abandoned property through Google Maps and planned her route so she didn't have to pass through any tolls. But one security camera at a gas station near the border caught her driving past in Bailey's car. The police were able to pull it a week after Bailey was found. It's a grainy image, poor quality.

But it was enough for them to arrest Jade for the unlawful disposal of a corpse and interfering with an investigation. She refused to say why she'd done it—how she could pretend to mourn her missing best friend after she'd left her body cold in a snow pile.

Then Cathy found Bailey's journal, stuffed in a slit in her mattress. The Hammonds had finally decided to clean out Bailey's room.

I knew it would be bad when Detective Burke called my parents and asked if we would come down to the station. Ellie Knepper had tea waiting for us; Burke's face was grim.

He didn't let me read the pages, but he told me of the plot to kill me inside them. Bailey had become obsessed with me, fixated on the idea that Andrew and I were in some sort of secret relationship. Burke said it wasn't clear who came up with the idea to kill me the night of the barn—but Lauren had undoubtedly saved my life by showing up and tagging along. She had seen the hunting knife in Bailey's bag. The knife Bailey had picked up from Cliff Grosso the week before—the same day a neighbor spotted her car outside his house.

Bailey had changed her mind about the plan after that night in the barn. She wanted to back out, and Jade was *unhappy about it*. (Burke's words—as if the difference between my living and dying could be compared to a customer's reaction to overcooked eggs.) That's why Cliff and Bailey were arguing the night of Sully's party—Bailey had tried to convince Cliff to take the knife back, but he said he couldn't sneak it onto the shelves of the hunting shop without his uncle asking questions. Then, when Bailey went missing, he was worried that the knife he sold Bailey was involved in the crime and could be traced back to him.

The investigators found the hunting knife locked in Bailey's glove compartment, not a trace of blood on it. They never found the knife from our kitchen.

With Jade refusing to talk about how Bailey had wound up dead—stabbed to death by my sister—the prosecutors came up with a theory with the help from criminal profilers.

Jade was worried that Bailey would slip and everyone would find out they'd planned to kill me. She was losing control over Bailey—something she'd maintained since middle school, when she lied about Val starting rumors about Bailey. Jade wanted Bailey to herself, to alienate her from all her friends.

Once Jade figured out that Bailey was serious about leaving Broken Falls—and her—she couldn't handle it. Backing out of the murder plot—the one thing that would bind them together forever—was the final straw for Jade.

We don't know what Jade said to Lauren to convince her to kill Bailey. After the night in the barn, Jade came to my house while my father slept and told Lauren *something*. I can only assume it was all about a torrid affair between Andrew and me. Somehow, she must have convinced Lauren that they had to get rid of Bailey to keep her quiet, or else I would get sent back to New York and Lauren would never see me again.

We do know that she told Lauren to steal a knife from our kitchen, one no one would notice was missing. She told her to leave Bailey's car and body at Leeds Park after it was done. After Tyrell dropped her off at home when the party ended, Jade left to pick up Bailey's car. Jade then drove an hour and a half to the Minnesota border, where she dumped her best friend's body. While she was there, Jade ditched the chef's knife and the bloody jacket Lauren left in the car.

On her way home, before leaving the car in the garage at the abandoned house, Jade stopped at the Leeds Barn to make the bloody handprint—to make sure that the police searched for Bailey in Broken Falls. There was so much blood in the car that sitting in the driver's seat drenched Jade's clothes in it.

Jade was the Red Woman Chloe Strauss saw in the early hours of the morning.

Jade drove up and down the winding roads of Broken Falls, ditching the clothes—a bloody men's sweatshirt, and a pair of pants that the police still haven't recovered—before leaving Bailey's phone at Cliff Grosso's house. She then went home, where she showered, cleaned her bathtub with bleach, and went to sleep until Cathy Hammond called her.

The judge decided that Jade had preyed on a young girl who was vulnerable to manipulation. A forensic psychiatrist told the DA that it was his opinion that Lauren had experienced a psychotic break as the result of the stress in her life. She didn't know right from wrong at the time of the killing, and suggested the minimum sentence.

They gave her eight years, to be served in a psychiatric facility. She still believes that Josephine Leeds, speaking through Jade, wanted her to kill Bailey.

They think that with proper treatment, she'll be okay. That she won't kill again.

The story is national news now. Jade's picture is on the cover of *People* magazine, along with the caption: *Pretty Little Psychopath*.

Her mother, Beth DiMassi—formerly Beth Becker—showed up for the arraignment. She was very surprised to hear that she'd been dead for the past twelve years.

EPILOGUE

I can't stop reading all mentions of the case. It's an obsession now, a need to know that Jade will stay far away so she can never hurt me.

I get my wish two months into the summer, when Jade accepts a plea deal on all the charges. Combined, she will probably serve the maximum. Sixty years.

I can't bring myself to show up for the sentencing, but Bailey has plenty of supporters in the courtroom. Val Diamond calls me after to tell me that Jade had a chance to speak—to make a statement, plead her case, and tell Bailey's family to their faces once and for all why she killed her best friend.

But she chose to say nothing. She refused to pin it all on Lauren, like she could have. All we have are questions. The biggest one: Why? Why keep protecting my sister when she's the one who drove the knife between Bailey's ribs?

The prosecutor thinks it's because Jade knows it won't make a difference. She's the one the public hates; she's the psychopath who manipulated a damaged, troubled little girl.

Her only unselfish act is not taking Lauren down with her. Or maybe she just doesn't care anymore.

Hours after the sentencing, we find out that it's the latter. The district attorney calls to tell us that Jade had been hoarding migraine pills and tried to overdose. Another inmate found her in the bathroom, slumped over the toilet.

She survives; days later, her attorney forwards me a letter. The handwriting sends me into a panic.

The letter is a page long, obviously written before her suicide attempt. Jade tells me she wishes she'd never met me. That Bailey was all she had, and I'd made Bailey so crazy it had ruined her life. Jade says she's going to kill herself because she has nothing left. She wants me to know it's my fault.

I think back to how she smiled at me when Bailey introduced us. The pain on her face that first morning we realized Bailey was gone. The way she slept in Bailey's bed the night after the vigil because she couldn't be alone. I wonder if any of it was real, or if the media is right—that Jade can't feel, she only mimics emotions to control and manipulate.

I wonder what was going through her head when she decided she wanted to die. I'd like to believe it's because she felt remorse and couldn't live with what she'd done.

Sometimes it's the only way I can live with myself.

. . .

Ashley is not leaving my dad. Lauren will need her parents when she gets out. She's not expected to serve the full eight years the judge sentenced her to. The thought of being able to hug her again someday, smell the hint of Froot Loops in her shampoo, makes my chest tight.

It also scares me. Because if she turned on Bailey so fast, who's to say I'll ever be safe?

Lauren killed someone. No amount of time in that place can undo that.

And who will she be when she gets out?

We're moving out of the house on Sparrow Road. Ashley and my dad are, at least. They bought a small house closer to Madison, only fifteen minutes from where Lauren is being treated. Andrew accepted the full ride to Madison—he couldn't turn down free college, especially in light of how much Lauren's attorneys cost—and I'm staying with my mom for the last couple weeks of summer before I come back to start community college not far from Andrew's school.

In the weeks after Jade was arrested, Ashley dragged me to Andrew's therapist. She suggested I write my mom and not send it, but I realized I needed her to hear everything. She wrote back. We've been talking on the phone for the past couple months. She sounds different—I don't know if either of us has changed enough. Ashley and my dad said they'd get me on the first flight back home if things get bad.

It's my first night back in New York, in my mother's new

apartment. It's a new construction—one of those places with a golf course no one uses and all white fixtures inside. When I walk in, feel my feet sink into the carpet, I stop. Inhale.

"What?" My mother looks nervous. "Did I forget to take the garbage out?"

"No," I say. "It smells like you. Just you."

That smell is almost enough to unglue me—it reminds me of a time when it was just the two of us and everything was good. I wonder if we'll ever get that back.

I want to believe it. I *have* to believe it.

I'm jet-lagged, so my mother suggests we order pizza. I think of gathering around the table at the house on Sparrow Road, over a sausage pizza with half pineapple for Andrew, and a pit opens up in my stomach.

"Why don't I cook?" I say.

"Cook what?" My mother looks concerned as I raid her kitchen for something to throw together. Her cabinets are modestly stocked, but she has the staples for grilled cheese.

I need to busy my hands, keep them occupied so I don't wind up on my phone, Googling our names.

Kacey Young. Jade Becker. Lauren Markham.

Everyone has something to say about the girls who caused Bailey Hammond's death.

"This is delicious, baby," my mother says after the first bite of grilled cheese. She licks away a string of orange from her lip. I'm staring, I know, but all I can think is, *She had cheese in the house.*

It's too much, that she bought my favorite food. My face is wet and I can't swallow the bite of sandwich in my mouth.

"Baby, what's wrong?"

I just shake my head. I can't say it, can't put into words how bad I am at this business of being loved. Some days it feels like a burden.

My father and Ashley don't blame me for what happened, but I don't think I can stand to see how they blame themselves. Maybe if they'd focused less on Andrew's issues and more on Lauren's. Maybe if they'd brought her to a therapist after the bullying with Keelie March. Maybe if they'd loved each other enough that Ashley hadn't made that phone call to Beth Schrader. Maybe they simply blame themselves for creating a child with a monster deep within her.

In my darkest moments, I blame myself. If Lauren had been at Emma's birthday party the night of the barn, I would be the one who's dead, not Bailey. She would be in jail along with Jade—or maybe Bailey and Jade would have pulled it off, and I would have been the girl who vanished. The one people would remember on anniversaries. The Markhams would miss me, I know they would, but they wouldn't be as broken as they are right now.

We. Not they.

Because that's the one thing Andrew was right about: that I'm one of them, and I always will be.

My mother lets me turn in early for the night without interrogation; she insists I take her bed in the master suite and says she doesn't mind the couch.

But when I wake up in the middle of the night, disoriented, my breath heavy, her arms are around me.

"You were screaming," she said. Her face is streaked with tears. I realize she's under the covers with me.

"I didn't want to leave you," my mother says. "I never, ever should have let you leave."

I cry into her, my nose mashed against her collarbone. The nightmare has followed me here: the one where my sister plunges the knife from our kitchen into Bailey's stomach and then turns it on me. I run from her every time. She never catches me.

I always manage to wake up in time.

I've taken to thinking about the engagement ring on Ellie Knepper's finger when my brain can't handle the weight of it all. I like to think I could have a life like hers someday. That eventually I'll be able to stop searching for home and make one for myself. I distract myself by trying to imagine a distant future. One where I'm a pastry chef or an art teacher like Mr. White, and I go out for drinks after school with the other teachers and forget everything that happened in Broken Falls.

It's better than the alternative, which is thinking about the last words Lauren said to me—the thing she whispered before I left her hospital room that day, when I asked her why she really killed Bailey.

She was going to ruin everything.

You were going to have to leave us.

ACKNOWLEDGMENTS

Behind every book is a village of dedicated people making everything happen, and this one is no exception. I have a bunch of people to thank for their endless support and enthusiasm.

First, Krista Marino deserves a crown (and a vacation) for her tireless work on this book in its many incarnations. I can't believe the new heights we have brought this story to. Thank you for guiding me toward the book I always wanted to write — and for doing so very patiently! Also, thank you for sharing my dark, twisted taste.

Suzie Townsend, my agent and champion. Don't ever go anywhere. I would die without you. (Just kidding. But seriously. Don't leave me.)

Everyone at New Leaf Literary and Media—Joanna, Sara, Pouya, Mia, Kathleen, Jackie, Jaida, Danielle, Chris, Hillary, and Mike—you guys are a dream team. Thanks for putting tape over your mouths for me.

Aisha Cloud, my publicist, who works continually to make miracles happen on my behalf. Aisha is also insanely cool.

The absolutely incredible team at Random House Children's Books: Beverly Horowitz, Monica Jean, Kimberly Lauber, John

Adamo, Mary McCue, Dominique Cimina, Adrienne Waintraub, Laura Antonacci, Alissa Nigro, Kate Keating, and Angela Carlino.

The Slackers—especially Lindsey Culli and Steph Kuehn.

My family and friends for putting up with the highs and lows of loving a writer, especially Kevin "Wonder Husband" Thomas.

And my psychiatrist, for keeping me sane long enough to finish this book.

Beware the Red Woman.

Turn the page to start reading
the original short story

Wrath

I *could be home watching* Saturday Night Live. Even in her head, Cassidy realized how pathetic it sounded. Here she was, hundreds of miles from home, at a party—a college party!—and all she could think about was the prospect of her own bed and the blue glow of the TV to lull her to sleep.

She snuck at glance at her cell phone. It was almost one in the morning, and they hadn't even been at the party very long. Meg had insisted that no one showed up to parties before midnight, but when the cab dropped them outside the Sigma Alpha Mu house, the line was already spilling onto the street.

"What if we don't get in?" Cassidy had whispered, inches from Meg's ear. Relief snaked around her ribs; if they couldn't get into the party, maybe they would head back to Meg's dorm and make microwave lava cakes and watch TV shows on her laptop like they used to before Meg left for college.

"We're *going* to get in."

It wasn't Meg who replied; Cassidy turned around in time to see Dani and Maureen, the girls they'd shared the cab with, roll their eyes at each other. She wasn't sure which one of them had said it. Beside her, Meg rearranged the hair falling over her shoulder, intent on pretending she hadn't heard anything.

Dani and Maureen lived across the hall from Meg. Cassidy had instantly retreated into her shell when Dani sauntered into Meg's dorm room earlier that evening, a bottle of Fireball whiskey in hand, and flopped onto Meg's bed like she lived there. Maureen had picked up the curling iron resting on Meg's desk and proceeded to wrap her sun-streaked hair around the barrel while making fun of Meg's weirdo roommate, who went home every weekend.

Meg had nudged Cassidy while they were piling into the back of the cab and whispered in her ear. "Can you at least pretend to like them?"

Cassidy hadn't said anything. And now here she was, mashed up against the wall of the Sigma Alpha Mu house, waiting for Meg and Dani to come back inside. When Dani had come up behind Meg, tapping her shoulder with an unlit cigarette, Cassidy almost lost her shit. "Since when do you smoke?"

"Only when I drink." Meg's cheeks went pink. Whether from embarrassment or all the Fireball shots they'd done in the dorms, who knew.

Maureen was supposed to wait with Cassidy, but she'd disappeared to take a spot at the flip cup table, snatching the first chance to ditch Meg's dorky high school friend from home.

Cassidy sipped from her cup of vodka and cranberry juice, only to make it seem like she was doing something besides standing by herself. No one was watching her anyway.

Or so she thought.

"Hey, pretty. Whatcha drinking?"

Cassidy lifted her gaze from the rim of her cup. The guy was in a blue-and-white-striped button-down, a Walker University T-shirt showing underneath. Brown hair, brown eyes.

Cassidy raised her cup. "Vodka cranberry."

"Nice." The guy grinned. One of his front teeth was crooked. Cassidy took another sip of her drink, desperate to look away.

"Name's Jacob." The guy extended a hand. Cassidy shook it. "Cassidy."

"You a freshman?"

"No," Cassidy said. "I don't go here. I'm visiting a friend."

Jacob's eyes lit up. "Are you in high school?"

Cassidy's insides squirmed. An alarm bell sounded in her head: *Lie.* "No. I go to community college."

Jacob's lips parted, one corner of his mouth tugging upward. "Oh yeah? What school?"

The room was filling up, forcing Jacob to take a step closer to her. Cassidy could smell weed and beer on his breath. She thought of how she'd taken a five-hour bus ride from Illinois to Wisconsin to see Meg, only to wind up alone with this creep.

"I have to find my friend." Cassidy wiggled away. "She was supposed to be back by now."

She waded through the mass of bodies in the living room, skirting the crowd that had formed around the coffee table. People were cheering, laughing, but Cassidy didn't stop to see what they were doing. Sweat was pooling beneath the gold crop top she'd borrowed from Meg, and her head was feeling hollow.

Cassidy stumbled out the front door, immediately getting edged to the side of the house by the crowd of people waiting to get inside. She dug her phone from her wristlet and called Meg. The line rang and rang until Cassidy heard a *click*, and voices on the other end.

"Meg." Cassidy glanced at the screen, just to make sure the call hadn't been dropped. "*Meg.*"

The line went silent. Cassidy blinked against the pressure forming behind her eyes and called Meg again. This time, it went straight to voice mail. Cassidy's phone beeped three times in succession.

The goddamn thing died.

A flutter of panic in her chest. She hadn't been able to charge her phone fully, because Meg had needed the outlet for her curling iron. Cassidy had meant to go into the hall to use the outlet there but she'd forgotten, and now her goddamn phone was dead.

She couldn't stay out here. The booze in her blood was doing little to keep her warm. She hadn't brought a jacket—none of the girls had, too much of an inconvenience—and the November night nipped at every sliver of her bare skin. She marched back up the steps to the house, using her hands to part the crowd. "Excuse me. *Excuse* me."

The guy manning the door hassled her until she convinced him she had *just* been inside and she'd already paid her five dollars. Cassidy tamped down a burp, swallowing away the sting of vomit from her throat. She tried to take inventory of the shots she'd done in Meg's dorm—three, maybe? The problem was that she'd barely eaten; Meg had promised to take her to the dining hall when she arrived on campus, but Cassidy's bus got stuck in traffic, so she'd just scarfed down the granola bar her mother had packed her.

Cassidy made the rounds of the house, eyes peeled for Meg or Dani or Maureen. They weren't in line for either of the two bathrooms.

Cassidy pulled out her phone, hoping that by some miracle it had been resurrected in her pocket. The sight of the black screen threatened to unglue her. She blinked away tears and stumbled back outside.

A cab. She'd find a cab to take her back to campus. She didn't have a student ID to get back into Meg's dorm, but maybe the building monitor would take pity on her.

The street was quiet, save for the crowd in front of the house. Cassidy wrapped her arms around her middle and headed for the corner, where she'd have better luck finding a cab.

Fucking Meg and her fucking friends. Cassidy shivered; she'd reached the corner, only to realize that the road was a dead end. She chanted the words under her breath as she headed back the way she'd come: *Fucking Meg.*

Cassidy kept her head down so she wouldn't have to make eye contact with the people standing outside the frat house. What if they noticed her walking back and forth? It was so pathetic it made her want to puke.

She noticed the patch of ice too late. Her tailbone smacked the sidewalk, her legs tangling around each other. A pack of guys gathered around a car parked on the street howled with laughter.

The tears blurred her vision. She rolled onto her side, wincing, as someone put a hand on her upper arm. "Are you okay?"

Cassidy looked up. Wide, warm eyes staring down at her. Someone laughed in the distance and the guy looked over his shoulder. "Shut the hell up. She could be hurt."

"I'm okay." Cassidy accepted the guy's outstretched hand. She couldn't help but notice how strong he was. He was wearing a Green Bay Packers sweatshirt, wavy brown hair peeking out from under his knit beanie.

"My friends are dicks," he muttered. "Are you sure you're all right?"

Cassidy's throat went tight. "Not really. I lost my friend and I have no idea where I am and my phone is dead."

"Do you want to use my phone to call her?"

"I don't have her number memorized. We came to the party together, but I think she left—" She halted, realizing her words were slurring together. "I just need a cab to get back to campus."

"You're not going to find one here at this time of night. This neighborhood is a dead zone." The guy's brows knitted. "You said campus—Walker, right?"

Cassidy felt her teeth knocking together. "Y-yeah."

"I live off campus," the guy said. "I'm heading back toward the school—I have to pick up a friend from another party, but if you don't mind making a quick stop, I could drop you off at the dorms."

"Are you sure?" Cassidy rubbed at the gooseflesh on her arms. She heard the threat of tears in her voice, and the guy must have too, because he gave her a sympathetic smile.

"It's really not a problem. Seriously."

Cassidy felt herself thaw a bit. As long as she had a ride back to campus, she could deal with everything later: getting into the dorm, her dead phone, Meg and her stupid friends. "Thank you. I can't thank you enough."

"Don't mention it. I'm Stephen, by the way."

"Cassidy." She followed Stephen across the street, where a green sedan was parked. Stephen held up his remote and opened it with a *blip*. Back on the other side of the street, the pack of guys hollered at them. Stephen gave them the finger and opened the passenger door for Cassidy.

"Thank you. Thank you." She didn't know if she was capable of saying anything else. Stephen started the engine and heat blasted from the vents. He pointed two of them at Cassidy; she leaned back in the seat and closed her eyes.

"How'd you wind up here?" Stephen asked, once he pulled away from the curb.

"My friend has a class with one of the guys," Cassidy said. She caught Stephen's smile.

"They're kind of the worst."

"I gathered." Cassidy paused. "Do you go to Walker?"

Stephen scratched the back of his neck, one hand perched on the steering wheel. "Yup. Graduating in May. You want the radio on?"

"Sure."

Cassidy stuck her hands in front of a vent, kneading her frozen knuckles, as Stephen tuned the radio. He skipped over a station playing a familiar, bass-heavy classic rock song before doubling back and turning the volume up.

"I love this song," Cassidy blurted.

"It's kind of creepy," Stephen laughed. "But a classic."

Cassidy tilted her head to the window, humming along with the song. Why couldn't she remember its name? She'd heard it dozens of times as a kid; it was one of her father's favorites. Even worse, Cassidy was getting the spins. Shit, what if she didn't sober up by the time she got to Meg's dorm? Would the building monitor write her up? The thought almost made her laugh. She wasn't even a student; how could he write her up?

"You okay?"

Cassidy swiveled to face Stephen. "Me?"

"Thought I lost you there for a minute," he said. "I think you fell asleep."

"Crap, I'm sorry."

"It's okay. I'm not offended." Stephen grinned. "We're almost there."

Cassidy sat up straight. Rolled her neck until it cracked. She glanced out the window, watching the trees, dusted lightly with snow, whiz by. The car passed a sign that said WELCOME TO BROKEN FALLS.

"Broken Falls?" Cassidy watched the sign retreat in the side mirror. "Isn't Walker in Middletown?"

Stephen flicked the turn signal on, his brow furrowing. "The house my friend is at is supposed to be around here. I'm gonna have to pull over and call him for the address."

Cassidy's stomach puckered as Stephen stopped on the side of the road. He leaned toward the windshield, peering out into the dark. Cassidy spotted a dirt path leading up a hill.

"I think it's here," Stephen said.

Cassidy swallowed, keeping an eye on Stephen as the car eased up the driveway. His face had gone slack. Cassidy's heartbeat quickened. On both sides of the car, there seemed to be nothing but woods for miles.

"I don't see a house," she said. "You have the wrong place."

Stephen rolled the car to a stop. Cassidy clutched the door handle, ready to yank it open. "What are you doing?"

"Hey, shhh. It's okay." Stephen leaned over, taking her face in his hands. When she jerked away, he tightened his grip. "What's the matter?"

Cassidy tucked on the door handle. It was locked. "Let me go. Please."

"Shhh, shhh." He kept saying it. *Shhh.* His hands moved to her shoulder and then to her arms, pinning them down as she tried to claw at his face.

"Let me go!" she screamed, before he clamped a hand over her mouth. He moved his free hand to the zipper of her jeans and she wiggled out of his grasp for just long enough to reach around him and lean on the car horn.

Stephen jerked back, surprised. Cassidy elbowed him in the nose. While he was shouting *you broke my fucking nose!* she leaned across him and punched the button that unlocked the doors.

Cassidy stumbled out of the car, bile rising in her throat. She ran back toward the road, the snow seeping into the sides of her flats. She patted her back pocket, remembered her dead phone, and pressed her fist to her mouth to muffle a sob.

Rustling in the woods behind her. She kept running, the cold air slicing through her lungs. The road should be close; she came to a halt at a half-frozen stream. Surveyed her surroundings. In the distance, under the light of the moon, she spotted the outline of a house.

That doesn't make sense—who would live in the middle of the woods

She didn't stop to think. She ran toward the house, away from the sound of Stephen's footsteps. Cassidy darted in and out of the thicket of trees, yelping as a branch sliced across her cheek.

"Cassidy? Where are you? You'll freeze out here."

She forged ahead, her feet numb. Several feet away from the house, she halted.

A barn. It was just a stupid, rotting barn. One that hadn't seen people in decades, it looked like.

Stephen's footsteps drew closer; he was faster than she was, bigger, stronger. Cassidy ducked into the barn, searching for anything to hide behind. Moonlight streamed in from a gaping hole in the roof.

I am going to die. He's going to kill me.

The sound of her name, again. Stephen promising not to hurt her.

She looked around, her heart rocketing into her throat—and there it was, hanging on the wall, on a rusted hook.

Stephen burst through the barn door at the same time Cassidy gripped the handle of the shovel. He whipped his head around, his jaw connecting with the wide swing.

Stephen stumbled backward, his elbow flying up to cover his face. He kept fumbling to regain his balance, until his foot connected with something on the floor. Cassidy thought she saw a flash of white in the corner of her eye before Stephen went down with a sickening crunch.

A whimper escaped Cassidy's throat. She cocked the shovel and took a step toward Stephen, who was screaming in pain. He rolled onto his side and she shrieked.

The rusted prongs of a pitchfork were wedged into his back. Stephen had stopped screaming; his face had gone slack, lips parted slightly.

Cassidy covered her mouth. She hadn't seen the pitchfork lying there—how had he fallen at such an angle? She *swore* it hadn't been lying there a second ago. She didn't have time to process what was happening: Stephen, still very much alive, was dragging himself forward, grasping for her ankle—

Cassidy brought the shovel down on his head. Once, twice, until blood splattered her flats and Stephen stopped moving.

She couldn't stop crying. She'd been sitting in Stephen's car for half an hour, debating what she should do. Would the police believe her, that it was self-defense?

Was it self-defense? She could have gotten away easily, once she'd knocked him out with the shovel. His eyes were closed, but he was still breathing, and she *kept hitting him*. It was as if something had taken over her—some entity, some other Cassidy, one filled with vengeance and rage.

The police would be able to tell how many times she hit him, right?

Cassidy wiped her face and started the engine; Stephen had left the keys in the ignition. The shakes had seized her body. She didn't feel drunk anymore. She sucked in a breath and backed down the hill, leaving the car's lights off.

Stephen's car had a GPS. She punched in *Walker College* and let the directions download; according to the map on the screen, she was on Sparrow Road.

A violent gust of wind shook the car, and Cassidy looked up. She caught a glimpse of the side mirror. The blood drained from her body: there was a *woman* on the side of the road. Cassidy froze, but the woman kept walking, stumbling, toward the hill Cassidy had just come down. She never stopped to look back at the car. Cassidy peered closer in the mirror—the woman was in a nightgown, and she was barefoot.

Cassidy pressed down on the gas pedal, peeling away from the shoulder of Sparrow Road. When she looked in the side mirror, the woman was gone.

Fingerprints. It was all Cassidy could think of as she pulled into the first empty parking lot she could find within two miles of Walker College. She parked Stephen's car behind a dumpster; she was behind some sort of warehouse.

Cassidy riffled through the center console, finding a balled-up Dunkin' Donuts napkin. She wiped down the steering wheel, the door handle—everything she'd touched.

She spied a leather wallet in the cup holder. She flipped it open and saw a driver's license for someone named Alexander Ports. The license had Stephen's picture; his birth date revealed that he was thirty-one.

Relief washed through Cassidy. Those guys outside the frat house—they hadn't been Stephen's friends. *Alexander's* friends. They probably hadn't gotten a good look at her face either.

Her feet were raw by the time she reached Walker College. She had no idea what time it was. When she stumbled through the doors to Callaway Hall, Meg was at the security desk, frantic.

She threw herself at Cassidy. "Where the fuck have you been? I've been calling you for two hours. We were about to call the police."

"My phone was dead." Cassidy's lips were numb. She looked down at her flats, which were splattered with blood. Alexander's blood. Her stomach dropped to the floor, but Meg wasn't looking at her feet.

"How the hell did you get back here?"

Cassidy mumbled about a cab and let Meg drag her up to her floor. She headed straight for the bathroom at the end of the hall. Yanked paper towels out of the dispenser and scrubbed her flats until Alexander's blood was gone.

She didn't want to clog the toilet, so she tore the bloody towels into pieces, flushing them one by one. Eventually, someone started pounding on the stall.

"Cass. What are you doing in there? You're seriously freaking me out."

Cassidy drew in a breath. Shut her eyes and leaned against the door. "I'm fine."

. . .

In the morning, there was nothing in the news about a body being found in Broken Falls. By the time Sunday morning rolled around, there was still nothing—not even a missing persons report for an Alexander Ports.

Meg was passed out on her bed, her arm thrown across her eyes. Cassidy left a note on Meg's desk saying she was going to get coffee.

She found a cab outside the drugstore a few blocks from campus. When the driver told her it would be twenty bucks to get to Broken Falls, Cassidy just nodded. "That's fine."

She had him drop her off a mile from Sparrow Road. It wasn't even seven o'clock yet; the sky was gray and pearly. Cassidy pulled her coat around her and let her phone GPS direct her toward Sparrow Road.

Stupid. So, so stupid to come back here. She knew it, but she had to see for herself. She had to know Friday night wasn't simply a nightmare.

And if no one had found him, she had to get rid of him somehow.

The barn looked even more dilapidated during the day. Even in her drunken state, how had she mistaken it for a house Friday night? Cassidy pressed one hand to her chest, willing her heartbeat to slow down.

She paused in the entrance to the barn. Covered her mouth with a hand, in case she got sick.

She stepped inside.

A small *oh* escaped her throat. The barn was empty—there was no Alexander/Stephen, no shovel, no pitchfork.

Cassidy had to sit down. *What the hell. What the hell.*

She started to stand, her knees threatening to give way beneath her. She held out a hand to steady herself, and she saw it: the blood staining the snow on the ground where Alexander/Stephen's body had been.

Cassidy tore out of the barn. *Impossible, impossible.* She had to have lost her damn mind. He was there—she freaking *left him there*—

She skidded to a halt when she reached the bottom of the hill. Doubled over, gasping for breath.

When she looked up, she saw the woman on the other side of the street. Staring at her. She was wearing the same nightgown she'd had on the night before, the midsection stained with blood. Her bare legs were splattered with caked mud, and her brown hair fell in strings over her shoulders.

The woman locked eyes with Cassidy, and very slowly, she raised a finger to her lips.

If you loved *Little Monsters,*
turn the page for a sneak peek at
Kara Thomas's new book.

"Sharp, brilliantly plotted, and engrossing."
—KAREN M. McMANUS, *New York Times* bestselling author of *One of Us Is Lying*

the
Cheerleaders

Kara Thomas

Author of *The Darkest Corners* and *Little Monsters*

Chapter One

This house was made for someone without a soul. So I guess it makes sense that my mother wanted it so badly. I can imagine how her eyes lit up when she walked through the five-bedroom, three-and-a-half-bath new construction. I'll bet she thinks this house is the answer to what's wrong with us.

When Tom, my stepfather, showed me the bathroom attached to my room with its own Jacuzzi tub, he said, *Bet you feel like Cinderella*, because he's an idiot.

I should be happy for my mother and Tom, because the old house took so long to sell that it nearly destroyed their marriage. I should be thrilled I don't have to hear the words *terrible real estate market* and *bad location* ever again. Neither they nor the listing agent had the balls to come out and say that no one wanted to buy a home on the street of horrors.

The worst thing about the new house is that there's no way to sneak into my room. The dining room is right off the front hall, so when I get home from dance team tryouts, I can see my mother at the table eating Chinese takeout with Tom and Petey, their "oops baby."

Petey is ten now. Mom married Tom when I was five. When I was a kid, I overheard her telling my grandmother that she and Tom both were done with children. Mom had Jen and me, and Tom had a college-aged daughter with his ex-wife. Four months later, Mom was pregnant with Petey.

So, totally an oops baby.

"Monica," my mother calls. "We're eating dinner."

In other words, *Don't you try to disappear upstairs.*

I plod into the dining room, the smell of the takeout souring my stomach. Everything hurts: standing, walking, sitting.

At the table, Petey is sucking up lo mein noodles. One slips from between his lips and falls on the screen of his iPad, because God forbid he perform a basic function such as eating without playing *Clan Wars.*

"Petey," Mom says, "please put the game down."

"But I have to harvest my crops."

"Do you want the iPad to go in the garbage?"

"You wouldn't throw an *iPad* in the *garbage.*"

"*Peter.*"

Petey's eyes go wide, because Mom only uses his full name when she's really about to lose her shit. I almost want to tell the poor kid it's not his fault that Mom is acting like a psycho.

"Monica." Tom looks up from his phone, finally noticing me. He takes off his reading glasses and breathes on the lenses. Wipes them on his shirt. "How were tryouts?"

"Fine."

"The new Chinese place gave us extra fortune cookies!"

Petey says, and I say, "Cool," which pretty much sums up the depth of my interactions with my half brother.

Mom's eyes are on me. I keep my own eyes on a carton of white rice. I grab a plate and spoon some onto it.

"What's wrong?" Petey asks. It takes a second for it to sink in that he's speaking to me. Tom is watching me now too. My mother makes a face as if she just swallowed down vomit.

"Can I go lie down?" I ask.

"Go ahead," she says.

When I get to the hall, I hear Petey whine, "How come she gets to do what she wants?"

I practically have to crawl up the stairs to my room. The over-the-counter painkillers my mom picked up for me are seriously garbage. I would call Matt, my ex-boyfriend, because even though he denies it, he's friends with people who can get the strong stuff. But Matt graduated and he's not in Sunnybrook anymore and we haven't spoken since July.

My heating pad is still packed in one of the storage tubs Mom and I bought from Bed Bath & Beyond before the move. I dig it out, biting my lip. The nurse at Dr. Bob's office said it would be like bad period cramps. But it hurts so badly I want to die.

I break into a sweat from plugging in the heating pad and flop onto my brand-new bed. King-sized, like my mom and Tom's. She insisted—the room would have looked too small with a queen.

They say you're not supposed to put the pad directly on

your skin, but I do it anyway and curl up on my side. I'd gladly take my flesh melting off over the pain in my gut.

A knock at the door. I grunt and Mom pushes her way in, holding a bottle of naproxen and a glass of water. "When was the last time you took painkillers?"

"Lunch," I lie. I popped four before tryouts.

"You can have two more, then." Mom perches at the edge of my bed. She might as well be a mile away. It's really obscene, how big the bed is.

I groan and pull my legs up tight to my body, into the fetal position.

"I told you that you should have stayed home today." My mother taps the naproxen bottle to her palm, shakes two pills out.

"Coach would have cut me from the team." I accept the pills. Swallow them greedily.

Mom is quiet. She drums her fingers—the nails rounded and coated with clear polish—on my comforter. Her anxious tic. Finally: "Have you told Matt?"

"No."

I can't tell what she's thinking—whether she actually *wants* me to call Matt at college and tell him.

"He could support you," Mom says, after a beat. "You don't have to go through this alone."

"It wasn't his anyway."

I stare straight ahead so I don't have to see the look on her face.

When she stands up, her profile comes into focus. She looks sad for a moment before she catches herself. "I hope you learn something from this pain."

My mother shuts the light off on her way out—or at least, she tries to. She can't find the switch at first, because it's opposite where it used to be in my old room. Finally, she gives up, leaving me under the glow of the top-of-the-line energy-efficient LED bulbs.

She's wrong, I think. Pain isn't supposed to teach you anything. It only exists to hurt you. And she should know that better than anyone.

I'm camped on the porch, rain plinking on the overhang, staring at the house across the street when Rachel pulls up in her cherry-red Volkswagen Beetle the next morning. No one lives there. The contractors had to abandon construction inside the house because the people who bought it ran out of money. Since we moved in, the empty house has been the subject of my mother's bitching. All the house is doing is existing, not bothering anyone. It's exactly the type of thing that offends my mother.

Rach and I have been best friends since we were kids. She turned seventeen in July, which means she got her license over six months before I will. Rachel had to repeat kindergarten, and kids used to make fun of her, because what kind of moron can't pass kindergarten? Then in the eighth grade she got her braces taken off, discovered a hair straightener, and grew B-cups, and everyone shut up.

Rachel lowers her sunglasses to look at me as I duck into the passenger seat.

"Do you feel okay?"

"I'm fine," I lie. "I woke up too late to do my makeup."

"I hope the list is up," Rach says, putting the car into reverse to back out of my driveway. She actually sounds nervous.

Of course we'll be on the list. Rachel, our friend Alexa, and I were the only freshmen to make the dance team two years ago. Rach's mom drove us all to school that morning so we could look at the list together. Arms linked, knees knocking under our new jean skirts for our first week of high school.

Seeing our names on that list made us feel unstoppable. I was naïve and thought being one of the dance team girls meant I wouldn't be known as the sister of one of the cheerleaders. But our particular tragedy isn't the type people forget easily; being Jennifer Rayburn's sister is like having an enormous scar I have to dress every morning to hide it.

A shot of nerves twists my stomach. Or maybe it's the naproxen. My sloppy performance at tryouts yesterday is reason enough for our coach to drop me, if she felt like it. Coach is not known for doling out second chances. Forget your dance shoes? Go home, and don't bother coming to practice tomorrow.

I wonder if I'll even care if my name isn't on that list. I tilt my head against the window. Rachel rolls to a stop at the sign at the end of my street. She looks both ways, counts silently to herself, ever the perfect, cautious driver, always looking twice at my house to see if Tom is watching.

Tom is the sergeant of the local police department. Having him for a stepdad is a really easy way to figure out how many people you know have a deep-rooted fear of law enforcement.

Rachel pulls into Alexa's driveway, and of course she isn't ready; she never is. I'm about to text her, ask why she has to make us late every damn morning. But her front door swings open, and she flounces down the driveway, wearing her Sunnybrook Warriors hoodie with skinny jeans.

Alexa pours herself into the backseat and immediately whips out her compact. She starts applying her Merlot-red lip stain.

"Seat belt!" Rachel yells.

I catch Alexa's eyes in the side mirror. "What do you even do all morning," I ask crabbily, "if you always have to do your lipstick in the car?"

Alexa rakes a hand through her hair, shaking out her freshly ironed waves. "Well, Monica's obviously getting her period."

I almost make Rachel pull over so I can walk.

We get to school with a few minutes to spare before the first bell. The side doors by the gym are propped open and we step into the hall and right into chaos. There are buckets scattered on the floor, catching steady drips of water leaking from the ceiling. A custodian is on a ladder, attempting to tape a trash bag over a hole in the ceiling. I hear him mutter something about all the goddamn rain this year so far.

"This place is so ghetto," Alexa announces, and I want to hit her, because she has no idea what the word actually means. Besides, we're one of the wealthiest school districts in the county.

A bunch of trophy cases outside the locker room have been moved into the center of the hall. We sidestep them, but not before I see her. My sister.

She smiles at me from the largest photo in the biggest trophy case. She's posing for the camera with four of her friends. Their mouths are painted cherry; their cheer pleats are blue and yellow. The photo is from the first home game of the season, five years ago when there was still a cheerleading squad.

A wave of nausea ripples through me. Every day after gym, after dance team practice, I go out of my way to avoid this picture.

I knew all the girls in it, some of them better than others. Juliana Ruiz and Susan Berry were Jen's best friends and fixtures in our house for as long as I could remember. When they made the cheerleading squad their freshman year, they became friends with two sophomores: Colleen Coughlin and Bethany Steiger.

They all smile at me: Jen, Juliana, Susan, Colleen, and Bethany. It really is a beautiful picture.

By the end of the season, everyone in it was dead.

Chapter Two

A small crowd is gathered outside the main office, where Coach said she would post the list this morning. As we approach the bulletin board, a pack of freshman girls walk away, dejected.

Next to me, Rach sucks in her breath. We step up to the bulletin board. I scan the candy-colored papers tacked to it—a list of people who got callbacks for the fall play, a flyer advertising the girls' soccer team car wash, information for a weekend SAT prep course.

"There's nothing here," Alexa says.

"Yeah, there is." A familiar voice. I turn around; the Kelseys are behind us, iced lattes from Dunkin' Donuts in hand. Kelsey Butler rattles the ice in hers. She points—her nails, painted apricot, popping against her dark skin.

I look where Kelsey is pointing—a sheet of paper tacked to the bulletin board. On it, a single line:

DANCE TEAM LIST WILL BE POSTED AT NOON

Kelsey Butler's best friend, Kelsey Gabriel, sidles up next to her to get a better look. Kelsey G's usually fair hair is sun-streaked even lighter, and her skin is freckled. "Ew. Why?"

"More people tried out this year," Kelsey B says. "Maybe she needed more time to decide."

The Kelseys walk off together. They'll be on the list; they're seniors, and both of them were in classes with me at the Royal Hudson Dance Studio when we were younger. The Kelseys, with their inhumanly high leaps and whip-fast pirouettes, are the closest things Coach has to favorites.

My friends and I stay close together and head for the second floor—we're Rayburn, Santiago, and Steiger, and homerooms are assigned in alphabetical order. As we file onto the stairs, I catch a glimpse of Rachel. She's picking at the corner of her mouth, where her lipstick is flaking.

"It's fine," I say, softly enough that only she can hear. "You've got this."

She's no doubt thinking about what Kelsey B said. Rachel is haunted by the triple pirouette she hasn't mastered—the one Coach threatened to put in our competition routine this year.

Before I can find my seat in homeroom, my teacher says my name. "You're wanted at guidance."

My stomach plummets to my feet. "Why?"

"Dunno. I'm not your secretary," he drones.

I take the slip from his grasp, eyeing my guidance counselor's almost-illegible scrawl.

I choose the longer route to the guidance office so I can pass a bathroom. I dig out the plastic baggie of naproxen my mother left on the counter next to my Tupperware of veggies and ranch this morning. She's doling out the pills to me four at a time, as if they're Oxys or something. I open the baggie and knock them back with a sip of water from my bottle.

Mr. Demarco is sitting with his back to me when I rap on the doorframe of his office. He swivels around in his chair, his face brightening when he sees me. He's in an ice-blue polo that makes his matching eyes pop. Rachel and Alexa call him a silver fox.

"There she is." Mr. Demarco sets his Starbucks cup, marked *PSL*, on his desk. "Sit, sit."

He drags a chair next to his desk. He moves a box of pamphlets off his seat; I catch a glimpse of a campus quad, bright with fall foliage. I sit down, pressing my chem textbook into my abdomen.

"So." Demarco smiles without showing any teeth. "How are you?"

"Fine." I grip the chem textbook. Press harder. Does he know? There's no way he could have found out. Not unless my mother told him, and I made her swear, my nails digging half circles into her arm, that she wouldn't even tell Tom.

Demarco takes a sip of his coffee. "I'll cut to the chase. Mrs. Coughlin is trying to put together a memorial ceremony, in the courtyard."

Mrs. Coughlin, the health teacher. Colleen Coughlin's mother.

Mr. Demarco doesn't give any further explanation; he doesn't need to. Colleen Coughlin was in the passenger seat of Bethany Steiger's car when she hydroplaned during a storm and drove into a tree. The car was so mangled that supposedly the coroner had trouble figuring out which girl was which. One of the paramedics at the scene vomited.

The first two cheerleaders to be killed that year.

"A memorial." I take off the ponytail holder on my wrist and wrap it around my fingers, cutting off the circulation in the tips. "Like a religious thing?"

"No, not at all," Demarco says. "Just a small ceremony in the courtyard. Mrs. Coughlin asked if you'd like to be a part of it."

At my stricken expression, Demarco picks up his empty cup, taps the base of it against his desk. "Obviously you don't have to say yes. Mrs. Coughlin did pick out some poems she thinks would be nice for you to read."

He hands me a stack of paper held together by a butterfly clip. I don't look at it. "It's just . . . ," I mumble. "It would feel weird. I didn't even know Colleen and Bethany."

"Oh no, we'd honor all the girls at once. Everyone thought it would be best that way."

In other words, get the memorial out of the way before homecoming, because my sister's two best friends died five years ago the night before *their* homecoming. It wouldn't be very nice to remind the crowd about the horrific way Juliana Ruiz and Susan Berry were killed when everyone just wants to watch some football. "Wow. Okay. Thanks. I actually think I have a quiz next period."

"Of course. I'll write you a pass."

While Demarco fishes around in his drawer for his stack of passes, I let my eyes wander. There's a Sunnybrook Warriors pennant over his desk, right next to a New York Giants calendar. Right above a framed photo of the Sunnybrook football team from six years ago, posing with the state championship trophy. We haven't won it since.

If you look at pictures of my family, you might wonder whether my sister was adopted. Mom, Petey, and I all have shocks of brown-black hair and blue eyes. Jennifer was blond, like our real father, and had his green eyes.

I remember a time when she liked me. There's proof: photographs of us trick-or-treating dressed as sister Disney princesses and videos of us putting on plays on the back patio, starring ourselves and Mango, our Jack Russell/rat terrier mix.

But we were four years apart, and once Jen started middle school, it seemed like my very existence offended her.

"That's just how it is with sisters," Mom would tell me when I was still small enough to climb onto her lap, face stiff with tears after a fight with Jen. Feel her fingers grazing over my ear as she played with my hair. "Aunt Ellen and I didn't become friends until we were in college."

Before homecoming her sophomore year, I gave Jen strep throat. It wound up saving her life. For a little while, at least.

Susan's parents were in Vermont for her cousin's wedding the night before the game, and Juliana and Jen were going to stay at her house with her. Susan refused to miss homecoming, even for the wedding, and besides, someone needed to be at home with Beethoven, the Berrys' beloved Saint Bernard.

Mr. Ruiz was going to pick them up in the morning so they could grab breakfast at the diner before the homecoming game. It was a tradition Juliana had with her family—pancakes before she performed.

It wasn't supposed to be a big deal, a bunch of fifteen-year-old girls spending the night by themselves. Sunnybrook was one of the safest towns in the country, and on our street, everyone looked out for each other. But when Juliana's father arrived to pick the girls up the next morning, both of them were dead.

They'd been strangled. Juliana's hands were sliced open, and one still held a shard from the broken mirror that hung in the foyer. She had fought like hell.

Susan hadn't seen it coming. She was on her back at the top of the stairs, staring at the ceiling. Across the hall, the shower was still on. She must have run out when she heard Juliana's screams.

If my sister hadn't been too sick to sleep over at Susan Berry's house that night, Susan's deranged neighbor would have murdered Jen too.

Lucky, everyone called her. *Blessed.*

In the end, though, it didn't make a difference.

Some people say a curse fell over our town five years ago. What else could explain the tragic deaths of five girls, in three separate incidents, in less than two months?

Some people think Jen's death was the most tragic of all.

Jen was in the top three in her class, beloved by everyone who was lucky enough to know her. She wanted to spend the summer before her junior year in South America, volunteering for Habitat for Humanity. She was planning on going to veterinary school, because as much as she loved helping people, her heart belonged to animals—especially the horses she used to ride as a child.

Jen wouldn't have done it. That's what they don't understand. My sister, with her pages-long to-do list of everything she wanted to do in life, never would have killed herself. Maybe it makes sense to them that she would do it, once they put themselves in Jen's shoes. Would living every day having to imagine what Jack Canning would have done to her if she'd been at that house be much of a life at all? Was life even worth living if all of her friends were dead?

I don't know if we're cursed. All I know is that my sister wouldn't have killed herself. And if she did, why didn't she leave a note explaining why?